The Question of Time

Samantha Wood Wright

iUniverse, Inc.
New York   Bloomington

iUniverse books may be ordered through booksellers or by contacting:

iUniverse
1663 Liberty Drive
Bloomington, IN 47403
www.iuniverse.com
1-800-Authors (1-800-288-4677)

Because of the dynamic nature of the Internet, any Web addresses or links contained in this book may have changed since publication and may no longer be valid. The views expressed in this work are solely those of the author and do not necessarily reflect the views of the publisher, and the publisher hereby disclaims any responsibility for them.

ISBN: 978-1-4502-5880-7 (sc)
ISBN: 978-1-4502-5879-1 (hc)
ISBN: 978-1-4502-5878-4 (ebook)

Printed in the United States of America

Library of Congress Control Number: 2010913326

iUniverse rev. date: 09/21/2010

I must thank Mama for teaching me respect for the dead, and for memories no one can take from me, and love I can tell of or wait for thirty years and stand as she does and weep. Someday that is all I'll have of her and in turn my children of me

For my mother Peggy (Happy) Williams Wood and for her father B. Williams

Acknowledgement

Many thanks go to my gracious and gifted friend author, Maria L. Whittington, my critic, my inspiration and the sane and encouraging voice through the whole process of getting this book to print.

She is also the artist who has given the book its beautiful face and is the architect of White House.

Table of Contents

Pretty Storms

1951

I had stared at the clock on the bedside table for nearly two hours still unable to sleep. So much had happened since Mrs. White's lawyer had told me I had inherited her house and her fortune. And as strange as that was when the lawyer, with the most unpronounceable name I had ever heard, was in my living room telling me this Mrs. White was still alive and in good health, and the next day she was dead and I was living in her house.

I only knew her through her writing and when I asked the lawyer why, he had been no help; he just kept saying Mrs. White has arranged or Mrs. White has requested. And if the strange room and the strange circumstances weren't enough it had to start raining; and damn funerals are depressing enough without getting soaked too.

Tired of tossing and turning and feeling very much like a character from one of her books, I decided that if I was going to be awake I was really going to be awake and went downstairs to make coffee.

I walked to the door as lightening lit up the room, thunder roaring so close on its tail I felt a chill go through me. I closed the bedroom door behind me to the sound of pouring rain and my pounding heart. The door creaked and I shook all over, and as the door closed the lights in the hall came on. I felt calmer with the light and looking around the ghastly figures in the darkness of a moment ago gave way to furniture, statues, plants, and lamps.

At the foot of the stairs I heard a clock strike one. At about that same time lights came on as I walked through to the dining room. I stood on the threshold to the kitchen and the lights were now on in both rooms. As I walked further into the kitchen the dining room lights went out behind me. I stepped back into the dining room and the kitchen light went out. I thought this was weird, about as weird as things could get in 1951. I wasn't too sure about any of it but I decided I liked my entry into rooms being announced this way especially since I was much braver in the light.

I was beginning to see my benefactor Mrs. White as a woman with a sense of humor. On second thought, eccentric might be a better choice of words; I had only met her once. Then I find out she has left her house and money to me with the only conditions being that I read the eulogy at her services and sleep in her attic bedroom in this old house with a half dozen other bedrooms. I couldn't begin to know why but then I loved a good mystery and I had plenty of time on my hands. I would figure it out.

I went to the kitchen setting the light game in motion again. It was a big white room with more windows than a conservatory and everything in it was old though well cared for. The cabinets and the walls looked freshly painted. A big double bowl, double drain board sink was as shiny as if it had just been installed. The refrigerator was hidden behind a door with hinges on it, reminiscent of old iceboxes, and the stove was an old wood burning stove that had been converted to electric. Everything was either turn of the century or made to look so, lending a certain charm to the room.

I found the percolator on the counter behind a roll top cover, along with the toaster, and a waffle iron. I made coffee, thinking to myself that I was going to love this old house and that I liked the strange old lady who had lived and died here more and more. I wondered what she was like, I mean, what she was really like. I had read all of her books and I was awed, to say the least, by her imagination, but the mystery surrounding her had grown with each new book

She beat out H. G. Wells when it came to writing about things in the future that had come to pass. It was if she wrote her books and the world followed her outline exactly. She had a trick or two up her sleeve that was certain, and maybe just maybe, I was the person who would "bust the case" as they say in old dime detective novels. I hoped, even if I didn't discover her secrets, I would at least come to understand why she had chosen me to inherit the mystery.

I looked around the kitchen for a cup and didn't see one. There were, and I just noticed this about the kitchen, no overhead cabinets. She was five feet tall, I remembered, and probably couldn't reach them but then I realized there were so many windows there was no wall space for cabinets.

I looked for a pantry and found it beside the refrigerator with only a small peg hole, big enough for a couple of fingers, for a handle. Inside were the cups I was looking for and other dishes too. A couple of shelves above what I would have guessed to be the everyday dishes were beautiful deep red glass dishes. I picked up one of the cups, which was tall and slender and had a stem on it like the glasses. They were even more beautiful up close. I turned the cup upside down to see if there was a name on the bottom, and I saw AVON in raised letters and the numbers 1986. The only Avon I knew anything about was the Avon that made cosmetics, not dishes, and I tried to tell myself the number couldn't be a date no matter how much it looked like one; it had to be a lot number or something else.

When the coffee finished perking I poured myself a cup and opened the door to sit on the porch and watch the storm up close. I sat down in one of at least a dozen wicker chairs lined up against the house. Lightning blazed across the sky again and again as if it understood my reason for sitting here and planned to give me a real show.

The porch was enclosed with glass panels that were hung from hooks near the ceiling and secured in place at the bottom with fasteners. Their shades were pulled all the way up to allow all the view possible. And one thing this house had plenty of was view, with its vast yard full of beautiful old trees, stone benches, statues, birdbaths and fountains. I had walked the grounds earlier and remembered that across the whole back of the property there was a flower garden and beyond it an orchard whose tall branches seemed to give the place an enclosed feel, even to the sky. She must have had some great need for privacy, but why, I wondered?

Beside me was a table, with a stack of National Geographic magazines and a single copy of a magazine called Victoria. It was too dark to read here, but the magazine looked interesting and I promised myself I would read it someday. For now I sat with my coffee and watched the storm. The thunder roared and rolled on and on shaking the ground and the house, even the sky it seemed, but out here in the half lit night (the kitchen light had gone off on its own when I stepped outside) I felt that I was at least eye to eye with the storm and in no danger.

I remembered a late afternoon at Lake Hopatcong when I had been caught in a sudden summer storm. I had sought shelter from the rain on a nearby porch. The owners of the house were not home and their cat, who was just as wet as I was, walked around and around me rubbing against my legs. A burst of thunder scared me and the cat half to death, and I picked the poor thing up, and stood on the porch holding the cat until the storm let up, which wasn't more than a few minutes, then ran home.

I remember seeing the tiny little white house with its pink trim and feeling so good. I went in by the side screened in porch where Mrs. Polidori, her mother, her father, and a neighbor lady were passing the afternoon in their favorite way over a game of canasta. The whole place was full of the wonderful smell of Mrs. Polidori's lasagna.

The summer here at the lake with my friend Marilyn and her family was a welcome respite from the heat of the city. We often spent days here at the lake in separate pursuits; and Marilyn had left early for the beach while I finished a book I was reading. When I started to the beach, Mrs. Polidori's mother had asked me if I were going to be a nun after I had announced that I was never going to get married. I remembered blushing with embarrassment when I told her I wasn't Catholic. She spoke only broken English, and always spoke Italian when she was excited, which she was now. Words were flying, and her old husband was laughing, and winking at me. "Now, now, Mama." he was saying to her; what she was saying, I never knew.

When I came back I was soaked through. She forgave me for being Protestant long enough to tell me to get into dry clothes before I caught a cold. I grabbed a towel and hurried to the room I shared with her granddaughter Marilyn. Sitting on the bed, I laid back and fell asleep, and dreamed of a Sunday when the smell of lasagna filled my parent's home, and I sat at the table barely able to swallow, fighting back tears of rage and humiliation.

I wrote about the storm for a freshman English project later, using a lot of imagination since I had never seen the lake out of season. I had snow blowing and the cat and me freezing and the Polidori house wrapped in snow, with icicles hanging from the trees and the roof's edge, and the windows frosted over. I remember the whole piece being so beautiful and expecting an A or an A+, but the teacher broke my heart by giving me a C and writing a note across the top saying my sentences were too long. I had argued with her about my sentences saying, "Elizabeth Windom White's sentences are long". Her rebuttal had been, "But you're not Elizabeth Windom White."

Now here I am sitting on the late Mrs. White's porch in the middle of another rainstorm. I remember thinking, except there is no cat, when I heard a soft meow and looked down to see the biggest, fattest longhaired cat I had ever seen. It was like a giant fur ball, so round and fleeting, that I wasn't sure which end was which, or that it was a cat, except I knew I had heard a meow. I didn't see where the cat ran off to and after calling it for several minutes with no luck, I gave up and sat back in my chair to watch the storm, trying to remember the words to Mrs. White's poem, 'Pretty Storms'.

> *The sky is aflame with many hues of gray*
> *the kitten draws nearer afraid of the thunder's roar*
> *and blazing sky, like Chinese New Year*
> *or our fourth only more beautiful and magnificent.*
> *the kitten draws still closer with the flashing and the roaring*
> *it's hard to believe creation is a strictly scientific thing*
> *amid such a spectacular display of temperament*
> *and the war is not that far away nor the hungry children*
> *frightened too perhaps by pretty storms*

About three-thirty the worst of the storm was over and I was pretty sleepy so I gave up my chair on the porch and went upstairs to bed, propping the attic door open, and crawled into the massive bed, the biggest bed I had ever seen (it was more like two beds really) wondering if it had been made for Jack's giant and his bride.

I lay awake for all of five minutes lulled to sleep by the gentle patter of rain on the ceiling windows above the bed and dreamed the whole house was made of glass, not surprising since I had never slept in a room with glass ceilings before.

When I awoke the next morning it was to the smell of coffee and I immediately panicked, thinking I must have left the coffee pot plugged in last night. I grabbed a robe and flew down the stairs putting it on as I ran.

The house was damp and chilly and the lights didn't turn off and on with my steps as they had last night. I know that was a dumb thing to be thinking of as I hurried to the kitchen but I couldn't help it. Everything was new and strange and I had half expected to wake up and find myself back in my drab little apartment in Jersey City.

I opened the kitchen door thinking the coffee sure smelled great and not the way all night coffee would smell, and there in front of me stood a strange woman. I let out a scream and we stood glaring at each other not sure which of us was the intruder.

"Hi. I'm Jennifer Stone," I said. She stared harder at me and said nothing; it was as if she hadn't heard me. I told her my name again and she walked away still saying nothing. I watched her pick up a small tablet from the long table in the middle of the room. She wrote something on it and walked back to me and handed me the tablet, on it she had written her name Blanche Ballard. I wrote my name and handed the tablet back to her. After some minutes passing it back and forth between us I learned that she was the housekeeper and that she came three days a week and had been doing so for many years.

She was tall with short curly white hair, looked to be about sixty and was rather pretty. I could tell she took pride in her appearance; her dress was cream colored with tiny red rose buds all over it and there was something about the way she carried herself.

At first I thought she was a relative of Mrs. White's or a very close friend but then I realized if that were the case she would be the heiress, not me. I was back to that old question of why me, and wondering if I would ever know. I felt sorry for Mrs. White for having no family; I knew well enough how that felt. I was an only child, estranged from my parents, divorced and alone. I wished so often there had been children, some piece of the marriage to carry away with me, instead of this emptiness I felt.

As I poured myself coffee I could feel Blanche's eyes on me, and I didn't blame her; she probably had more questions than I did. I turned to sit down at the table with my coffee and I caught her eye, inviting her to get a cup and sit with me.

She smiled, got her cup and picked up a small white bag from the counter top. I hadn't seen the bag until now, probably because of its color; white seemed to run into white everywhere in this beautiful old room. The bag was full of chocolate donuts. This time I smiled and I made sure she was looking straight at me.

I got up from my chair once she was seated and walked across the room for the tablet we had used earlier to communicate. Writing as I walked back to her, I handed her the tablet. She read my note. Tell me about yourself, I had written. She ignored my request and wrote back, where is Mrs. White?

I nearly fainted when I read her question. How could she not know the old woman had died? But, I learned, it wasn't that she didn't know Mrs. White had died but that she thought the body would be on view in the house.

We sat for the longest time exchanging notes. I got up once to pour more coffee and Blanche got up once. The pot of coffee and the bag of donuts emptied at about the same time and still we sat passing the tablet back and forth. After a while it was time to get ready for the afternoon service. I asked Blanche to go with me and she cried while I stood there feeling dammed uncomfortable that I couldn't. Blanche obviously loved this woman I had barely known and again I was left wondering why I had inherited a stranger's fortune when this dear faithful woman here with me had not?

The clock struck ten and at almost that moment a strange chime went off. I was still trying to identify the sound when I heard a knock at the door. I hadn't seen Lawyer P come up.

"Did you sleep well?" He asked, but his tone told me he could care less how I had slept. He was only checking to see that I had fulfilled my part of the will's arrangement and he was disappointed to find I had. Then he asked a few of yesterday's questions over again, trying to give this visit the appearance of a professional call. And after a few minutes he left but lingered on the steps. When I went out to see if he wanted anything else, he shook his head no and hurried to his car.

He had as many questions as I did, the biggest one being why I was the new owner of the house he achingly wanted for himself. A lot of what I thought he was thinking might be conjecture, but I knew I was right about that one point. He couldn't hide his disappointment about the house. It was in his voice, in his eyes, and when he looked at the place he almost seemed to drool. I could see him swallowing hard and often as he told me about the house that first day in my apartment and today when he stood on the steps looking around the grounds, his pain seemed to fill the air

I stood on the steps where he had stood a moment ago and looked out across the huge yard surrounded by a tall metal fence. On the fourth side, which was south and straight ahead of me, there was a dark board fence and an old barn of some sort. The house itself stood back off the road. I looked up in time to see the wide gate across the driveway open automatically and Lawyer P drive away. I understood now that the chime was connected to the entrance to the property and with the incredible size of the house and Blanche's near deafness that it would have been needed to alert Mrs. White to the fact that she had company.

Not until two days before Mrs. White's death did he find out about me. The will and papers with instructions on where to find me were given to Lawyer P then. And here I stood having beaten out the faithful family maid and the faithful, I hoped, family attorney for the estate. More questions. I was looking forward to the day when some of them would be answered.

Merlin in the Mist

1922

The old shop was the deep brown of aged wood and stood back off the road at the end of Main Street. The sign was the same dark wood and hung on end by a single nail, which caused it to beat against the building with the slightest wind; the word BLACKSMITH burnt into it years ago was barely legible. Board fences enclosed the yard on all sides and a wide dirt path led to double front doors that stood open whenever possible inviting fresh air and friendly faces; with hitching posts running north to south in front of the big doors. Smoke always coming from both chimneys, the fire in front was for shoeing or melting metal to pound into tools or hinges for some new barn door; the stove in back near Old Ned's sleeping rooms boasted a coffee pot on even the hottest summer days and a skillet of meat and potatoes or a pot of stew in the evenings.

Eight year old Morgan ran around the shop to the side door so as not to distract Old Ned from the fire and cause him to get burned or to mess up his work. He had heard the old man yell at other boys for that very thing. Since he meant to keep on old Ned's good side he was mindful of everything he heard him say. He had it all committed to memory and could tell when asked just where Old Ned stood on everything important. He loved him like a father and indeed he was more of a father to the young boy than he realized.

Morgan's father T. Williams, a railroad inspector, was gone all the time with his job. Daily problems that couldn't wait were taken next door to Old Ned, the wisest man in town all the boys' agreed.

Morgan was barely six and almost got in a fight with a much older boy the day he realized he loved Old Ned and half the town's children with him. He never felt bigger or prouder of himself than that day, though he had won the fight with words, not his fists. Words were all he had against a kid twice his size and words had served him well.

"Words are a gentleman's weapon," his father had said when he told him about defending Old Ned and waiting for the punch from Henry that never came. Instead the other boys had agreed with Morgan and patted him on the shoulder and he had walked away feeling great leaving Henry standing there without a friend.

Today he was proud and excited and he just knew that when Old Ned heard the good news he would be excited too. Morgan burst through the double side doors, closed against a cold March wind and quickly closed them again behind him. Old Ned was pouring himself a cup of coffee, heard him come in, and held up an extra cup gesturing to the young boy. Morgan nodded a hearty yes and walked over to the old man. They sat down on a couple of big stumps shoved against the shop's inner wall. Frequent visitors to the shop had polished the stumps and the wall behind it to a high shine.

Four horse stalls lined the south side of the shop filled with the sweet smell of fresh straw. It was a town joke that Ned trained any horse left with him to do its business outside or the shop wouldn't smell so nice; but in earnest he cleaned it up almost as fast as they dropped it. If a horse stayed long enough they probably got the idea, Morgan figured, because the sweet smell of grain, smoke from the fires, and a strong pot of coffee were the shop's smell, not manure.

A horse's occasional whinny, the old man's deep voice, and the pounding of the hammer were the shop's sounds. Some days boys would come by after supper or during the day if the news couldn't wait, and their voices would mingle with Old Ned's. Morgan's heart always fell at those times for he wanted the old man to himself.

His cold hands warmed quickly with the cup he held and he sat waiting for the warmth to flow through him. The fire was blazing and the coffee smelled great. He loved the smell of it and the strong black color, though he knew his parents wouldn't approve.

Old Ned mumbled something to him about business being slow today. "I'm caught up," he said aloud, "and I put on that old pot of coffee hoping to draw some boy to visit me to talk away the day."

Morgan smiled and looked about the shop savoring the moment and the warmth that flowed through him from head to toe. He truly did love the old blacksmith and he knew every corner of the shop as well as he knew his own room. He brushed a loving hand along the stump beside his leg where he had sat listening to the tall black man all his life.

Old Ned laughed aloud and Morgan looked to him startled. "Why did you come runnin' in here awhile ago - is there something you forgot to tell me? You sittin' there all warm and curled up by the fire like an old mama cat."

Morgan blurted out, "We're going home!"

"But boy you just live next door," the old man teased and waited for the rest of the story. All the boys could tell you that Old Ned had the best pair of ears in town. He always listened no matter how strange or how silly, he always listened and he was listening now. He was listening as much to what Morgan was saying as to what he was not. Morgan had studied that about him until he could copy every gesture of it. The way his eyes got perfectly still as if he was searching for the words with you. The way his ears perked up and a smile stole across his face as you began to speak.

"We're going to England, Papa's home," Morgan said excitedly, and they spent the rest of the cold March day around the fire talking about the planned trip.

In late April, Morgan and his family except for his sister Theresa, who was newly married, boarded a train to Louisville where they would change trains to New York City.

The train station in Louisville was the biggest building Morgan had ever been in. He walked around staring at the magnificent ceiling, falling over everything. His mother called him down till she was hoarse and still he could not stop himself. She finally gave up in disgust warning his sisters to watch their feet and to try and keep him from killing himself in his many falls.

He loved the trip. The countryside they passed through was so much like his hometown of Glendale, Kentucky; he waved to the boys with hats in their hands standing at the depot of almost every town. He shouted back and forth out the window with a boy named Billy, in a little town in Ohio, until his father pulled him back in the window by the seat of his pants.

The excitement of the train stood out in his mind. He loved it. He felt he understood his father better than he ever had. He understood why his father was always on the trains and never at home. He was going to work for the railroad himself when he grew up, he decided, but he would not have any sons. Girls were okay they didn't need a father like boys did. But then he might have a boy, and he could let his boy go see Old Ned the way he did.

He loved the dining car with its white linens and black waiters scrubbed clean and wearing white jackets. He had never seen Old Ned scrubbed and he was sure he didn't own a white jacket or he would have seen it. The food was wonderful and he ordered frog legs the first night for dinner. He'd seen them stuck but had never eaten them and was more than a little troubled by how much like a person they looked, even to what seemed like a tiny hand on the hip. He had to force himself to eat them and thought they tasted enough like chicken that he would stick to eating chicken from then on.

The part he liked best of all about the train was passing from one car to another. Here he could feel the vibration of the wheels running against the tracks and hear it so loud it pushed everything else from his mind. He passed from one car to another pretending to barely escape falling under the wheels or from the top of the train while being chased by bank robbers he had discovered hiding out on the train.

He woke that night terrified by the sound of total silence. No clickity clack, no screeching of metal on metal, no whistles blowing. All the sounds he had grown used to, he now missed. Sitting up in the top berth, he bumped his head on the ceiling in the dark. Rubbing his head he climbed down to look out the window. It was pitch black outside. No movement, no sound, no people, no lights in the distance. Panicky he ran out the door of his room to find his father and straight into the arms of a porter. He screamed!

The man spoke softly but firmly. "Everything is okay. Be careful you don't wake up everybody on the train with your racket. We're outside a town in Pennsylvania. The town is behind us; that's why you can't see its lights. We're waiting for another train to pass through so we can change tracks." Morgan sighed with relief and tried to look brave though he was scared to death.

"Come with me and I'll show you everything okay, but promise me first, no more screaming."

Morgan promised and followed along as they stepped down from the train by a light the man held. The rocks along the tracks were sharp and rough on his bare feet. He crossed over them and onto the grass alongside. He could see lights in the distance. "That's the depot there. Do you see it?" the man asked Morgan, pointing toward the lights.

"Yes sir," the boy answered. "Yes sir I see it."

"Your first train ride, ain't it, boy?"

"Yes, sir, but my Papa works on the trains," Morgan said proudly.

"I know son. I know your father. Well we better be getting back before they leave us standing here. We'll be starting up again real soon," he said holding the light up to the watch he had just taken out of his pocket.

Morgan slept late the next morning and missed breakfast. When the shouting of the conductor woke him he thought his family might have left him behind, but looking around he saw his sister Sarah's doll and her bag. Reassured but still feeling an urgency to hurry, he dressed quickly, packed his pajamas, gave his hair a quick brushing, and hurried to find his parents.

The narrow aisles were full of people squeezing past each other dragging bags and children. One very big lady had a basket with a tiny wet nose sticking out of the top. He pushed his way through and patted the tiny nose. A grateful tongue licked his hand. He smiled and hurried on.

He soon stood outside his parents' room and braced himself against the scolding he knew he would get. His father's loud voice could be heard through the closed door. He knocked lightly and opened it. His sisters sat lined up on the bed, Kay holding Julia and Deborah holding Sarah, with Happy and Bea sitting between them half hidden among starched dresses, their dark hair hidden under big straw hats. Poor Sarah, he thought, she can't possibly see; her hat is nearly as big as she is.

Morgan, the misfit, the only boy and the only one of the children with blond hair and blue eyes stood waiting nervously for his father to speak. Mr. Williams turned and gave his son a stern look. "Morgan, I thought we had an agreement," he said.

"Yes, Papa, we did. I mean we do, sir!"

"Then why haven't you been helping with the younger children? Your sisters Kay and Deborah both tried to wake you and you would not get up. We could have left you home with Theresa and been none the worse off."

Papa had a way of making Morgan feel very bad when he wanted to. Now was one of those times. To make matters worse, his sisters sat smugly enjoying every bit of his misery. It was hard being the only boy. The girls had no imagination. They didn't understand him. He looked up startled from his thoughts. His father had him by the shoulders and was shouting to him. "Did you hear me boy?"

"Yes sir," Morgan mumbled.

"Then go get yours and your sister's things and hurry back here. We have only a few more minutes. Bea, you go with him to be sure he finds his way back here or we shall end up losing him."

"Yes, Papa," she answered, following Morgan out of the room and down the still crowded passageway.

Morgan was angry and rushed past the people as fast as he could. He opened the door to his room, went in and slammed the door hard again. Bea was close on his heels and the door slammed in her face. She reopened it almost as angry with Morgan as he was with Papa but quickly calmed herself, deciding it was much too nice a day to be upset.

She knew how her little brother felt. She felt that way a lot herself. She didn't quite know what the feeling was but it had to do with feeling like she didn't belong, a feeling of somehow being different. Everything came hard for Bea, the way it did for Morgan. They were different and yet somehow the same. He was smart and yet he fell all over himself sometimes when he got carried away with his play. She was not so smart and she fell all over herself trying to hide it from people. Morgan and little Happy were the only ones in the family that she felt accepted her the way she was and she was afraid that when Happy got older she would not love her the way, she felt, the others didn't love her now.

"Morgan", she begged, "Don't be upset. It's such a pretty day and we're in New York City. Papa says there is a lot to see and do here. Let's be happy, please."

Morgan smiled with the funny face Bea made and agreed to be happy just for her. He never could stay mad anyhow. There was this wonderful adventure ahead of him. He was glad Bea was the one Papa had sent to help him. She was not like the others. She got no joy out of seeing him miserable or in seeing anyone else miserable for that matter. She seemed young like him and like Happy and he wondered how she could be when she was clearly one of his older sisters. He dropped the thought and hurried with his packing while Bea gathered up Happy's, and Sarah's things. One last look around the room convinced them both that they had everything and they left the room, bags in hand.

Morgan noticed the quiet of the aisles and worried that they had been left, as his father had threatened, and hurried Bea along. When they arrived back at their parents' cabin the whole family stood in the hall lined up, bags and babies balanced on every hip. "Let's go," he heard his father say and the parade of Williams' began to leave the train.

This station was even bigger and grander than the one in Louisville and Morgan found he was being pushed along in the biggest crowd he had ever seen, unable to look around the way he would have wanted to. At first he had trouble seeing his father and mother in the crowd but his father soon passed the word along for them to join hands. In this way they made it through the crowded station and out onto the streets.

The crowd was still everywhere around them. They came to an abrupt stop several feet from the door and stood for a while. Morgan wondered what was going on and then they began walking again. Cars backfired and smoke billowed as cars came to a halt. Horses reared up and whinnied; loud and angry voices shouted above it all telling some unknown person to watch where they were going. They walked on and were in the middle of the street with cars, carriages, wagons and bicycles stopped all around them. The voices grew louder and Morgan realized they were the reason for the big stir, his family, hand in hand, parading across a New York street as if they owned it. While Morgan was excited and anxious about the traffic, he saw his father wave to the crowd smiling despite their outcry.

"Damn Catholics!" a man shouted, and his father shook his finger at the man and warned him to mind his tongue in front of the ladies, and they continued their trek. Morgan was relieved when they were on the sidewalk again, glad the traffic had started up and the shouting had faded. He had never seen so many people in his whole life, and to have them all looking straight at him and his family was just too much.

Both the babies were crying at the tops of their voices. Happy had pulled away from Morgan and gone to their father. Morgan ran after her and grabbed her hand as she looked up to Papa and asked, "What is a damn Catholic?" Mother and Father looked to each other and burst out laughing. "Never mind, Happy," Papa said. "Let's get a carriage and go to our hotel. We need to get rid of this baggage so we can see the town."

Their stay in New York was a whirlwind of activity. Papa took them to see everything of any importance, the zoo proving to be a real disaster for poor Morgan. He got too close to the camel's cage and the camel spit all over him. His father had insisted that he now smelled too bad to be a part of their company and made him walk behind all of the girls. They naturally enjoyed this, his latest mess, and the discomfort it caused him, but he ended up enjoying it too once he got past their taunts.

He pretended to be a French Foreign Legionnaire who had been talking to his camel about their next campaign against the bandits infesting the desert. The camel had misunderstood his plans and had spit at him in disapproval. They were more in agreement now and he rode the camel past the cages of the other animals and his silly sisters. The smell of the camel was not unpleasant to him and it would make a good disguise against the sharp-nosed bandits. They would not know he was a Legionnaire, but think him a camel trader. When he was close enough to capture them it would be too late. His family would join with the grateful inhabitants of the dessert city in congratulating him when he brought the bandits in single-handed.

He loved the whole trip and used his imagination when his sisters and their propriety tried to pen him in and make him march along with them in their silly hats and prissy dresses. Too soon their trip would be over and the fun would run out for him. Too soon, he feared, he would be a papa too with a parade of giggling daughters following him everywhere. He decided he would have fun now where and when he could. Let his sisters tell on him; they seemed to enjoy doing it so much.

Happy and Bea were his only friends among his seven sisters and Bea couldn't be trusted if the others got to her first. She would look a little sad as he squirmed under Papa's or Mama's gaze and go right on agreeing with the other girls. He knew she was unhappy in the middle like this and he always tried to show Bea he didn't blame her. He knew the others were stronger and smarter than her. She was at their mercy as much as he was. As for little Happy, she had just turned five and there was still time for her to turn sour like the rest. Though admittedly Julia was younger and was already much like the older girls. This gave Morgan great hope that Happy would be his one true friend among his sisters while Sarah, not quite three, was much too young to be siding with anyone.

Their fun filled week ended all too soon. Papa woke them up early on the last day in New York, a beautiful warm April day. Morgan thought he must have been feeling good for Papa had roused them with a happy boisterous voice and a big smile. Morgan heard him singing as he left the bedroom and he could never remember having heard him do so before.

"He must be happy to be going to see his family," Deborah whispered to Bea. "It's been over twenty years since he's been home you know."

Morgan stopped short; no he didn't know - he had no idea. He began figuring the ages of his sisters up on his fingers and must have lost count or Deborah was wrong. Not likely, he reassured himself and tried figuring the years again. On the third try he remembered his dead brother, Harvey, who had died at seven long before he himself was born. Harvey was older than Theresa by two years. Theresa was seventeen and married now. That would make Harvey nineteen if he had lived. Morgan found the years really did come to twenty; twenty-one to be exact, and of course as always Deborah was right.

The hotel fixed a picnic lunch for them and they went to Central Park where they spent the early quiet of the morning enjoying the day and each other's company exactly the way they did at home on a Sunday morning.

When they checked out of the hotel on Monday they had bought so many new things in New York, they looked worse than they had when they arrived, bags and babies in tow parading single file out to the street to their waiting taxi.

When they arrived at the ship the smell of the ocean was the first thing that caught Morgan's attention. It was the most inviting thing he had every encountered. He was looking forward to this trip and he planned to go deep-sea fishing as soon as they left. He had read about it in the hotel lobby brochures on the South Seas. He would catch the biggest fish ever caught if he could, and if not for real then at least in his imagination.

Boats and ships of all sizes could be seen near and far. Their own ship huge and gray before them was the biggest of them all. They boarded and settled their things in their cabins and hurried to the deck where everyone was gathered. People stood leaning over the railing waving to the crowd below. Morgan, with Happy by the hand, pushed his way through the crowd. He could see hundreds of people below and pretended they were all cheering and waving to him. He, their prince, and his royal family were going to visit with the King and Queen of England. His middle name was Edward and he knew he had been named for Prince Edward, the son of King George and Queen Mary. Prince Edward would be king some day and he too would be king. Of course his captive audience knew all of this and he waved and waved wishing them well until his family's return.

The voyage that had promised young Morgan so much joy turned sour very quickly. According to his parents they were traveling with an international crowd and it was imperative that he remain as quiet as possible, keep out of the way, speak only when spoken to, and never under any circumstances bother the crew. With all these rules and the threat of dire consequences if he broke even one of them, the only thing left for him to do was stare at the four walls of his cabin or out to sea. He faced spending the whole voyage doing just that and dying of boredom.

Even his imagination failed him until one day he was walking around and overheard a tiny little drawn up man speaking German. He immediately took off on a grand spy adventure and spent the rest of the trip following the man around listening to what he said. He paid great attention to who the man talked to and wrote it all down in his notebook, then would go to his cabin where he would try to decipher the code the German and his friends were using so he could tell the authorities when they got off the ship.

Morgan didn't see the German spy again until they docked in England and was relieved as he had run out of space in his notebook and was trying to remember everything he heard.

A crowd was once again gathered waiting for the ship. He waved for a few quick moments to his adoring fans before he was dragged away by Kay, who kept insisting that she was not going to get in trouble because he had run off, and that he better get his things together and grab Happy's hand. She meant to have Papa in a good mood when he introduced them to his family. Morgan, seeing where there could be a real advantage to that, left the railing and followed Kay to where the rest of the Williams children stood waiting for their parents to join them.

Papa and Mama, arm in arm, led them down the gangplank into the arms of their own parents. Morgan recognized them from their pictures in the family album though they did look much older. So did his parents for that matter and he tried to imagine being twenty-one years older; he could see himself white haired for his father had been white haired since he had a fever at eighteen, but he could not see himself any bigger. He wondered if this meant he would be a midget and immediately thought of joining a circus. Once again he felt Kay pulling him along and calling him "short stuff" like she did most of the time. Morgan now convinced of his career plans for the future smiled and tried to ignore his older sister. He knew what lay ahead for him. He would only have to wait a few years.

Soon it was Morgan's turn to be introduced and hugged by a half dozen relatives. The first man he met after his Grandparents was his Uncle Edward, his mother's youngest brother and his namesake. "I thought I was named after Prince Edward," he shouted and they all laughed.

Uncle Edward tousled his hair and hugged him again. "Don't worry, lad, we both are," he said smiling.

Bea, Julia, Morgan, and Happy rode with Uncle Edward and Grandmother Butler and Grandfather Jim as they drove through London past the castle where Morgan thought the guards looked like toy soldiers, and out into the country. Behind them the rest of the family rode with Grandmother and Grandfather Williams in another car.

Morgan sat quietly holding Happy's hand for support, studying these strangers called family. He saw some of his mother in his Grandmother Butler though his mother was shorter. They had the same short hair worn the same way, the same full figures, the same stern look that somehow prevailed even through the biggest smile, and (Morgan was soon to learn) the same firm way of handling people.

Grandfather Jim was big and jolly and soft spoken. He too had white hair but not much of it, Morgan noticed, and he patted his own hair with the sudden dread that he might lose his, not sure what caused it. They were family, that's all he knew, and family had a way of taking after each other. Grandfather Jim didn't talk much but when he did it was pleasant, sometimes funny, and it almost always made Morgan feel good.

Uncle Edward was young, tall, and tanned with an infectious grin and dark hair and happy eyes. He held a pipe that seldom made it to his mouth because he kept waving it about using it to point out things of interest along the way.

They would be staying at the Williams house he learned as both cars drove past what was pointed out to Morgan as his mother's family's place. His parents had been neighbors he realized for the first time and he wondered if he too would marry a neighbor girl, shrugging off a feeling of dread as he thought of the girls his age in Glendale.

They had lunch at the edge of the garden in a huge glass house with intricate white metal trim. The furniture, not like anything he had ever seen before, was stone, while just outside the house on brick walkways there were metal chairs with glass-topped tables. Fortunately the food, "enough to feed an army," Kay had mumbled nudging him, was familiar and he ate till he made himself half sick. Had it not been for stern looks from both parents he would have, no doubt, finished the job. He excused himself, and to escape further glaring looks, decided to investigate the yard beyond the garden. Almost immediately he bumped into his Uncle Edward who offered to walk with him around the grounds.

He quickly decided that his uncle was wonderful and came to see him more as a big brother than an uncle. They talked about everything, even the trip over, and young Morgan ended up telling him about the German spy and showing him the small notebook he had tucked away in his pocket.

They spent quite some time sitting under a big tree trying to decode the notes the boy had taken. Young Morgan explained to his uncle that he had written the words the way they sounded since he didn't know German. In the end they were left to their imaginations, which soon caused them to see they had more in common than just their names. Uncle Edward, a much later child than his many sisters, was also an only boy and had relied on his imagination too. During the month long visit they shared many wonderful hours together. Of all the relatives the boy met, that until now had only been faces peering back at him from the pages of the family album, he learned to love Uncle Edward best.

Of all the strange and wonderful customs of the British he most enjoyed tea, especially since his Grandparents ate dinner so late he would have been starved without it. He had to dress and sit and listen to the grownups talk and that was awful. But the scrumptious cakes, the endless variety of cakes, and the hot tea to wash it down were wonderful.

Tea was over early on one particularly beautiful warm afternoon. The adults were not home, having gone to visit someone. This left Morgan and his younger sisters in the care of the servants. Tiring of the endless giggling and squealing of the girls he had gone out on his own.

The estate ran on for miles in all directions. Acres of beautiful lawns immediately surrounded the grand old house that his family had lived in for generations. He ran through these fields and turned to look back at the house. It was the biggest one he had ever seen. It seemed like a castle to him though his family assured him it wasn't. He argued that it looked like the king's castle he had seen on the way here, only smaller. They had told him that it was much smaller and they were not the same at all. Still it was a castle to him and he ran and played in the fields about it imagining knights fencing with bandits and rescuing maidens in distress.

Soon he saw a dragon spewing fire on a band of travelers who ran and hid behind the trees. He imagined himself one of them and ran to hide too. He ran from hiding place to hiding place acting out the grand battle with the dragon until he killed it and a knight happening by saw his heroism and knighted him too.

In his play he lost sight of the house. The vast lawn with its many trees had become a thick dark forest. It was growing late. The sun low in the sky shone between the trees in long warm streaks. Morgan was cold and sought out a patch of sun to sit in to get warm and he looked about for something familiar.

It grew darker almost before his eyes. Frightened he stood up and ran from place to place like a trapped animal. He wondered if he would be missed at the house. Would they search for him? How long would it be before they found him? Would they even look? Would they wait till morning? How late would his parents and his grandparents be away? Questions filled his mind. He had to calm himself. He had to think about what to do. He sat down in the waning sun, cold, tired, and hungry.

He sat quietly and watched fog appear and the trees take on a ghostly gnarled look. He heard the screeching of a night bird, an owl, he presumed. The cold wet wind brushed his cheeks and chilled his bones. He wished he could warm himself by a fire and suddenly smelled a campfire burning and heard the loud pop and crackle of a log being added to it.

He looked toward the sound and saw a bent aged figure hooded in a dark woolen cloak against the wind and the rain. The old man stood tall and moved like a man much younger somehow catching Morgan when he fainted.

The smell of wet wool permeated the dazed boy's senses. When Morgan opened his eyes he found he was in some kind of crude shelter out of the rain. It was a heavy blanket stretched from some low hanging branches. The old man stood stirring the fire and talking to some unseen person. Morgan sat up and looked around. Seeing no one he called out, "Who are you talking to?"

"Ah boy, you are awake are you? Old Merlin gave you quiet a scare didn't he?"

"Yes, yes you did, sir," the frightened boy answered.

"My, my, a boy that tells the truth when the time is perfect for a bit of bragging is a rare lad. I'll tell you this!" Merlin said brushing his hood back from his head for a closer look at his new companion.

The rain stopped with a flick of Merlin's hand and a look to the sky. A heavy fog lay everywhere but between the boy and the man walking toward him.

Morgan noticed the delicate features especially the eyes; they were as blue as his. They were also somehow hypnotic and he found himself unable to break away from them. They seemed to see right through him and to know every bone of his body and thought of his mind. But they were also warm, smiling eyes.

Morgan was no longer afraid though admittedly this all seemed like a scene from some great mystery. How did the rain stop at the old man's command? How could they be surrounded, as they were, by a heavy fog, so heavy that the full moon shone through as if it was a waning candle, and yet the night air within that circle remained crystal clear?

The man had called himself Merlin, had he not, Morgan recalled. Perhaps he was Merlin, the magician of King Arthur's day. He remembered reading of his great powers and of his long disappearance and then his resurfacing years later. He remembered the rumors that he had not died but had only gone to his cave to rest, perhaps to reappear again. His father's family home here in England might be near where Merlin had lived so long ago. He didn't know. And if it wasn't, he reasoned, a man like Merlin could pretty well go wherever he liked. Was this the same Merlin, the Merlin of the stories he had heard so much about? He wondered and before he thought he had asked aloud.

Merlin's laugh echoed through the forest and bounced off large stones with a flash like a ricocheting bullet. Morgan stood up amazed following the flash and the sound.

"You are the magician!" Morgan shouted excitedly, and Merlin entering into the spirit of the moment tossed the light about with more bravado. It went from tree to tree, then within the boy's grasp and as he reached for it into the sky above them and out of sight.

Morgan laughed and chased after the light until he was exhausted, forgetting his fears and his predicament. Merlin had planned it that way. There would be time enough to see the boy home when they tired of each other's company. In the end the light would lead the way for the boy and Merlin would once again retreat into obscurity waiting for another time, another lost boy to work his magic on.

Back at home Morgan ran in through the open French doors of the dining room flushed, out of breath, and shouting about how he had gotten lost and sat down in the woods, and about the old man that had come and helped him home. The adults listened and tried to calm him down but he would not be hushed. In the end his father sent him to his room without supper saying he had heard enough of his childish nonsense.

The boy went upstairs broken hearted. He could not believe his good fortune in having met the old magician but no one believed him. He was not in the habit of lying; why did his father think he was doing so now? He climbed the steps hungry after his hard running. His shoes and stockings were soaked through and he was cold. But he was glad for one thing. Here he had a room to himself. The last thing he wanted now was to have to deal with teasing sisters. He needed privacy very badly to figure out just where he had gone wrong. He had seen his Papa angry before but not like tonight. He could remember having been called down for being too imaginative before, but never had his father accused him of lying.

Entering the dark room he fell across the bed and cried. He must have dozed for awhile because once again he could see the old man and the light and then he heard his Uncle Edward calling him. He sat up in bed and looked around. Uncle Edward turned on the lamp on the bedside table and held a plate of hot food for him. Young Morgan smiled and anxiously reached for the plate. He was starved and the food smelled wonderful.

"You must keep quiet about this lad or we'll both be in trouble. I sneaked into the kitchen and got cook to fix you a bite. A boy can't be missing his supper after an evening with Merlin, now can he?"

The grateful boy looked up to his newfound friend and tears came to his eyes. "They didn't believe me, Uncle Edward, they didn't believe me." He said.

"I believe you lad, I believe you. Did I ever tell you about the time I met the old man myself?"

Jennifer Stone

1951

At eleven thirty when I heard the gate chime again, I was in the tub soaking and hurried out. Throwing on a robe I ran to the window at the end of the upstairs hall. Lawyer P was coming up the drive and behind him were two dark green trucks with black lettering on the side. Without my glasses I couldn't read the names but I guessed they were the caterers. I turned back to the bathroom and got back in the tub again. I had plenty of time; all I had to do was dress and walk across the yard, and the services weren't until twelve. Judging from Mrs. White's generosity with me, I was more than certain that the lawyer was being well paid for his trouble.

The phone rang after a few minutes and I got out of the tub to answer it. It was a wrong number. I gave up on my bath and went to the attic room to dress. Mrs. White had provided a beige turn of the century dress and shoes for me to wear. How she knew what size I wore was as much a mystery as everything else. The dress itself was long and flowing with long sleeves, a high collar, and a lace bodice. The shoes were low heels; she had known too somehow that because I was five foot five I only wore low heels.

Along with the dress and shoes there was a long heavy cotton slip and a beige rain cape with a hood, in case of bad weather. How in the

26

hell did she know it would rain today? Pearl earrings and combs for my hair lay on the vanity. Were they hers, I wondered, picking them up to admire them for the one-hundredth time?

I looked around the strange attic room feeling sad and confused and thought of how lonely it must have been for her in this big old house, wondering why had she picked me to replace her insisting that I sleep in Jack's giant's bed as she had done? Was she family I had never known? If so why hadn't she told me years ago? Why was I here in this room with its gray cast and windows bathed in gentle streaks of rain? Shadows played with the rain teasing me; I walked to a nearby window and wrote why in its mist.

It was a long room sparsely furnished, with the glass ceiling pitched high on the east side. The walls were a soft white with oak floors and trim. The bed was brass and white filigree with posters nearly touching the ceiling. There were two bedside tables and by the window overlooking the front lawn there were two wicker rockers with a small round table between them. The table was covered in a floor length lace cloth with two books and a lamp in the same filigree pattern as the bed.

The vanity was oak too, though so cluttered with combs and brushes, hand mirrors, and makeup, you could hardly see its top. It struck me as odd that an eighty-eight year old woman would wear makeup until I realized that the colors and the brands were my own. Again I wondered how she knew.

Standing in front of the vanity looking at the room, behind me in the mirror I realized for the first time that the room was devoid of anything that might have been Elizabeth Windom White's. It was as if the room weren't hers at all and never had been.

Then my eyes fell upon the huge framed picture hanging over the bed. It was of a breathtakingly beautiful blonde woman with a mole on her cheek and the most haunting eyes. Her lips were caught in a half smile as if a sad thought had come to her mind at the same instance the photographer had snapped the picture and her smile had just started to fade away. I loved the picture and I was happy it had been left for me and, I wondered too, if Mrs. White had known that I would like it?

I crossed the room to the big oak chiffarobe and flung open the double doors. The clothes were all in my size. I sat down on the bed to get a grip on myself. The clock on the table by the window struck a single time indicating the half hour; it was eleven thirty. I had thirty minutes to get dressed and out in the yard.

I stood up, took off my robe, and put on the long cotton slip. It smelled wonderful like flowers of some kind. Potpourri, I supposed; old ladies like potpourri. I remembered my grandmother had it in all of her drawers.

I put on my stockings and shoes and the dress that had about thirty tiny fabric covered buttons up the back. They were hard to handle and I was beginning to panic and pictured Lawyer P having to come to get me, which was motivation enough because suddenly the buttons were all done and I was at the mirror looking for a brush. I brushed my long brown hair into a bunch, twisted it into a big loose knot and secured it with hairpins, then put in the beautiful pearl combs. When I finished putting on my makeup I stood in front of the mirror looking like I had stepped out of the pages of some history book.

Again I wondered why, but there was no time for questions; they would have to wait. I would have my answers, I vowed to myself as I stared back at my own reflection in the mirror. The very determined look on my face made me laugh and wonder whom I was trying to impress. I turned from the mirror toward the bed, picked up the rain cape, and started downstairs putting it on as I walked.

Blanche was waiting at the bottom of the stairs for me. She had changed her dress; it too was early twentieth century and white. Was this a costume party or a funeral, I wondered, as I helped her with her raincoat and we walked together out the kitchen door?

The driveway was lined with cars and the lawn was full of women in brightly colored dresses and men in spring suits all from the turn of the century. There was nothing on the grounds at that moment that was black except for some of the cars and they wore festive streamers as if to apologize for their dreary color.

The rain had stopped. The sun was trying hard to push the clouds aside and put in an appearance. Scattered across the yard in huge pots were white roses with delicate wisps of baby breath. The grass was green and birds hopped about on the wet ground searching for worms, chirping their thanks.

It was warm for this early in the year, or so I heard; being new to Kentucky I didn't know if they were right or not. When I left Newark Airport yesterday, snow was coming down, already on the ground, and an icy landing strip very nearly cancelled the flight. Now everything here was greening and lush and beautiful.

The driveway was brick with intermittent patches of grass popping up, fighting the same battle for space with the bricks that the sun was fighting with the clouds.

I suddenly felt very proud to be here. "Elizabeth Windom White, you are some lady," I said aloud as Blanche and I walked toward the crowd of people making their way to the many blue canopies scattered around the garden's edge, my words floating away on the wind as there was nobody to hear me.

Soon we joined the crowd and walked along catching bits of laughter mixed with regrets and Mrs. White's name. I wondered what their stories were. One tall good-looking man bumped against me and hurried on without apologizing. What's the hurry I wanted to shout but I stopped myself. This was her day and I would behave myself even if Lawyer P pushed me, and I knew he would love to; the only thing stopping him was that he hadn't found a cliff high enough to make it worth his while.

We neared the many canopies and people began to leave the path and mill around. The smell of roses filled the air and blended with the smell of food and coffee. I walked to a nearby urn and poured myself a cup.

I saw Lawyer P. and tried to duck away but he saw me and called my name. I walked toward him reluctantly knowing I would have to deal with him sooner or later and that I might as well get it over with. As I neared him I noticed the red carnation in his lapel and it looked strangely out of place. Then it hit me it was the only non-white flower here.

I was only a few feet from the lawyer when a young man, probably in his early twenties, passed between the lawyer and me, carrying a huge tray, shoulder high. He fell against the lawyer and regained his footing barely in time to keep the cups and saucers from falling off the tray. He apologized many times over to the enraged little man and finally walked on at the lawyer's insistence. I could have sworn I saw the boy smile as he moved away.

When the lawyer and I stood in full view of each other again I saw the red carnation crushed at his feet. Now I was smiling too and I took a white rose from a nearby urn and breaking the stem shorter I put the flower in the lawyer's lapel. He said nothing but I could tell by his expression that he was boiling inside.

"You wanted me, Sir," I said after a moment.

"Yes," he answered. "I wanted to introduce you to some people."

Just then a man walked up and said, "Excuse me but I need to talk to him", and led Lawyer P aside. I could hear him telling the lawyer about the great trouble he had gone to getting the allotted number of roses. The lawyer quickly brushed the man off and returned to where I was standing.

"Sir,' I said, "I couldn't help but overhear what that man said to you. Could you explain what he meant by the allotted number of roses?'

"Mrs. White specifically requested (there was that phrase again) two thousand forty-one roses here today. The man was probably trying to justify the preposterous bill he will be sending."

"Why two thousand forty-one roses?' I asked.

"Never mind, there isn't time for that now; we'll discuss it later," he said as he took me by the arm and led me to the nearest canopy.

We walked up to two women, both about forty years of age. The one he called Sandra Smith, was brunette with subtle streaks of gray and dark searching eyes. She was thin, taller than me, and wore high heels. I found myself having to look up at her or I would be staring straight at the beautiful pink shell brooch she was wearing at the throat of her dress. The second woman Brenda Jones was a redhead. She was much shorter than the first woman and a little heavier. She wore high heels and even with them she was probably making the same choice between looking up to me or at my throat; I was almost sorry I hadn't worn a brooch for the occasion. "These two dear ladies are Mrs. White's agent and editor respectfully," Lawyer P said.

I was thinking about their names Jones and Smith and smiled; in fact, I almost laughed out loud. They must have read my mind, because they interrupted each other with comments about the names before I could say a word. I wondered if Lawyer P was buttering them up because he thought of writing a book, possibly one about the late Mrs. White. He wasn't being nice to them without a good reason; this I knew from watching him with other people. I hoped if he was planning a book that he would wait until he got over being upset about losing out on the estate or, I was afraid, he would not do the old lady justice.

When he told them my name was Jennifer Stone, both of their faces lit up and they fell all over each other trying to be the first to shake my hand. Did they know something I didn't know? Why did my name set them off like that, I wondered, but we didn't stay with the ladies long enough for me to find out before he excused us and led me off to meet some other people.

This went on for a while and everybody was reacting to my name pretty much as Sandra Smith and Brenda Jones had done. Lawyer P was either enjoying himself at my expense or he wanted me to meet all these people to show them he was not upset about losing out as he had.

Word quickly spread among the crowd that I was Jennifer Stone and everyone was looking at me and talking in hushed voices. I managed to slip away from the lawyer at one of his intended introductions and hide behind a giant coffee urn. I was tired of his game whatever it was and besides my feet were killing me. I found a chair and sat down still out of sight of the lawyer and took off my right shoe and began rubbing my foot.

"Are you really Jennifer Stone?" A deep male voice asked from behind.

I turned toward the voice and asked rather sharply. "Who wants to know?"

"My name is Michael Black and I'm not asking for myself but for my readers. I'm a reporter for the Times," the man said stepping around the table and walking toward me.

"What's the big deal about my name, anyhow? Have I missed something here?"

"Miss Stone, if you are Miss Stone? You know what the big deal is."

"I am Jennifer Stone!" I said getting more and more frustrated by this whole thing. "Now do you mind if I ask you a question? What is all this fuss about my being Jennifer Stone?"

He laughed out loud and I drew back my shoe ready to throw it in his face. I must have looked really funny but he managed a straight face and I put the shoe back on in case of further temptation.

"Let's begin again, shall we?" he said softly. "I am Michael Black."

"And I am Jennifer Stone," I replied.

"You really don't know, do you?"

"Don't know what?" I asked him.

"The importance of you being who you are," he said as he pulled a worn copy of a book from his trench coat pocket and held it out to me. "Read the dedication," he said, watching me closely for my reaction.

I took the book from his hand and looked at the cover. It was an Elizabeth Windom White book, an early one judging from its condition, or he had been carrying it around with him for quite some time. The title was not one I recognized, and I had read and reread her books all my life. "She doesn't have dedications in her books," I said as I opened the book.

The copyright date was 1912; it was indeed an early book. "I didn't know that she had written anything before 1915," I said aloud. He said nothing but continued to watch me. Curious I turned to the dedication page as he had said to do and read the words slowly, *I dedicate this and all future books I may come to write to Jennifer Stone.*

I must have fainted because when I opened my eyes again I was on the couch in the living room and Michael Black was standing over me. Remembering the book he had handed me and the dedication I had read, I reached for his hand. He moved closer and stooped down beside the couch

I hadn't realized before how handsome he was with his long, straight blond hair and his tan. His eyes were green and warm and his laugh, for he was now laughing at something someone in the room had said, was the most haunting laugh I had ever heard. He looked like something from the same page of the history book I had stepped out of earlier in his old style suit and his stiffly starched shirt with its wide deep green tie. The tie brought out the green of his eyes perfectly. I felt so comfortable holding his hand, like I had known him for years instead of the few minutes it actually had been. Mrs. White would have said we had known each other in other lives; perhaps we had. It was a romantic enough notion and it suited the clothes we were wearing and the old lady we had come to put to rest.

Lawyer P stepped from behind the couch where he had been trying to shush Michael and to get my attention. I wondered how much longer I was going to have to look at his disappointed face. If having the estate meant he would be hanging around I would take back any idea I might have entertained of Mrs. White having a sense of humor. This man was anything but funny.

One thing I had caught between shushes, that the lawyer was repeating now that I must read the eulogy; it was a condition of the will. I sat up and felt weak; at Michael's urging I lay back down. The room stopped spinning after awhile and I pulled Michael closer. "Go to the attic; there is a box there very near the attic steps with some books in it. Get Mrs. White's 'Helena' and bring it to me, please."

Michael stood up, let go of my hand and turned to leave the room. Lawyer P took him by the arm to stop him. He turned and spoke sharply to the lawyer. "Let go of my arm."

Lawyer P. did so but then looked glaringly at me and said, "I will not have him roaming freely about this house; he has no right."

"He has every right," I said. "Have you forgotten I am the owner of this house and unless I am mistaken you work for me, not the other way around?" The room grew quiet. All eyes were on me. Lawyer P. stood red faced with his head bowed for the few minutes until Michael's return.

I sat up slowly as several people reached out to help me. I said thank you to Michael and took the book from his hand. I searched for the scene of Helena's impending death and noted the page number, then I stood up and carrying the book I walked past the lawyer. Michael came to me and I leaned on him as we walked out to the waiting crowd together. We crossed the lawn and people applauded as they saw us coming and stepped aside to clear a path.

Michael walked with me until I was very near the podium and then tried to break away. I begged him not to go and he walked beside me up the few steps to the microphone and sat down in one of the chairs behind me. Lawyer P had sullenly followed us and sat down in the end chair as far from Michael as he could get. I stood leaning on the podium with the book laid out in front of me and turned to the page I was to read. I looked out over the crowd of people all seated now in chairs that had been arranged in rows during my absence. Everyone grew quiet. I waited and thought of what to say.

"My name is Jennifer Stone," I began and they all stood and applauded. Tears came to my eyes and I reached in my dress pocket for a handkerchief. It fell to the floor and as I bent to pick it up Michael put it in my hand. I squeezed his hand gratefully and stood up. My head was pounding and everything grew blurry. I closed my eyes and prayed for the strength to finish. When I opened my eyes again I lowered my head to read.

"Helena found herself thinking about her father and her brothers who had died with the sea and felt all the more a part of it, though something felt different about it all, as of late.

She wondered if she was getting old. The aches and pains her old mother had talked about for years were starting to be her aches and pains. Yes, she must be getting old, she decided, and to think about the others who had gone on before her was only natural.

Perhaps her own time was near; if so, she would be ready. She preferred the sea to being an old woman in a rocker on shore again. She would never give up the freedom of the open sea with the wind and the smell of the salt air. She might only be able to mend the nets or carry the meals to the men at their post, but to be on shore again waiting for death or boredom to kill her; never, she vowed. She would throw herself overboard first and let the saints worry about her soul. She had never believed that strongly anyhow.

What had the church done for her or hers except take the little bit that they did have in times of bad catches? What had they given in return but threats to their immortal souls? While she didn't doubt that she had a soul and that it was immortal she wasn't too sure about any of the rest of it. She was especially doubtful that the church had some kind of magic that would save you from your fate in the hereafter.

The more she thought about it the more she was certain that her time was near and she meant to be at sea when it happened if she had to crawl. She had waited too long to get to sea and she had earned her right to be there as surely as any of the men. She would keep quiet and hold on a little longer and the sea would be hers forever. She knew it meant too much to her to be otherwise.

The rain started as they came in one evening and by morning the skies were black. The winds were cold and strong and all of the boats stayed in, the men taking this time to mend things that needed mending.

Helena was urged by them to take the day off and stay at home with the women, which she finally agreed to just to quiet them. After only a few hours of listening to her old mother groan and her sister-in-law complain about her work, she dressed and went down to the boats. She had been fishing too long; she was not for sitting around the kitchen any more getting old and forgetful.

She was teased by the men when she came in sight of them and for a moment she saw herself as a young girl walking with her papa and she was begging him to take her to sea with him. She could hear all of her brothers laughing and teasing her and she could feel herself growing angry and yelling at them. They would tease her all the more when she got red faced and loud and she knew this but still she couldn't help it. The visions faded with papa making them leave her alone.

She realized now that she had only a day or two at most to live, and that it was all happening for her the way it had happened for her papa and others she had heard of. There was always this very real remembrance of something from long ago. She would not mention it to anyone and she would be at sea when her time came; she promised herself this. The storm would pass and she would be at sea.

The next morning she was up with the others, dressed and ready with an urgency she hadn't known since her first days at sea. After listening to her mother and watching her totter about with her mind on things and people that were years past, she was glad for the feeling she was having about her end being near. To her anything was better than giving up the sea and growing old.

She patted her old mother on the head, kissed the sleeping children, and said good-bye to her sister-in-law. Her brother was just putting on his boots; so she left the house and started the walk down to the waiting boats.

She stopped outside the gated yard. The morning was quiet, light just beginning to clear the distant hills. She could see the outline of the many boats casting eerie shadows against the sky. She stood locked in the moment and felt the presence of the only god she could ever accept.

Here in this beauty, on this hillside, the breeze slightly stirring, here was her church. She believed this might be the last time she would see her village and hear the laughter of her people. She could stand on this hill forever but she would be forgotten. After today her name, Helena Ostoroff, would only be whispered in the tiny chapel among the candles and the prayers.

I put the book down and looked out at the crowd. "I'm sure you all recognize this as an excerpt from her book 'Helena'. There is also a letter I am supposed to read to you. It begins…

Dear Friends,

Thank you for coming today to see me off on my next adventure; I would ask that you remember me not for my works, but for myself, and the times I have spent with each of you, for that is what I will be remembering until we meet again. Perhaps the next time you will write the stories.

Each of you carries a part of me with you and for that reason I know I will never truly die.… we are just parted for a while and we will know each other again in another life or two. Treat the world kindly, take special care of her forest and, yes, even the lowly tree in your own field of vision.… Until then, good-bye for a little while.… Elizabeth.

I stepped down from the podium and joined the crowd. And we said our good-byes after awhile. As the last of the guests began to drive away I caught Michael's attention and asked him to stay. He agreed but at Lawyer P's insistence was to wait in the house.

Now the private service was to begin; only a young man named Travis, Blanche, the lawyer and I remained. Together we walked along a shaded brick pathway towards the southwest corner of the property to a small fenced in area. I noticed very old stones, some with no dates given. I wondered about one pair of nicer stones bearing the names, T. and Ellen Williams; I knew they weren't her parents; the name was wrong. Two smaller ones belonged to Harvey and Bea Williams, and a still smaller set read Mark and Nancy. More questions, ever more questions.

Before us there was a canopy with a handful of chairs and the ever-sickening sight of piled dirt. I grew anxious and nauseous. Funerals brought out the worst in me. It was all so final. Letting go was something I had done all my life until I had nothing to hold to. felt empty and alone, always alone.

There were two silver caskets framed on three sides with white doves and lilies. Close beside each other they formed a single picture. Both caskets were new and clean, sparkling in the little sun shining through the now budding trilogy of trees. Damn! Now I realized there were two caskets and that meant two bodies, and I had no idea who the second one belonged to.

Soon the silence was broken by a soft male voice to my right and I was drawn to it. I looked to see who was speaking and saw that it was Travis, the young man who had so graciously landed Lawyer P's red flower on the ground earlier. His hands were gesturing as he spoke. I watched and listened. He was reciting the Song of Solomon and telling Blanche with his hands.

The service was over in a few minutes. The others began to walk away and lost in thought I hadn't noticed, so I was the last to leave the small family cemetery, closing and latching the gate as I did. Lawyer P was a few feet in front of me so I ran to catch up. "Who is in the second casket?" I asked.

"Her son, Joey, he died two days before her," was his answer. Then handing me the device that opened and closed the gate, he added, "I can't be angry with the dead; it isn't fitting," walked to his car and drove away.

Boy in the Picture Girl up a Tree

1926

It was the first day of the new school year and twelve year old Morgan was not happy; he had just had the worse summer of his life. Everyone in town knew about Merlin, and the kids had haunted him until he had retreated to the house and the orchard to escape them. Now with school starting he would be at their mercy and so far, he felt, they had showed no mercy.

Dressed and ready he sat down on his bed and waited for his mother to call him to breakfast, remembering the night four years ago when he had seen the old magician. How could he forget? If not the exciting and magical man himself, then certainly the teasing even the adults had engaged in. His life had changed since that night; just how much he himself could not believe.

His Uncle Edward had told him of a similar encounter with Merlin when he was a boy. He had also given Morgan the book *Time Travel* by H. G. Wells to read on the ship coming home, and that book had begun his search. He would prove to himself if not to the world that he had met Merlin. He believed to do that was somehow tied up in the subject of the book, which he had read on the ship coming home and at least a dozen times since.

When he had written to Uncle Edward about the book, his uncle had sent books about Merlin. Young Morgan had studied these and begged for more and always his uncle sent them, never once saying he was too young for this book or that book. Morgan loved him most of all for this. In some ways his uncle was as young as he was, but in other ways they were both as old as time.

To escape the town's children, Morgan had spent the summer reading and studying Merlin and time, and a new subject his uncle had introduced him to, meditation.

His uncle and Old Ned were the only two people who believed he had seen Merlin. Even Happy, who had grown to become his dearest childhood friend, thought he had made it up, like the legionnaire and the camel, the German spy on the ship, and the dragon on their Grandparents' lawn. He had long ago stopped talking about it to anyone, but it was too late. The children, who had always found him different, now had a very effective weapon against him.

"Morgan," his mother called and he went down to breakfast meeting Happy, Julia, and Sarah on the stairs. It was Sarah's first day of school and she was as excited as he was depressed. Morgan sat sullen at the table barely eating; only Happy knew why. A knock at the door saw him on his feet and away from his plate. Being too upset to eat, he welcomed any excuse to leave the table.

Opening the door he found himself face-to-face with Andrew and Rebecca Hays, and speechless. Maybe today wouldn't be so bad after all, he thought, unable to believe his good luck. He had been watching eleven-year-old Becky all summer wanting to meet her and there she was standing at his front door.

Bea came up behind Morgan before he could say a word. "Hello Andrew," she said softly and Andrew turned beet red as all the Williams children stood looking at him. Minutes later they started out with Bea and Andrew leading the way to school. Morgan, Becky, Happy, Julia, and Sarah side by side walked behind them.

Happy kept walking into Becky to get her closer to Morgan while Morgan kept looking daggers through Happy to get her to stop. He was embarrassed and red faced and falling all over himself trying to maintain some sense of dignity. A horn honked and they separated, running to the side of the road to get out of the way. When the car passed, the three young girls ran on ahead trying to catch up with Bea and Andrew, to bother them for a while, Morgan hoped. He also hoped Bea would know how to handle the little cupids so he could walk to school in peace.

He and Becky were quiet the whole way. When they reached the schoolyard Morgan could see the others whispering and pointing. Laura Jenkins grabbed Becky by the arm and pulled her away. Someone shouted, "Merlin," and they all joined in, repeating it over and over till the bell rang and their teacher appeared at the school door to welcome them.

It was the same thing at recess though they kept their voices down so as not to be heard by the new teacher. Coming home they were louder and running after him. Happy, big for her age and twice the fighter most of them were, jumped out of the path in front of them; scared half to death they stopped and walked home the long way.

Later when Happy caught up with him he wanted to thank her but he couldn't find the right words so he started talking about the new teacher. They walked home together and to school together the rest of the year. The kids not daring to tease him where Happy could hear them, soon lost an active interest in him and Merlin and lost themselves in their love affair with the new blond teacher, Melanie Ferguson.

Becky forgotten in the excitement, he had gone to Old Ned with questions that had no answers, or so the old man said. He had tried to understand love, he told Morgan, ever since he had first felt the pangs of it himself many years ago when his cousin Nell visited with her parents from North Carolina.

Later in the school year when Miss Ferguson announced that she was going to marry Reverend Barker, all the boys moaned aloud with the pain of a dozen hearts breaking. Morgan shot up out of his seat and ran from the classroom.

Outside in the cold wind of a promised winter storm he stopped and thought of his coat and hat. He shook his head no, deciding not to go back. He never wanted to see her again. Tears filled his eyes and his heart ached. There was nothing to do now but go on home. The kids would laugh at him if he went back; Miss Ferguson would laugh. No, Morgan was sure she wouldn't laugh, but what she would do he didn't know.

When he came in the kitchen door of his house he was half frozen. Only moments after he shut the door snow began to fall. Dipping himself a cup of soup from the pot kept hot on the back of the stove, he held the cup in his hands for warmth, backed up to the fire, and tried to warm himself.

He hurt everywhere, and tears once again filled his eyes. He vowed never to fall in love again; it hurt too much and besides that there was the embarrassment when you couldn't think or talk straight in her presence. All of it hurt too much.

An hour later when his sisters came home from school he still stood before the fire with the cup in his hand, mourning his loss. The girls were unusually quiet and seemed sad. He wondered what this had to do with them and then as if answering his thoughts, little Sarah shouted, "Who will be our teacher now?", and burst into tears.

Bea held Sarah and turned to Morgan. "Miss Ferguson wants to talk to you. She's waiting for you at school. We brought your coat and hat home for you; they're hanging on the back porch. Oh, and Morgan, better not mention coming home without them to Mama or she'll grease you up and give you cough medicine, and all of us too."

Morgan sat the cup down on the table, thanked Bea half smiling, and went out the door remembering how the mixture of possum grease and kerosene used on them for colds blistered poor Happy; and how their mother would put even more on her, swearing the whole time that Happy had blistered on purpose just to get out of wearing the stuff. The home made cough medicine was just as bad. Bea was right; he would keep the coat and hat business to himself, and he knew the others would too. The cure was much worse than a cold.

The day had grown colder and his coat and hat were wet with snow. He put them on and tried to forget the cold and turned his thoughts to Miss Ferguson, wondering what she wanted with him and how he would be able to face her.

Miss Ferguson walked the floor from her desk to the window watching for Morgan. She hoped she hadn't made a mistake asking one of her students to come out in this weather. She had no idea what she would say to him when he got here; she only knew she had to talk to him. The hurt in his eyes when he left today was something that haunted her. Yes, she told herself, she had been warned that one of her students might have a crush on her from time to time, but how was she supposed to cope when every boy in class seemed to be in love with her? She certainly hadn't been prepared for this. Besides, Morgan showed more promise than a hundred boys and she had to be sure he returned to school. Glendale was a small town, and word would get out; and she feared the dear, sweet, sensitive boy would once again be the butt end of a joke.

Her thoughts were interrupted by a repeated thumping sound. She walked to the door and opened it. Morgan stood on the small porch trying to stomp the snow off his boots and brush it from his shoulders. Taking his hat off and giving it a good hard shake, he looked up too late. The snow flew right in Miss Ferguson's face and he was once again apologizing. It seemed to him that all he was ever doing with her was blushing, stumbling, and apologizing.

"Come in and stand by the fire," she said. Morgan hesitated. "Never mind your boots; the floor will be nastier than this tomorrow when everybody gets here. I'm sorry to call you out in all of this but we have to talk."

Morgan came in and closed the door behind him. He looked around the empty classroom grown dark now with the stormy day. It looked different to him, as if he'd been away for years instead of a few hours. He walked to the front of the room to get what warmth he could from the dying fire. The wood box stood empty and the trash can full; and today's assignments were still on the blackboard.

It felt so strange being alone here with her. Morgan half expected Reverend Barker to come barging in the door pointing his long thin finger at him shouting, "Thou shall not covet..." He stopped himself short with the unnerving sound of floorboards squeaking loudly as he walked, making each step more frightening to him than even the prospect of the preacher putting in a sudden appearance.

How many children, he wondered, had been scared out of their wits over the years by those same squeaking boards when they had jumped to their feet upon hearing their names called, terrified they would not be able to answer the teacher's question. How many boys had acted out tonight's scene over love of a pretty schoolteacher? He walked on, trying to forget the sound of his feet hitting against the squeaky boards.

He stood in front of the stove now. To avoid her eyes he kept his head turned away from her, looking instead at her desk and the neatly folded flag on it. A stack of thick, dark books lay in the far corner.

She spoke and he tried to hear her over the pounding of his heart. Looking around the room he noticed the rows of empty desks and the papers on many of them. He tried to remember who sat at each desk and to picture them there reading the carefully graded papers but his imagination failed him. He was alone, alone with his teacher and he wanted to cry.

"I don't know where to begin," he heard her say.

"Miss Ferguson, I'm sorry about leaving the way I did," Morgan blurted out.

"It's okay, Morgan; that's only part of what I wanted to talk to you about. I know that some of the boys like me; they like me a lot. I know that you are one of those boys and I'm sorry I hurt you when I told you I was going to be married. I hope that you and I can remain friends.

The boy stood staring at the floor and said nothing. His heart was breaking; what was there to say? He was only twelve years old; he couldn't compete for her love. He wouldn't know how or where to begin.

"Morgan, did you hear me? I said I hope that we can be friends."

He remained silent. She watched him and waited for some sign that he was listening. The snow had grown deeper and was now up to the low sills of the floor length windows of the school. The wind was up too; she could hear it whistling around the door. She knew they needed to talk and get home.

"Morgan," she said sternly and with a new urgency. "I know you're disappointed, but you're so young. Don't you see how very young you are? You still have so much to learn. You are different, Morgan, not like the other children. You are very special and dear to me. Hate me if you must but please don't stop coming to school. You have a great mind. You can be anything you want to be. Please don't let this, don't let me or anything else stand in your way."

"I'm alright," Morgan said. "I never planned to quit school. I'm going to be an archeology professor like my Uncle Edward, or maybe a history professor."

"Then you will return tomorrow."

"Yes, ma'am, it will be awkward but I will come." the boy answered.

"You are so dear to me; you are like a little brother. Can we still be friends?"

"We can be friends," he said, "but Miss Ferguson, I have seven sisters; I don't really need another."

She laughed softly at his words. Oh how he loved her laugh and the way she threw her head back. He loved the way her eyes sparkled and her upswept hair with its wisps of curls on the back of her neck, her walk, everything about her. He stopped himself. This would be the last time he would think of her that way. He would think of other things. He would keep busy and study hard. In a few more years he would be going to England to study, perhaps to stay.

"There will be other young ladies for you to care for, Morgan, girls your own age."

"I'm sure there will be," he answered, "but I must go home now; my family will be worried."

"If it's any consolation, the other boys were as upset as you were. You have plenty of company on this it seems. I doubt they'll tease you about this the way they do about Merlin."

"You know about Merlin?" he asked, surprised. He stopped on his way to the door, looking straight at her for the first time.

"Yes, Morgan, and I think it's a beautiful possibility. The world is full of beautiful possibility, never forget that."

"I won't," he mumbled, opening the door to a strong wind and struggling to keep hold of it. Together they fought to close the door behind them as they went out into the storm and on their separate ways.

The wind was blowing hard in his face taking his breath away. He could barely stand up and fought to see in the swirling snow. A wide field lay before him, and in the near distance he could see the snow covered trees of the orchard like white lace against the night sky. Everything was blanketed in the fine white blowing powder, even him. He thought that he could lie down now in this and be covered over and give up. He could give up to the taunting of the town's children, or he could push on. Push hard against the wind, against life, against time itself, until he had his answers. He walked on remembering her words; the world is full of beautiful possibility.

The Williams house stood tall and as white as the snow beyond the orchard. He was almost home now with only the acres wide yard before him. Old trees with ghostly snow laden branches towered above the roof of the big house. It was a welcome sight although strange and unfamiliar with the storm's handiwork, which had left everything blanketed in white. He knew it was the biggest house in town but he hadn't really noticed before how truly big it was or, he thought, perhaps it just looked so big because he was feeling small, tired, beaten, and chilled through by the force of the wind.

Opening the screen door he stood partly shielded from the wind. He shook the snow from himself and kicked his boots against the wooden door that still lay between him and warmth. When he opened the door the heat from the kitchen hit him hard in the face. He felt faint and braced himself against the doorframe for a minute before closing the door behind him and succumbing to the warmth of the room and the much needed break from the wind.

Papa was sitting at the kitchen table with a pot of hot tea and two cups, Morgan noticed. A plate covered over with a clean dishtowel was in the center of the otherwise empty table. "Get out of your wet things," his father said. "There are warm dry clothes for you on top of the firewood."

Morgan was anxious to do just that. He was frozen through but he also questioned the motives behind his father's friendliness. He sat down to pull off his boots and wet socks first. His slippers, warm and dry before him, looked more inviting now than he ever would have thought. He was by nature a boy who liked to go barefoot and had been reprimanded more than once for running around the house without slippers, but tonight the slippers, with their soft woolen linings, beckoned to his half frozen feet. Soon his wet clothes were on nails behind the stove to dry and he was in warm woolen underwear and a thick heavy winter robe sitting at the table with his father.

He prayed someone would come into the kitchen to break the long silence, but no one did. A closed door separated them from the rest of the household. He was sure his sisters were all whispering over their sewing and their schoolwork in the front parlor, as afraid of breaking the silence as he was; though break it he felt he must. "Papa, when did you get home?" he said, almost choking on the words.

T., who was called by his middle initial, which didn't stand for anything, smiled at his son. "I arrived about the time you set out on your return trip to school. Didn't you hear the train? Of course you didn't," he said, answering his own question. "You had other things on your mind. Did you and your teacher settle matters between you?"

"I think so," Morgan mumbled, bracing himself for the lecture he knew was coming.

"Then will you be returning to school tomorrow, son?"

"Yes, Papa, I'll be returning. I'm truly sorry for walking out like I did."

"Did you tell your teacher that?"

"Yes Sir, I did."

"Then the matter is settled. Eat your supper; your mother has saved you a plate. I will pour the tea and you and I will talk about something else."

The shocked boy reached for the plate his father had uncovered and pushed toward him. He was in no mood for teasing and it looked very much to him as if his father was. The night wasn't over yet, he told himself, tired as he was, still half frozen despite the warm kitchen and the dry clothes. The food looked wonderful as he took the fork from his father's hand. He wanted to inhale it. Lunch had been hours ago, he noticed looking at the clock on the shelf beside the kitchen door. They both held the fork now, as his father had not let go; his hand was now over Morgan's, and the boy trembled.

"I have teased you long enough, son," he said letting go of the fork. "I have a story to tell you. It's a long story. Would you be interested in hearing it, or are you too tired?"

"I would be interested," Morgan said, relishing any time his busy father could find for him.

"I can well remember my own first love. Would you care to listen to an old man reminisce? Perhaps you will draw comfort from the story knowing that first love is all a part of becoming a man." The boy and his father were a long time at the table talking. Morgan was warm, full, and happy, though tired through.

The next four days he was in bed with a terrible cold. He needed the time; he welcomed the time to get over Miss Ferguson. When he was well he went to Old Ned for some magic because he felt nothing less than magic would ease his pain. He explained his problem and the old man disappeared into a back room without a word. Morgan sat waiting lost in thought. After awhile he heard the door open and close again. He looked up. His friend handed him a potion, wrapped in a bit of cloth, which he said was to be mixed in a hot cup of tea and drunk down fast. Morgan thought it sounded a lot like the medicine his mother gave all the kids for a cold and he told Old Ned so. Ned laughed and agreed that they were somewhat alike but it was all he could do for him so take it or leave it. Morgan took the potion with gratitude, promising Old Ned the moon in exchange, but the old blacksmith settled for a little help in cleaning up the shop. The dirty, tired, grateful boy, potion in hand, ran home at dusk.

Putting a pot of water on to boil he gathered up the cup and a teaspoon of loose tea, emptying the potion into the tea. Hiding the rag it was tied up in deep in his pants pocket, he sat dreamy eyed at the table staring out the window. It was a clear cold February night, the sky covered with stars, the moon full. School was almost over for the year. He thought of Miss Ferguson a lot and found himself wondering if she was watching the night sky, like him, or perhaps grading his history paper.

He loved history, he loved the past but she brought it alive for him. He could almost smell the ink the Declaration of Independence was signed with, hear the debate of the signers, and feel the warmth of the July day so long ago. He could hear the muskets firing, the horses' hoof beats, and the men crying out in battle. No wonder he loved her; she was so much like him, as blond, as blue eyed, as excited about history.

She was the one who had presented him, and of course the whole class, with the notion of interviewing an older person about some important historical happening they had witnessed firsthand. Until then he had not realized the gold mine of information living in his own town. There were many older people who had come from other countries with different histories; things that were not found in his American History book, Old Ned's Jamaica, his parents' England, Mr. Kruger the miller's Germany.

Summer came at last and beginning when the children were quite young, a photographer had come every year in early summer to record their growth. Morgan being the only boy always had his picture taken alone and then with the whole family. He arrived at the foot of the stairs this year holding a book in his hand, as the photographer was just setting up his camera; the photographer thinking it an interesting touch included the book in his picture.

When the children gathered for the group picture Happy was nowhere to be found, and the other children were dispatched to different parts of the house to look for her. Morgan totally disregarding instructions from Mama on where to look had gone to the orchard and Happy's favorite tree where he found her hanging upside down.

"You came to read to me," she shouted to Morgan as he approached with the book still in his hand.

"Maybe later," he shouted back to her; "right now you are wanted in the house to have your picture taken."

"Promise," she pleaded and he did promise as they raced back to the house together. After the pictures were taken they spent the day as they often did with Happy hanging from a tree in the orchard, and Morgan sitting on the ground reading to her.

Two Days in March

1951

I stood in the yard watching the lawyer drive away thinking about Mrs. White's son. It started raining again and I pulled my hood up and the cape tight around me; as I looked around the yard I saw that the canopies were being taken down.

Turning toward the house I saw Michael on the porch patiently watching me, giving me time. He had taken off his suit jacket and his tie. His collar button was undone and with his suspenders showing he looked more comfortable. The casual look became him, unlike the starched toy soldier look he had earlier. I hurried inside.

"Mrs. White died on the 6th so her son would have died on the 4th. Is there any significance to those dates?" I asked him as soon as I came up on the porch.

"What son?" he questioned.

"Joey," I answered

"How do you know he died on the 4th?"

"The private funeral I just attended was for her and her son."

"I had forgotten that she had a son named Joey; I thought he was just a character in a book."

"The book you have?" I asked him.

"Yes, Jennifer, in the book she used her own name and she had a son named Joey. He had some kind of mental problem. She explains it better than I ever could."

"You mean he was crazy? Can I borrow your copy?" I asked, though I didn't like borrowing or lending books.

"No, not crazy - slow, strange; she had a name for it. There must be a copy of the book here in the house somewhere," he said, avoiding my question about borrowing the book. "Which room is hers?"

"The attic; will you help me look?" I asked, taking off my cape and hanging it on a hook on the porch to dry. I led the way into the house; it was growing dark so of course the lights came on in the kitchen and the light game commenced. When we left the dining room the lamp in the upstairs hall came on, and by this time I could tell Michael was as confused as I had been last night though he didn't say anything. I propped the attic door open by pushing a nearby box of books against it and led the way up the few steps to the attic.

At first glance it seemed there were no books in the room. There were no shelves, no desk, nothing that would give this room the appearance of having belonged to a writer. We were ready to give up and leave when Michael noticed the two books on the little table under the dormer that I had forgotten.

I followed him to the table and we each picked up a book. Mine was a copy of *A Place in Time*, the book we were looking for. I opened it and inside Mrs. White had written, "Jennifer, I have waited nearly forty years to give this book to you, I hope you like it. Love, Elizabeth Windom White, March 4th 1951." According to Lawyer P that would have been the day her son died and I wondered if she had penned the message to me before or after his death.

I continued to turn the pages, looking for the dedication page, hoping somehow I would not find my name there. Michael had been reading over my shoulder and must have also read my mind because he laughed. To get his mind off the dedication I asked him the name of the book he had and he showed it to me; it was *The Journals of Louisa May Alcott*. Now I remembered why March 4th and March 6th, the dates of her and Joey's death, had seemed so familiar to me but it would be months before I would know the real significance of these two dates. I put the

Alcott book down and took *A Place in Time* downstairs with us. Since Michael had read the book, I hoped we could discuss it over supper. "Are you hungry, I asked?"

"Yes, and supper is in the oven; I fixed it to have something to do while I waited," he said.

We started through the dining room and I could tell he was trying to ignore the lights but I knew from my own experience it took more time for it to feel natural. "It's a lot like having an invisible maid, isn't it?" I said, and he laughed and shrugged it off. He wasn't going to say a word if it killed him so I changed the subject.

"Supper smells good," I said as we opened the kitchen door but it was lost on him because when the lights went out behind us, he turned and gave the dark room the most ridiculous look. I burst out laughing. He turned red and I laughed harder. Finally he laughed too.

"It's spooky," he said of the lights. "I wonder what turns them off and on and why?"

"No spookier than anything else around here, like a son that even her best friends don't know about. Maybe she was afraid of the dark," I added.

Michael interrupted me at this point, "I am not one of the old lady's best friends. I met her when I was a junior in college and she came to speak. I did some research for her on Hungary for her Sandor book. I never saw her again after that but I loved her books so when I got an invitation to come today, I came as a reporter and as a fan, nothing more."

"When did you get your invitation, Michael?"

"I got it about a week ago. Why?"

"Didn't it strike you as funny that you received an invitation to a funeral days before the hostess died?"

"Now that you mention it Jennifer, it is odd. But at the time I was flattered that she asked me to her 'farewell party' as she called it; I didn't think beyond that. You know yourself her books are futuristic. She's always known things no one could explain. She's almost never wrong and when she has been wrong she hasn't been off by much."

"You're right. She probably thought by getting the invitation early people would be too flattered to think about the oddity of the whole thing; that's why so many people showed up."

"Jennifer, I talked to the lawyer about the guest list; everybody showed up."

"You've got to be kidding."

"Scouts honor, everybody showed up. I have it from the man himself." Michael said, as he opened the oven door and pulled out a pan. "Its tuna casserole, the best I could do. Did you know there's not a single piece of meat in this entire kitchen?"

"I didn't know but then I haven't cooked since I came. Yesterday afternoon Lawyer P and I ate on the plane and today I had donuts and coffee with Blanche."

"Where did she find you that you had to fly in?"

"Jersey City. Let's eat. I'm starved," I said, as I got plates out of the pantry. I stood there holding the white everyday dishes for a moment and decided to put them back and get the pretty red ones. This was not every day to say the least, my first hot meal in the house with Michael, whom I swore I'd known for eternities, the unread mysterious book, and a thousand questions.

I asked for Michael's matches and lit candles on the table. He smiled and went to the kitchen for the coffee pot. We sat down together and as we did it seemed for just a moment that we had done this many times before. "The house has a strange effect on me sometimes," I said aloud.

"How so?"

"Just now as we were sitting down I felt as if we had done this many times before."

"Silly girl there's nothing strange about that. We have all of us sat down many times before." I sensed he was having the same thoughts but I would come to learn that Michael often kidded to hide his feelings.

"You know what I mean, this house, and this room with you." He looked uncomfortable so I asked about the book.

He got up and went to the kitchen to get it off the counter where I had placed it earlier and he came back thumbing through the pages as if looking for something. I waited and watched him as he sat back down.

He began eating again and continued to look through the book. After awhile he found what he was looking for. "Here it is, in chapter ten. *'She welcomed the quiet for Joey's sake. He would need time to adjust to his surroundings and the countless relatives that would be here soon. He would need time to remember this yearly reunion and to remember that he would be okay here as he had always been okay here.* And again in the same chapter she says, *'Uncle Morgan, every day is a battle for Joey, a different kind of battle but war just the same,* following a conversation between Uncle Morgan and her about a war."

"What war is she referring to there?" I interrupted.

"Vietnam, and from what she is saying in the book America was in the war."

"I've never heard of Vietnam."

"I hadn't either when I first read the book so I looked it up on a world map. It's real enough; it's in Southeast Asia. Do you want me to go on?"

"Yes please," I said, warming our coffee and sitting back down.

"*He fights to understand, he fights to cope, and he fights to fit in. Almost daily I see the pain of those battles on his face, and yes even on mine. Mother says I worry too much but it's there every second, you can't ignore it. He's so beautiful and yet so fragile. Loud sounds, a harsh look from someone, physical touch, all potentially explosive situations I must be there to explain to him.*"

"Do you need more?"

"Find out if she gave his problem a name. You mentioned that earlier."

"Here at the end of that same chapter, she says, *'She doubted there would be so many self appointed experts on autism back then when the problem didn't even have a name.'* Autism, that's the word. I looked it up when I reread the book about four years ago. There really is very little known about autism. And she's right about the name. It wasn't given a name until the forties."

"What else does it say about him? Come on, don't be bashful; read it to me."

"In chapter nine she says, *'Joey always saw sameness, he loved repetition, sought out the familiar to reassure himself that all was well in his world.'* And later on in that same chapter she says, *'Joey covered his ears and gritted his teeth. I rushed to him knowing the noise would set him off. I had to distract him and looked around for something. Joey's books lay on the ground where we had met up with Uncle Morgan and helped carry the trees. I gently took his hands from his ears so he could hear me. "Son, go get your books; see them on the grass. Take them to the porch; I'll join you in a minute."'* And at the end of chapter nine it reads. *'I looked to Joey contented in the back seat of the car with a Seven-Up, his magazines, and a black 4 by 4 like the dragon he had just taken from his pocket for the first time. It had been there all day, I knew, despite me repeatedly telling him to leave his Hot Wheels at home.'"*

"It was a form of retardation I guess."

"I don't think so, Jennifer. Some of the things she says about him make him seem pretty smart to me. Why don't you read the book and we'll talk about it again after that?" Michael said, closing the book. "It's late and you need to get some rest. I'll call you tomorrow. He got up to leave and tears came to my eyes. I didn't want to be alone but he was right; I was tired and I couldn't very well ask him to stay the night. He would say something practical and he would be right.

After he left I went back to my attic room taking the book with me. I laid it on the bedside table and walked to the window. Looking down I could see the tiny town of Glendale between the still empty branches of the trees; at least I could see her rooftops and imagined the rain glistening on her streets. I longed to walk those streets and become familiar with them and her people. I wanted neighbors I could wave to that would wave back. The shopkeepers on Jackson Boulevard in Jersey City were the only people I knew there. I sometimes walked that busy street buying nothing or some small thing just to see a familiar face. I had noticed when I drove here with Lawyer P. that there were very few shops and they were all at the far end of Main Street. I hoped I would know more than shopkeepers here. I had read that people in small towns were friendly. I hoped they really were and that they wouldn't be standoffish because I talked like a 'damn Yankee'. I would work on my accent though I wasn't too sure I wanted to sound like Ma and Pa Kettle. I thought of Travis, the boy at the funeral, who had read Blanche's hand signals so beautifully. He talked very nicely; maybe I could spend more time with him and learn to talk like him.

I wanted so much to belong here in this tiny community tucked between all these beautiful trees. I wanted to know this place where my comings and goings would be noted and I would be asked to help out in times of need. But I wondered if the fence would keep people out, people

I desperately wanted to get to know. I looked toward the gate at the end of the drive and saw that it was still open and decided to leave it that way. Maybe I would throw away the electronic device and let the gate hinges rust in the open position. Maybe take the fence down to show I wanted to be a part of the town; I had no one to protect like Mrs. White.

Questions filled my mind, I thought about the book and hoped it would help; I walked over to the bed and picked it up. The book's deep gray and white cover reminded me of a wintry night with White House surrounded by tall old trees, immortalized on leather and held still in time.

I got into bed still holding the book, afraid if I let go of it now I would lose it forever. The cover read, *A Place in Time by Elizabeth Windom White*, and showed a snow covered misted over picture of what was definitely this house. I turned the pages slowly once again noting the copy write date of 1912 and the dedication to me, Jennifer Stone, and I read *A Place in Time chapter one. . .*

One Boy Alone

1932

On Morgan's last visits home from college Old Ned had told him he was the one boy alone who had continued to come to visit him, the only boy who had not outgrown him. The other boys' visits had started falling off about the time they discovered girls and by the time they were men they only came if they had work for him. Children he had helped onto their horses or down out of trees were uncomfortable shaking hands with him today. They were sending their children to him now and he was telling his tales of the strange and magic to their sons knowing they too would grow away from him. Old Ned had insisted that Morgan was the only boy who had continued to come visit him as if the years had never happened and now Morgan was holding a letter from home saying he had died.

He wadded the letter up and tossed it across the room. Grabbing his coat he ran out of the building with tear filled eyes, got in his car, and drove to Uncle Edward's. He needed a friendly face, someone who understood.

He sped along the narrow curved roads and minutes later turned into Butler Lane, jerked the car to an abrupt stop, and ran up the massive stairs to the house.

When he reached for the doorknob the door seemed to be pulling away from him by some unseen force; the monstrous thing that always took a lot of handling to push aside now seemed to be floating. As the opening widened the dazed Morgan found himself face to face with his Uncle Edward, who held out his arms to him. Young Morgan fell into them and cried. "Old Ned is dead," he managed to say after awhile.

"I know, I just got a letter from your mother. I've been expecting you. Let's go outside to talk. It's a beautiful day and the sun will cheer you up. I'll have some tea brought out. Have you eaten anything?"

"No, Sir, I don't feel too hungry, but tea would be nice," Morgan said as they walked through the house and out the dining room doors to one of several tables with chairs scattered along the edge of the garden.

They sat in the shadows of the big house for a long time saying nothing. Morgan studied Uncle Edward, thin and tanned from his time on archaeological digs, noticing how his uncle's dark brown hair now streaked with gray made him look more distinguished; remembering back to times in the blacksmith shop when he had studied Ned in just the same way he was now studying Uncle Edward. Both men he loved like fathers. Both men he could not spend enough time with. Both men seemed to have something about them he very much wanted to integrate into his own being; but study as he did, he could not make it his. They were both heroes to him, each for a courage he did not have except in his childish imaginings of duels with dragons. There was a peace about them as if they knew something about life he could only wonder at. He felt empty; he always had felt empty; something was missing if only he knew what it was. They lived life when he only seemed to be going through the motions.

He needed warmth; he needed the sun, and the garden called to him. He stood up and started toward a familiar brick path circling through the endless patches of rainbow colors and haunting scents. "I've been trying to think of life in that town without Ned," he said. "I simply can't imagine it. He's always been there for me. He was my friend."

Edward stood up and followed him hearing the sound of the tea service being placed on the table behind them. "I know he was, Morgan. You have written so much about him over the years I feel I know him too, and I feel a personal loss. Did your mother say how he died?"

"He died alone," the young man replied bitterly, turning to face his uncle.

"Son, we all die alone."

"You know what I mean, I wasn't there. No one who loved him was there. Prejudice, what an ugly word; how can color separate people? He was not a color; he was a man who helped everyone, never mind their color or their prejudices. If color meant to him what it meant to some people I know, Old Ned would have hated all the children and he'd have chased us from his shop instead of drawing us to his big smile and his gentle ways. Once you sat and listened to his magic, his wisdom, you forgot color. You felt safe and good inside."

"Did people make race an issue with the old man?"

"In subtle ways yes."

"Prejudice is learned, Morgan."

"Then I'm lucky my father was not there to teach it to me."

"Morgan, child, it only takes a moment to say "colored" in that way. Your father never said those things because he was not taught it, nor was your mother. I once heard your father say. '*The color of a man's soul is what is important and I think their soul is as white as our own,*' Your father was a good man; he would never have taught you to hate."

"Hate is something we sometimes learn on our own. How did I escape it?"

"To begin with Morgan, prejudice is not always hate. Sometimes it begins as fear and as the fear deepens we hate ourselves for being afraid and we end up saying we hate what we are afraid of. You have faced your fears through the years; I have been a witness to that. I was there to see the eight-year-old boy run to his father and shout out the grand adventure of Merlin in the woods. When it happened to me I crept in the house and up to my room afraid of telling anyone for fear they would think me crazy. I was twelve, not eight; these were my woods, and I grew up on stories of Merlin. But I locked it away never telling anyone until you."

"I had to tell someone."

"Yes, but don't you see you had far more reason to be afraid than I did. Yet you faced your fear by trying to talk to your father about it, and when that failed you told me. Don't be too hard on the people back home; fear is contagious; even the bravest of us can catch it."

"Uncle Edward, there wasn't one damn thing about that old man to be afraid of."

"Not for you but for others. Maybe they hope their sons will do what they couldn't do, look beyond color to the man. The years make all of us strangers to ourselves; I lost the child in me years ago, the good we all begin life with. You have held on to some small part of that. How I don't know. Perhaps your search is responsible. You are looking for the past and it is in the past that these things lie."

"No, Uncle Edward, my search has emptied me. I think without it I would cease to exist. It has consumed me. There is more to life; there must be but I can't let go. I don't feel for people; I don't relate to people unless they can serve me in my search."

"If that is so, lad, then why are you here today? You feel for Old Ned. You love him?"

"Yes, I loved him. And I wonder if it isn't myself I mourn here today?"

"See the meadow over there." His uncle pointed to a wide stretch of open ground at the outskirts of the garden. "That field is for children and kites and the wind on a summer day. It is where the wind and the kite tease each other as the real of the kite and the dream of the wind, something felt but not seen, come together in a perfect blending. You are the eternal boy and the wind and the kite are for you to run with. Your search has not emptied you; it has filled you and I hope it always will.

"When you get too old to dream as I have, as your father has, as the boys from your youth who stopped listening to Ned have; that's forgetting the feel of the kite and the wind pulling you along in their play. Morgan, remember the dream. Remember it for me; remember it for your father; remember it for the boys you grew up with and forgot.

"Let's go back now and have our tea before it gets too cold. You really should eat something and while we eat, you can tell me about Ned's family and how they came to settle and live such a long way from Jamaica."

Realizing he was hungry, Morgan turned at his uncle's suggestion and they walked back each lost in their own thoughts. "Have you ever been to Jamaica, Uncle Morgan?" he asked as they walked past the white lilies, his favorite of all the flowers. He breathed deeply taking in the scent and the color of the fragile whites. "You know, Uncle Edward, if I were to ever plant a garden, I would plant only white flowers, especially lilies and lots and lots of roses."

"That is the most wonderful idea I've ever heard. A white garden! Can you imagine the flowers in the moonlight, like ghosts of every size and shape? Jamaica is a lot like that; it's mysterious. I doubt that I would ever have wanted to leave such a birthplace."

The two men looked to each other and their pace quickened, smiles spread across their faces. The promise of a long and very rewarding day stood before them like the table of waiting food. Young Morgan hurried to the table and stood over it pouring tea with one hand and reaching into the dish of fresh strawberries with the other. His uncle had excused himself and gone into the house to order another pot of tea. Unlike his young American born and raised nephew, he could not endure warm tea.

When he reappeared at the table he carried a large book with the word Jamaica sprawled across the front in tall letters. Young Edward's excitement grew when he saw the book, and he realized for the first time how alike the two men, Old Ned and Uncle Edward, were both eager to learn and to share with others what they had learned, both ready to listen to the boy. He loved them both and he was glad that he had been able to share each of them with the other. Today would be his tribute to the old man of magic he had loved and known all of his life. Today here in this garden thousands of miles away from Glendale, with its grave behind the blacksmith shop, a grave with fresh earth and dying flowers spilled over it, he would plan a white garden in honor of the white souls of all men, most especially the old Jamaican.

Uncle Edward cleared a place for the book and they opened it pouring over pictures of Ned's homeland. The many pictures proved that what his uncle said was true; the cities and the land were clean and well tended and the people with the varied browns and blacks of their skin wore beautiful, richly colored clothes.

The mystery was there too in the legends of a people steeped in magic. The healers, the story tellers, the listeners, all somehow reflected his beloved Ned who with his family had left there at about the same age that Morgan himself had first traveled to a foreign land.

Oh how he wished he too could have stayed in the new land. He wished it then with all of his heart and it was, he knew, part of the pain that stood between him and his father. He had wanted England and his Uncle Edward and his father had said, "No." He had yelled, "I hate you," over and over and clung to his Uncle. His father embarrassed had pulled him away. He thought he saw tears in his father's eyes and he had stopped. He cried the whole way home and tried to draw comfort from the book his uncle had given him there on the lawn that day, inscribed to my little brother Morgan, much, much older than his years, love, Uncle Edward.

He looked up to his Uncle, his older brother, turning pages now in the big book. He talked on about some little known facet of Jamaican life that would not be in a book but typical of the sort of things his uncle could tell him about any number of places he had been to.

The last of the dishes were cleared away, and the book on Jamaica now lay buried beneath a tablet and pages of papers torn from it filled with sketches of proposed white gardens. The wind had grown strong and young Morgan was holding down the corners of a fresh piece of paper on which his uncle was busy drawing yet another replica of the garden's brick and stone paths.

"We must find just the right spot. The garden is quite old you know. We don't want to disturb the tranquility of it by uprooting some long-standing plants. Now lad, tell me about Ned. I assure you I am listening and I very much want to know."

Ned's family found its way to Glendale over sixty years ago and while they had never been the social center of the town, they lived in relative peace. Ned had grown up at his father's side and taken over the business when his father died. At twenty he married Lily, a farm hand's daughter, who though she didn't love him was grateful to him for getting her out of back breaking field work -- work she had seen make old women out of her mother, aunts, and cousins before they were thirty.

"Where is Lily now? Funny but I don't remember you ever mentioning her before." Uncle Edward said looking puzzled.

"She died before I was born and they had no children, except the town's children and Old Ned made friends with most of them sooner or later," young Morgan answered.

"How sad, that a man who loved children so much could have no children of his own. But then it seems that has been my fate too, now that I think about it." Uncle Edward said sounding very distant and staring off.

"Why Uncle Edward I didn't know you were so fond of children. One would never think so the way you avoid certain nieces and nephews." Morgan teased his uncle.

"If you mean my sister, Margaret's children; my God, Morgan, they are so snooty even the queen would not be comfortable with them, but regular children I like well enough."

"Well then, my dear uncle, what about the gardener's three boys?"

"Those three cannot be children; that would not give them enough time to have learned such bad manners. I don't see how the poor man stands them himself."

"They take after their mother, don't you think?" Morgan continued teasing his uncle.

"I say, lad, are you trying to make a point? You know, you may be right. I don't believe there are any children I know that I am that fond of. So it would seem that fate was unkind to Ned and yet kind to me. Thank you for reminding me; for a moment there I was feeling sorry for myself. I have had a good life really, Morgan. I have you, I have work I love, good health, friends; I make a comfortable living; I have family money, and the ancestral cottage."

Morgan frowned at his uncle's words. "Ancestral what?" he asked.

"Does that offend you, lad? It is a bit big to be a cottage, you're right. When you were a boy and you came here, you thought this house and the Williams house were castles? Do you remember that?"

"Yes, yes I do," young Morgan said smiling at his uncle, his face aglow with the wonder of those years.

"It could be called a castle, I suppose. It has enough rooms, enough history, but the true definition of a castle isn't really about size; it is a house that is fortified and has seen battle and so Butler House it remains.

Would you call it something else if it were yours?" Uncle Edward asked staring very intently at his nephew.

"There is no chance of that, but if it were mine, no, I don't think I would."

"Good, then that is settled; it is as I have always suspected; you love the house and I shall pass it on to you." The two men were face to face now, one smiling smugly, the other looking like he had just been given the moon. "Don't look so surprised, lad. Who else would I leave it to, though hopefully I won't have to move out too soon? I'm young yet; thirty-six is young, you know?"

"Yes, Uncle Edward, thirty-six is young, and I hope you live to be a hundred and six. I just never thought you would." Morgan was speechless. How could he tell his uncle that he had dreams both awake and asleep of the house being his one day? Had he studied metaphysics too long; was he becoming psychic? "I have dreams about the house," Morgan added.

"What kind of dreams?" his uncle asked.

"I am in the house and I am in a soldier's uniform. I seem to be hurt and I am trying to get to the north tower. It doesn't make much sense does it?"

"Why not? You could join the service."

"Not this service, Uncle Edward, the uniform is one worn during the First World War," he said staring at his uncle, wanting to know what Uncle Edward thought. He had wanted to tell him by letter when the dreams startled years ago, but he thought the dreams just a childish expression of his yearning for England and his uncle's company. There was nothing either of them could do about that until Morgan was old enough to leave home and move back to England. He continued to study the man's face looking for that first reaction to the impossibility of the dream. All he saw was puzzlement and he had hoped for more.

Uncle Edward was a long time studying the boy's words he had no ready answer though he could see Morgan had expected instant words of wisdom. "Give me a minute, lad. You have had years to study this thing and you have not resolved the matter. Give your old uncle a minute. Let's walk to the center of the garden; I think I have at least one of our problems solved. Come along and bring the papers."

"All of them?" Morgan asked puzzled.

"No, just the one we had last. Come along, now, come along." Uncle Edward repeated.

Morgan grabbed the paper and a pencil for safety's sake. His uncle seemed a bit rattled at the moment and he could see himself being sent back for the pencil or something else before this thing was through. Still it was his white garden they were planning, and putting his dreams aside for a bit wouldn't hurt, he thought, as he hurried after his uncle who was already out of sight. Entering into the spirit of the moment he hurried to the center of the garden, which was a vast circle of brick, all paths leading from that point. He found his uncle on his knees running his fingers along the bricks in the exact center of the circle when he arrived.

"See here, lad, it is just as I thought. Look at the bricks here; they are not like the others. They have been placed here at a later time. See how they come together? They're not uniform like the others. We shall have the gardener dig up these bricks and put your white garden in the center of the whole garden. What do you think? Is that a grand idea or not?"

"It's an excellent idea, Uncle Edward, but are you sure you want to disturb the bricks?"

"But of course, lad; the bricks are not part of the original garden. We won't be disturbing them; we will be putting things right. Just think all these years they have been there in that unnatural way. Do you think the gardener knew and said nothing?"

The two men spent the rest of the day with the head gardener charting out the proposed white garden, the dream forgotten.

The Search

1951

I had finished the book late and planned to sleep in but the sound of birds chirping woke me at ten. I turned over and tried to go back to sleep but found I couldn't. I got up and put on a beautiful tan skirt and white blouse I found in the chiffarobe and passed up all the shoes I saw, not because I didn't like them but because I liked going barefoot. I remembered having read that Kentuckians don't like to wear shoes and laughed thinking maybe I was going to fit in better than I thought.

I picked up my glasses, put them in my skirt pocket, and went downstairs to put on a pot of coffee. It was a beautiful bright sunny spring morning and I felt great despite my late night. While the coffee finished perking I sat on the porch looking out over the beautiful yard and reflected on what I now knew about Joseph White and what he had meant to his mother and the meaning of the white roses strewn over both graves as if they were one.

I knew that love could create such a feeling of oneness between people. I had read it often enough but I had never experienced it for myself. I envied Mrs. White and wondered if I would ever know how she really felt. I wondered too if she might have poisoned herself or something to follow her son so soon to his grave; though I thought it more likely that she had willed herself to death after he was gone.

After awhile I got up for a cup of coffee and began a systematic search of the house. Knowing a writer has to have books and a desk and possibly even a working manuscript, I headed for what was the library though with the doors to all the rooms closed I had no idea of where it might be.

A Place in Time had said it was on the first floor. It also said the first door was locked and that the second door was only a few feet away, so I began by opening doors. The first one was a bedroom; a spacious room in white and oak like the attic, with beautiful peach and white wallpaper and accessories. It looked like it hadn't been slept in for a long time, if ever. The next door was to the bathroom, spacious and all white. I left this door open. Next there was a closet full of linens and lastly a locked door, and the only one left, so it had to be the library. Now I needed to find the key.

I went to the living room. There was in this room, as in all the others, an uncluttered look, giving it a quiet and relaxed feel. Two white sofas faced a giant square coffee table in front of the fireplace. The table held a large vase of white lilies, a pyramid shaped crystal, and a book on Greek Mythology. I picked the book up and glanced through it. It was written in Greek and I remembered having read somewhere that Mrs. White spoke and read Greek.

Along one wall there was a tall oak cabinet. On the shelves were a couple of vases with Egyptian artwork on them. I looked in the vases and found no key. The only other things in the cabinet were large, clear, beautifully shaped crystals, a single statue of an Oriental woman in a black, beige, and red kimono, a small stone replica of the arena in Rome, where Mrs. White had written about dying as a scribe in 79 A.D., and candles of many sizes and shapes, all of them white.

In front of one window were two chairs and a small round table with a linen floor length spread. A single crystal lamp sat on the table. In front of the other window there was a large clay colored pot with a tree that towered to the ceiling. The leaves gave off a soft sweet smell, a hint of which hung in every corner of the room. Until now I had thought incense or even the candles might have been responsible. In the pot at the base of the tree, a tiny bit of white was showing and I stooped to brush the dirt away. It was a small piece of plastic with the word eucalyptus printed on it. I remembered the tree now; Mrs. White had written in one of her books about having them throughout her house. At Christmas instead of a cut tree, she would hang lights and drape ribbons from these trees, saying she could not bear to see so many trees cut and used for such a short while only to be thrown away. She had always been obsessed with a need to plant and preserve trees; no one had understood her urgency. Perhaps I would find the answer here.

Hanging over the fireplace was a painting, in shades of grays and blacks, of the heavens with planets and stars spiraling, sometimes touching each other then appearing to spiral on past and out the other side.

The only furniture here that wasn't white or oak was the shiny black baby grand piano. A book of music was open on the piano to a song I'd never heard of called, 'The Shadow of Your Smile'. I read the composer's names, Paul Francis Webster and Johnny Mandel, and the copyright date 1965. Unlike the numbers on the bottom of the Avon dishes, this was clearly a copyright date. I wondered who played the piano and what the songs in the book were like as I thumbed through it catching titles, like 'Friendly Persuasion,' 'The Green Leaves of Summer,' and 'Anastasia'.

The overall feel of the room and, in fact, of the whole house was one of calm and openness. This must have been for Joey's sake, remembering that she had written in *A Place in Time* that the world of the 1990's had been too much for him, too noisy, too busy, too complicated. She had yearned for a quieter time, she said, and she had found it in this house.

As I started to leave the room my eyes fell upon two large portraits, one of Mrs. White and one of Joey. She looked to be in her late fifties and Joey in his thirties. Her deep auburn hair was up as it was in all of her pictures. She held a big floppy hat with flowers on it and wore a white blouse cut low in the front to show a heart shaped birthmark just above her left breast. I'm sure she never got out in the sun without her hat, which was the style of the day, and she was pale to prove it, but she seemed also to defy the style with cheeks that were a little too rosy to be anything but rouged, and her eyes were dark and round with a faraway look in them.

Joey was small and pale like his mother. His brown hair streaked with gray was worn a little long and parted in the middle as she had mentioned in *A Place in Time*. He wore a white shirt with the collar button undone, his tie knotted very loosely about his neck, a vest, and a double breasted suit coat. His smile was the innocent smile of the very young and his hazel eyes were very green looking at this moment. His youth had been captured in this picture that must have been painted by someone who knew him very well, not just an artist that had been hired for the occasion. I looked closely for a signature and was surprised to find the letters FWW. It could only have been Mrs. White's mother and Joey's grandmother Frances Williams Windom, the woman who had been the little girl in the orchard. Mrs. White had said in her book that her mother drew.

White House stood in the background in both pictures, tall, spacious, and regal. This was a beautiful fairyland of some sort and I felt like Alice. In this one room I closed the door as I left. There was something almost sacred about the feel of the room. It was her room I was sure. More than the attic, more than the library, this room spoke of her. I wanted to preserve the feel of her here, as she had written that Morgan had wanted to seal in the memory of his father.

I went to the dining room and went through all the drawers of the massive china cabinet that hugged an entire wall. I even took a chair over to it and climbed up to look in the bowls and glasses that filled the shelves. I reached behind every upright plate that rested against the mirrored back and felt under the corners of all the lace scarves. Then I reached up on top and brushed my hand back and forth until I felt sure I had covered the whole top. Something I felt very foolish about doing later, since I could not see to do it and Mrs. White at eighty-eight and only five feet tall could not reach to do it. There was no key there.

I stood trying to think of where I would have hidden a key and thought of the attic bedroom but shook my head, no. Going up steps for a key would be too much trouble. Which set me to wondering how the old woman had managed the two flights of steps to go to her room? I considered the possibility of her having made it a little easier on herself when she got older by settling for a room on the second floor. One flight of stairs would be a compromise and it might explain why the attic room looked so bare, so unlived in.

I ran up the stairs to the second floor and started flinging doors open as I hurried down the hall. These rooms were the same uncluttered light oak of the ones downstairs, only the wallpaper was different and the colors of the accessories and pictures.

The bedroom nearest the attic door was done in white and a soft green. I immediately recognized it as Joey's. Shelves lined the walls and on them were rows and rows of tiny cars and trucks. I had never seen anything like them before and walked over for a closer look. I picked up the first one I came to and on the bottom noted the words HOT WHEELS and a date 1968. How escaped me for only a minute, my first thoughts being of the love the boy, Joey, had for them and how exactly aligned they were on the shelves. The dates finally began to sink in and I picked up car after car checking them all the way up to 1990 and none earlier than 1968. I left the room to look for the key elsewhere, feeling confident that I would not find it in Joey's room.

I left all the doors to the rooms open on this floor too, finding none except Joey's that looked as if t had been occupied in years. Mrs. White had not changed rooms so the attic was the only logical place left to look.

I walked upstairs thinking about the dated HOT WHEELS, forced to consider the possibility that Mrs. White was telling a true, although impossible, story in *A Place in Time*.

The only drawers here were in the vanity and the chiffarobe so I began one by one to empty them. I put everything back a piece at a time; unfolding every handkerchief, scarf, and opening every potpourri pouch, I found no key.

I went downstairs for another cup of coffee and a bite to eat. It was then that I noticed for the first time that the dirty plates on the table had been licked clean. My mystery cat had put in another appearance.

I took the tuna casserole out of the refrigerator and put it in the oven to warm. A weird breakfast, yes, but I never ate real breakfast food because I didn't eat anything at all till I had been up for awhile and by then it was lunch time.

I realized I needed to go to the grocery when I looked for milk, thinking I would put some out for the cat, and I found none. With no car I had no idea how I would get there or where the nearest one was. Once again I went to the porch to wait and think. The day had grown warmer and I went out on the steps and sat down. I needed to feel the wind and the sun on my face. I needed to think about being here in this wonderfully peaceful place, though my good luck had been at the expense of two lives. I wondered more and more about their deaths and the cause.

Noticing the front gate was closed, I stood up shocked. How had that happened? I had the only device. Lawyer P had said so when he handed it to me, warning me not to lose it. The gate looked too heavy to have blown closed with the wind, and I hadn't heard the chime. I walked out and tried to open it but found it was locked. I was angry and for just a moment I was afraid. I felt like a prisoner. I went back in the house and got the device out of the kitchen garbage can, wiping coffee grounds off of it with a dishcloth. Back out in the driveway I pushed the button. The chime went off as it had yesterday and the giant gate swung open. I walked back to the house and started inside when I heard my name called.

Trey was running across the yard toward me. I smiled and waited on the steps. "Did you open the gate?" he asked out of breath before he was hardly close enough to be heard.

"Yes, Trey, I did; why?"

"We never leave the gate open, ma 'am."

"Why not?" I asked.

"No reason," he said, lowering his head as if he was afraid he had already said too much.

"Because of Joey?" I asked, waiting for his reaction to my question more than his answer.

He smiled. It was the same smile I had seen yesterday when he had so skillfully removed the red carnation from the lawyer's lapel. He was an intelligent boy, I could tell, and he had the answers to a lot of my questions. I would earn his trust and get my answers. I was sure that he could be trusted for he still had not answered my question about Joey; I respected him for this.

"Trey, "I said, "Joey is dead now. There's no one left to protect. I don't have the need for privacy that the White's had. Okay?"

"Okay," he said smiling again.

Changing the subject, I asked him if he drove and he said no. This complicated things a bit. I thought all young boys drove and I still needed a way to go shopping. I must have looked worried because he asked me what the matter was.

"I need to go to the store for a few things; there is no milk for the..." I stopped myself feeling embarrassed.

"There's a car ma'am. Do you drive? Mrs. White did and I went with her and Joey; I could show you around if you like."

"I'd love that, Trey; when can we go?

"I have a couple of hours of work to do first. Is that okay or do you need to go now?"

"Later is fine, Trey. I need to eat a bite of lunch first. Would you like to join me?"

"No thanks, ma'am, I really do need to be getting back to work." He smiled shyly and started back to the garage. Turning back towards me after a few steps he added, "Joey was allergic to milk. She never bought it."

"Thank you for sharing that with me, Trey, I'll see you later." I went inside and ate, did the few dishes from last night and today, then went upstairs to put on makeup and shoes.

I rechecked my purse to be sure I had the money that Lawyer P had given me at the Newark Airport. Along with receipts for personal debts that had been paid, there was the remaining cash and a checkbook on a local bank. The last entry in the book was dated March 2nd and was a withdrawal for the money Lawyer P had given me on March 5th, the day after Joey's death and the day before Mrs. White's.

She had clearly planned this but from what vantage point I didn't know. Had she killed the boy too, I wondered, perhaps knowing her own death was imminent? I couldn't really believe what I was thinking; a dear sweet old lady like Mrs. White, murder someone, never. Everything she wrote was of the beauty of life, all life. She would not have wanted to leave Joey without a caretaker, but I reasoned, if she was leaving me the house and the money and seems to have planned to do this for some time, why hadn't she asked me to take care of him? But I knew Joey would not have taken the loss of his mother so easily.

She was up in years; she might have planned both deaths knowing she couldn't live forever, and not wanting to wait until she couldn't think clearly enough to take care of matters. And take care of matters she had; they were dead within two days of each other. She had lived just long enough to see him out of harm's way. Still murder and suicide were so foreign to everything Elizabeth Windom White stood for I was back to asking myself if she might have willed it all.

The doorbell rang and I grabbed my purse and ran downstairs. Trey was cleaned up and standing at the door. Behind him in the driveway was a beautiful old Ford, as shiny as a new penny. I smiled proudly as I came across the kitchen and out onto the porch. "Hello," I said.

"Hello ma'am, do you have the gate box? We will need to close it while we're gone." He said shyly.

"Yes, of course," I agreed, and went back for the little black box.

We got in the car and drove out the gate. I paused at the road while Trey turned and pointed the box at the gate and closed it. I turned left as Trey directed me and found myself in beautiful farm country almost immediately.

As we drove along he was chattering away nervously. He seemed married to the earth somehow as he spoke of nothing else but farming. It was refreshing to see someone so obviously untouched by ambition and greed as to be able to do what they loved instead of breaking their neck to reach some career goal they weren't happy with in the end. I had done this and wound up miserable.

Trey had asked me a question about smelling the earth this time of year and I had missed part of it and asked him to repeat it. He seemed uncomfortable so I stopped the car at the first plowed field I came to and asked him to show me. He was so excited he jumped out of the car before it had hardly stopped and lost his footing, sliding down an embankment into the grass at the edge of the field. He got up quickly brushing his pants and shirt vigorously with his hands.

I could tell he was embarrassed so to put him at ease I slid down beside him. He laughed and helped me up. He had seen through my little act but we were friends. "That's exactly what Mrs. White would have done. You remind me of her in some ways." Trey said as he reached down and picked up a hand full of rich black earth and held it to my nose.

"It smells wonderful," I said, inhaling deeply. After a few minutes at the edge of the field with me asking questions and him patiently answering each one, he reminded me about the store and we climbed the embankment and got back in the car. No one had passed us on the road or if they had, unlike Jersey drivers, they hadn't honked their horns because we were in the way.

There was such a laid back way about the people here; I loved it. It was just what I needed to get my bearings after a lifetime of chasing the big brass ring, which reminded me of the carousel at Asbury Park. I had loved to go there when I was a little girl and I asked Trey if there was a park here and was disappointed that there wasn't.

Almost immediately we entered the outskirts of a small town, Trey referred to it as E town. We turned left and I was just about to ask him what E stood for when I saw a sign welcoming us to Elizabethtown and boasting a population of 5003.

We drove another block or so and came to the courthouse which the road circled as it became two lanes. We completed a half circle when Trey told me to turn. We were once again on highway 31W which we had been on since just before the welcome sign. We drove past some beautiful old buildings. I especially liked one called the Taylor Hotel. As we were coming up on another light just past the hotel, Trey told me to turn left. I had enough trouble changing lanes here to remind me of home and how aggressive Jersey drivers were. I pulled a few fancy maneuvers I doubt this town had seen before and ended up in the left lane ahead of everybody else. Horns honked all around me and two men in a red pickup truck loaded with sacks of something yelled, "women drivers". I smiled and waved.

Trey was tied in a knot in the front seat, whether out of fear of us crashing into something or of being recognized I wasn't sure. I laughed and told him everything was okay, but he refused to look up until the red truck had gone on.

"Mrs. White would have been very upset if the car had been wrecked." he finally said and immediately blushed and stammered; "I'm sorry I keep forgetting."

"It's okay." I said. "Is that why you don't drive, Trey?"

He surprised me with his quick, "Yes," and how fast he changed the subject by pointing out the store to me when I was already turning in the parking lot.

"Trey, I hope you know how to drive because you're driving us home." I said as I handed him the keys. He beamed and fell all over himself trying to get out of the car and around to my side to open the door for me. He did the same thing at the door to the grocery, walked in and took the cart to push for me, as if I had just given him the keys to the world.

Later inside the bank I felt very nervous; I had to keep reminding myself I was not here to rob the place, or to embezzle funds. The bankbooks both had my name on them so why was I so scared?

I walked up to a teller's cage and waited in line behind a woman with two small red headed boys. She was arguing about her balance while the two boys looked all around, one holding on to each side of her skirt; letting their eyes have the run of the place they couldn't have. They looked at me and I smiled; they giggled and looked away. They looked again a time or two in the five minutes we stood there but mostly they seemed to stare at the ceilings. I thought this odd until I realized it was the one unobstructed spot in the whole bank for them, as short as they were. Everything else was walls, and legs, and desk, and plants that were taller than the boys themselves. I needed something to keep my mind off my visit here so I joined them in their search of the ceiling which I found to be covered with a beautiful mural. I was happy the decorators had thought of children and nervous adults when they had built the bank.

The poor woman soon lost her argument with the teller and left the bank in tears, hurrying the boys along. I turned to watch them go, wishing I could help. The boys waved good-bye and I waved back. It was all I could do, or was it?

I handed the teller my checking account book. "May I order some checks?" I asked. She looked at the book, turned pale, and ran to the back of the bank and inside an office door with the book in her hand.

Everybody was staring at me now the way they had at the lady with the two little boys earlier. I felt sick inside. I wanted to run but the teller had my bankbook. I looked around to where Trey sat reading a magazine he had bought at the store. He was too engrossed in what he was reading to notice me. Besides he couldn't help, I knew this; I was mostly looking for a friendly face.

I heard someone call my name and turned toward the voice to see the friendliest face I had ever seen attached to an outstretched arm that for a moment I was afraid was going to grab me. It belonged to a big, big man who lowered his hand, and now stood directly in front of me. "I am the president of the bank; I have been expecting you, Miss Stone; won't you please come into my office?"

I followed him down the narrow hall to the same office the teller had disappeared into earlier. I sat down in the cramped little room, with its desk far out in the middle allowing almost no room for visitors, and watched him edge his big torso around to his chair behind the desk. He talked about Mrs. White for a while and expressed sorrow at her passing. He also seemed to know almost nothing about her and kept asking me to confirm his suspicions about different things. It was pretty funny really, him sitting there knowing nothing and me sitting there knowing nothing, each of us trying to get something from the other.

I got up to leave after a few minutes, satisfied that everything was in order. I really was a millionaire and my checks would be ready in about ten days. He stood up to see me out of his office and suddenly remembered keys he had for me in his desk drawer. I watched him carefully maneuver the crowded space to his chair again wondering how he did it.

He opened the drawer and handed me a sealed envelope. I opened it hurriedly thinking one of the keys might be the key to the library. He dashed my hopes immediately by telling me they were keys to the late Mrs. White's safety deposit box and asked me if I wanted to open the box now. He seemed very anxious for me to do this and secretly I was just as anxious, hoping to find the library key and some answers.

He led me out of his office and down a short hall where we stopped in front of a metal crisscross kind of a door that reminded me of the inner doors of the elevators in some of the buildings in Jersey City. He unlocked this door and we stepped into a small room with safety deposit boxes lining the walls on either side of us. He stopped in front of a box and stepped aside. "This is, I mean was Mrs. White's box here, number 33. You have the only keys to the box which is, I know, a bit irregular but Mrs. White was a very persuasive lady."

I was thinking, I bet she was or her money was, but I said nothing as he took it out of its slot. He led me to the door at the end of the rows of boxes and opened it. It was a small paneled room with a table in the center with six chairs around it. He excused himself closing the door behind him.

I was alone now with the mystery box, which I put on the table unlocking it with the same key, I noticed, that I had used before. I laid the keys on top of each other, they were identical and I understood now why Mrs. White had both of them. Her privacy was very important to her and just as important to the inquisitive banker.

The box contained a single sealed envelope and several contracts. I looked through them and saw they were contracts with her publishers for her various books. I counted them; there were twenty eight, the missing one being for '*A Place in Time*' I was sure. I would check later but for now the long white envelope with my name on it was what I wanted to find out about. I opened it and began to read.

Dear Jennifer,

I know you are most curious about your part in all of this. You will discover the answers at White house and I leave this chore to you, knowing that you wouldn't believe me if I did tell you at this time. Time is the key; that is all I will say; time to reflect, time to discover, time to search.

You are by now entertaining ideas of my being a murderer and my own death a suicide. I know I would be if I were in your shoes; you are wearing your shoes, aren't you? Ha ha, just kidding. Rest assured that I did not murder my beloved son; I could not have done that no matter what blow fate might have dealt me. He died of a heart attack, and I of natural causes. Check with Dr. Holbrook if you doubt what I am saying.

I know that the dates of Lawyer P's visit to you, the prearranged farewell party, the bank withdrawal, and yes even this letter raise certain questions, the answer to all of them being I knew when we were going to die. Read the two books I left in the attic room for you until you find the key. They will keep you busy and they will bring up other questions that you will be ready to learn the answers to when you enter the library. The truth is in the library; look for it.

Trey and Blanche are old friends of mine and I'm sure they will serve you as faithfully as they have me.

I know you are more curious about our relationship than you are about anything else. For now I ask you to enjoy your newfound wealth and save this question for the library.

Your friend, Elizabeth

P.S. I bet you thought the keys at the bank were to the library. I wish I could have seen your face at that moment.

One thing I was sure of; the old lady's sense of humor was in perfect working order when she wrote the letter, which was dated March 2, the date of her last withdrawal. She was sewing up a lot of loose ends that day, I thought, and then it hit me. I went back over the letter to the part about their cause of deaths; she had listed the causes before the fact. One of two things was happening here. Either the old lady had exerted the same influence over this Doctor Holbrook as she did the banker, though admittedly I could think of nothing off the top of my head that she could hold over a doctor that would have the same leverage a fortune would have over a banker.

The only other possibility was that the futuristic writer Elizabeth Windom White was from the future and she had known the causes and the dates ahead of time. And I realized even I was getting ahead of time. How did you die and yet live to move back in time to tell the past when and how you died? How was that for a question for the library? I put the contracts back in the drawer and the letter in my purse. I was ready to leave and I bet with myself that I would open the door and bump into the honorable but slightly nosey banker.

He was there smiling the same big smile he had worn earlier in the lobby. I put the locked box in its slot and handed him a key. He sheepishly took it and I bet that he would be in that box at the earliest opportunity. Like Mrs. White had said of me in the letter, I would like to be able to see his face at that moment.

"Can you ask the teller who the woman was with the two little boys in line in front of me earlier?" I asked.

"But of course, anything for you," he said. "Please feel free to wait for me in my office. I'll only be a moment."

He was back with the name before I had a chance to sit down. I told him to transfer a thousand dollar from my account to the woman's account and to call her and tell her the bank was in error about her account balance. He agreed and did the necessary paper work and called her while I was still there as a show of good faith.

I walked away from the bank not remembering the president's name though I doubted he would be forgetting mine. One thing he said as I was leaving did stay with me though, "You are just like Mrs. White, so generous. Are you related? But of course you are; I can see the resemblance," he said, answering his own questions.

When I got back to the house the phone was ringing as I came in from seeing Trey off to the garage, and I hurried to answer it. It was Michael asking me out to dinner. I accepted and promised to be ready by seven.

We Were Strangers

1939

Morgan had remained in England after his graduation from college living with his Uncle Edward in the old Butler House. He loved everything about the house from the thick oversized oak front door, big enough for two men to go through abreast, to the dark musty cellar he had pretended was a dungeon when he was a boy. The twin towers, one on each side of the big stone house, brought back remembrances of childhood fantasies of the house being under threat of a siege with Merlin and him being the lookouts in the towers. It was the perfect place for a boy with an imagination to grow up in and he envied his uncle having done so. Some of his best fantasies of the house had come from his uncle and he despaired of them both having been only sons pretending in the same ways and not being able to grow up together. They had been like brothers from their first meeting so many years ago and they had remained close.

He loved the house, especially its ghosts. He would die here himself, fate willing, and join them in their nightly walks through the massive rooms and halls of the grand old house; in that way he would never have to leave. Having once thought of that, the idea excited him so much he had spent months researching the likelihood of Merlin having been a ghost those many years ago.

Reading everything he could find on ghosts and hauntings, researching first person accounts of encounters with ghosts and trying to communicate with them, he had come to know the ghosts here and their separate stories. Actually there were three ghosts and two stories.

Little Alice was his favorite and he could often hear her singing. She was always happy; perhaps that was why he liked her so much. Such happiness was beyond anything he could imagine and because of it he had targeted her as his first study.

Alice had fallen to her death from the hall window outside Edward's room some few days before her seventeenth birthday in March 1722. Her mother had died when she was eight and her father had immediately remarried. His second wife bore him a daughter Sally, and a son Jeremy. Then he married a third time, that marriage ending with the birth of a son Andrew and his wife's death.

Edmund now past forty, alone, and the father of four, left Alice to tend to the other children while he tended to his gardens. The happy, fragile, and extremely sensitive young girl, having been at the mercy of two unloving stepmothers, had learned to keep her fears and wants to herself.

Her brother Jeremy learned early from his mother of Alice's delicate nature and the ease with which power could be had over her. He enjoyed tormenting his older half sister with anything and everything, a particular favorite being frogs, which abounded on the grounds of the great house and which Alice was deathly afraid of.

Alice became a prisoner in her own room where she would quickly run and lock herself in as soon as her chores were done. Sally and baby Andrew played together and left her to her room, where she read and dreamed away the hours by looking out the window at the surrounding fields in search of a knight to come and rescue her.

Often when Alice left her room and Jeremy was around he would chase her with a frog or a garden snake. Her room became her sanctuary, her haven, not only from her brother but from a second person, the ghost Morgan knew as Uncle Albert, the brother of baby Andrew's mother. According to Alice, Uncle Albert was a half-wit who tried to touch her in ways her Papa would have killed the smelly old drawn up man for, if he ever found out. On the day of her death Jeremy was chasing her with a frog he had teasingly called Prince Dread. She had lost her footing on the highly polished floors at the top of the stairs and had fallen out the hall window to her death.

Two hundred plus years later the room was still her sanctuary from Jeremy and Uncle Albert. Outside the door of her room on the landing at the top of the stairs Uncle Albert, who had been trampled to death by a wagon some few days after Alice died, could be seen from time to time pacing back and forth as if he was waiting for the young girl to come out of her room.

A third ghost, baby Sarah, had awakened Morgan on more than one occasion by climbing into bed beside him while he slept. Studying the child who seemed frightened and in need of comfort, he sensed she could not speak or hear him as she seemed to study his face long and hard when he tried to talk to her but responded in no other way. When he was unable to learn more about her he approached his Uncle Edward with the story of the child.

They were sitting over the morning paper having finished breakfast. It was a Sunday and they had the day to themselves. No work, no planned trips, no lectures to attend or to officiate at, no opera this evening, just a beautiful summer's day to read and relax.

"Uncle, a young girl named Sarah has been getting into my bed at night and I hoped you would talk to me about her. All I know is her name as she seems to be deaf or something and that she is a ghost." Morgan said timidly, afraid of what his uncle would think.

"The little girl's visits have been reported over the years by more than one overnight guest in Butler House," Uncle Edward said looking up from his newspaper. "She was a mute as you suspected and about the age of three. She was the daughter of great, great, great Uncle Basil's and a household maid, Sarah Bingstrom."

"The child's mother had hoped Basil would marry her though this did not come to be. By the time little Sarah's problem was recognized her mother had grown to hate her and had been caught one time too many mistreating the little girl. She was sent from the employ of the family and plans were made to raise the child and make her as comfortable as possible."

"Rumor has it that Sarah sneaked back into the house one night and threw the little girl down the stairs, making it look like she had wandered from her bed half asleep and had fallen. It was supposed that the mother thought, with the child safely out of the way, she might return to Butler House and ultimately to Basil's affections. She went mad and was locked away in an asylum, where she died years later."

The ghost question having been freely discussed between them Morgan felt he could ask the question that was really on his mind. "Was Merlin a ghost?" He thought not but sought confirmation from a man who had shared the experience. There was nothing to do but to ask, unsure as he was of where the answers would lead.

Uncle Edward looked surprised by the question and quickly shook his head. "No, Morgan I don't think so. What made you ask?"

"You know that I have studied every facet of that night; time, magic, Merlin, imagination, and more. To me this is just one more thing to consider. There must be an answer and I have to find it. I have gone back to those woods countless evenings trying to find him again to ask him."

"Why is this so important to you, Morgan?"

"I don't know if there is an answer to that question anymore. At one time I wanted to prove to my father I wasn't lying. It was the first time, in fact, the only time he ever accused me of doing so and I wanted to prove I wasn't. You remember the night; I was wet, cold, tired, and worse yet, I felt betrayed."

"Betrayed?"

"Uncle Edward, my father was always gone, always away. I grew up waving goodbye to him. Honestly that is the bulk of my memories of him. Today if I were home it would be no different; he's never home. That first trip here to England was the most time I had ever spent with him. If I could add up the minutes here over dinner, the minutes there walking him to the station and standing at the depot seeing him off, all of those stolen minutes over the years would not add up to the thirty-one days in May that year; days when I could see him at breakfast, at lunch, at tea, at supper, at bedtime, and again at breakfast for a whole month. It was the only vacation he ever took. He was hardly home long enough to make babies and see them born, never mind seeing them grow up."

"You're angry with him?" Uncle Edward questioned somewhat surprised.

"Sometimes yes, but mostly I feel sorry for him. He is a stranger to his children. He never really knew any of us, though he favored Happy when we were small and he gave her that nickname. He knows little or nothing about us. That particular trip was the most time I had ever had with him. At a time when I needed him to believe me, to comfort me if he could, he called me a liar in front of relatives I hardly knew and then sent me away."

"Did that night do so much to you?"

Morgan bowed his head and didn't answer.

"Lad, I had no idea. I would have done more for you. I would have spent more time with you."

"Uncle Edward, you couldn't have done more if you tried."

"I love you, Morgan, and I am happy we have had this little talk. For years I have said I had no son, and now I see I have been wrong. As for Merlin, I don't believe he was a ghost. I urge you to continue your study and to consider what happened from every angle. Someday you will find what you're after."

"Do you really think so, Uncle Edward?"

"Yes, lad, I do. Let's compare Merlin and young Sarah. You've touched them both. Do you believe they are the same type of experience?"

"You're right! How could I have overlooked something as important as touch? When I fainted Merlin caught me as I fell. I remember the smell of the rain on his woolen cloak. I remember his wet whiskers against my cheek. Sarah on the other hand feels neither cold, nor warm, nor solid. She is like a mist I can pass my hand through and feel nothing but a chill at having encountered the unexplainable. No, they are not the same. Merlin was real. Sarah is not."

"Oh Sarah is real enough, lad, for a ghost, that is. She has scared more than one guest of Butler House out of a good night's sleep," Uncle Edward corrected him laughing.

"I agree with you, Uncle Edward; the three ghosts are real enough. Alice's fear fills the whole room sometimes and at other times her joy is just as overwhelming."

"Three ghosts?" the older man questioned getting up from his chair with a start.

"Yes Sir, Sarah, Alice, and Uncle Albert."

"You have met them too. You must have a way about you, lad. They don't show themselves to just anybody."

"Are they family?"

"Alice is. Her mother Elizabeth was the daughter of Gwendolyn Butler, who married Arthur Brown. Let's see now; Gwendolyn was the daughter of the elder Gregory, brother to, never mind all that it's enough to say Alice was a Butler."

"What about her father; she says he was a gardener."

"Oh, he was to be sure but a most unusual gardener; educated, genteel. Rumor was he was royal, the son of a princess. Unmarried though she was, the dear girl loved her son so much she insisted to her brother, that she would tell all the world the babe was hers if he didn't educate him and keep him near her. And it was done, or so the story goes. As to how I don't know. Usual court intrigue would have called for the murder of the princess and the baby. Perhaps it's all just a grand story."

"Perhaps so, Uncle Edward, but it would explain Elizabeth being married to a gardener."

"Not really, we were not so grand and pompous then as some of us have become," Uncle Edward said.

"You wouldn't happen to be referring to my cousin Gregory, would you now?"

"I might be," Uncle Edward answered adding, "but enough of this talk. There is still the matter of Merlin. We have time enough before supper to walk over the grounds a bit, perhaps as far as the woods."

"Let's go!" Morgan shouted excitedly.

"We're scientists of a sort, aren't we? We examine facts, collect data, and draw conclusions. Perhaps the answers you seek are in the place itself." Uncle Edward said, putting on his hat and leading the way out the front door of Butler House. The boy hat in hand followed close on his heels.

They crossed a vast lawn, immaculately groomed with hedges trimmed to an unnatural finish, the scent of flowers occasionally drifting past them carried from some far corner of the yard or the garden. Morgan breathed deeply; nature his most favorite thing in the world surrounded him. His heart swelled with joy; his eyes looked across the land trying to gather acres of wonder and beauty all up in one sweep.

He loved the English countryside the way he had loved the fields of Glendale before time stripped them of their openness and left houses, roads, and stores in its wake. He drew comfort from knowing that the land he now walked upon would not be sold off in parcels as long as any one Butler descendant lived and they numbered in the dozens. The acres about him were alive with the essence of his forbears having belonged to his mother's family for hundreds of years. Generation upon generation of them living, dying and buried here. The estate next to them, the Williams, belonged to his father's family, the same long line of people that were part of him. There was such a feeling of belonging, such a comfort, and such a peace here. If he found Merlin's secret here he could go back hundreds of years and be with family, Butlers and Williams like himself.

They walked on with Uncle Edward leading the way lost in thoughts of his own, perhaps remembering his encounter with Merlin, Morgan thought. He would leave his uncle to his memories and continue to soak up the peace the land offered him.

They walked into scant woods where the day grew dimmer and into thicker woods where evening seemed upon them almost with a step. Uncle Edward stopped and pointed to a spot in a clearing a few feet in front. "There," he said.

Morgan surprised interrupted him, "No, not there; we have a ways to go yet."

"Yes, here is the spot; see, I carved my initials on the very tree I was sitting under when Merlin appeared."

"That can't be," the young man argued as he went to the tree his uncle was pointing at and together they searched and found the name carved those many years ago, though Uncle Edward thought it was much further up the tree than he had remembered.

"This is not where I saw him, Uncle Edward; he was much further along in the woods, another mile perhaps."

"You were staying at the Williams house that evening. Why didn't I remember that before? I always assumed you saw him where I did; now I see the whole bloody woods belong to Merlin." his uncle said, and they laughed, pushed back their hats, and scratched their heads almost in unison. "That ruins my theory of a possible time portal," Uncle Edward added.

"A place where Merlin might step from one time to another at will; I've considered that before, Uncle, and I've searched the woods where I saw him, hoping to step through myself or catch Merlin in the act again. I've marked everything on a map I've compiled of the combined grounds of the two properties."

"Let me see it, Lad."

"It's back at the house in my room. I would love to have you look it over and make any corrections you find necessary."

"What are we waiting for?" Uncle Edward said, and they turned back walking briskly and talking nonstop.

When they got back to the house they found a telegraph had arrived addressed to Morgan. He opened it, read it, laid it back down on the hall table he had taken it from, and excused himself walking upstairs to his room. His uncle, concerned for the boy and knowing telegrams were seldom good news, picked it up and read, "Morgan, your father died 3:15 p.m. today August 21st. Come at once. Signed, Ellen Butler Williams.....

Edward sat down to think what the boy would do now. Of course he would go to America to bury his dead but would he return to his beloved England after that? He would be missed dearly for however long he was away and Edward hoped it would not be long.

Taking his pipe from his vest pocket he put it in his mouth unlit. The pipe, an extension of him, was one of his greatest pleasures. Reaching in another pocket for a pouch of tobacco, he filled it and lit the strangely shaped bowl. His mind wandered to his first pipe, a gift from his father on his twentieth birthday, and ultimately to his own father's death. They, unlike his brother-in-law and his nephew, had been extremely close. "Wild horses couldn't part them", they had always maintained, neither of them allowing for the greater might of death.

His father had died in a fall from a horse at a young sixty-two. "The fox certainly got away that day," he heard a spinster aunt say later. But she was quick to add, "That was the only one that ever had," and so it was with his father.

They loved each other though they had never actually said so once the boyhood years were over. While the feelings they had for each other had not changed except for the better, they had reached a point in time where men did not say such things. How sad he thought. He still missed the robust old gray haired man with his insatiable appetite for life and wished he could see him once more and say the forbidden words, "I love you, Father." Words he now said aloud to his memory.

Morgan returned following the smell of his uncle's pipe surprised to find him sitting in the hall where he had left him. He thought his uncle looked pale. Uncle Edward stood up at the sound of his nephew's approaching footsteps. He held out his arms to the lad and was taken aback when the young man placed a large paper, folded many times over, in his outstretched hand. The look of surprise on Uncle Edward's face prompted Morgan to remind him of their earlier conversation about a map. Uncle Edward looked confused as he began to unfold the map not sure what to say.

"Don't grieve for me, Uncle; we were strangers," the boy said.

With his heart stretched between two continents and two time frames he went home. He didn't arrive in time for the funeral of his father, and wished he had not arrived at all. The house and the grounds were left to him, the only son, and provided for his mother, to continue living there until her death. He felt trapped now, caged like a wild animal in a town that reeked of his beloved Ned, a town with train whistles many times daily to remind him of the stranger he had called father.

The Mirror

1951

Michael came at seven on the nose. I was ready and we left within minutes. When I got in the car I put the black box in the seat beside me.

"What's in the box?" he asked.

"It's the control for the gate; I want to close it when we pull out."

"I didn't know little towns had such modern devices," he kidded.

"For your information, Mister, we have running water too?' I teased.

"I know but not hot running water, at least not at my hotel."

"Which hotel are you staying at?"

"The Taylor."

"That beautiful old thing, I love it. Is that where we're going to eat?"

"Not likely; a gentleman never takes a lady to his hotel on their first date. Besides how do you know about the Taylor?"

"Trey and I were by there today on our way to the bank and the grocery."

"Who the hell is Trey?"

"He works for me; the groundskeeper I guess you'd call him."

"When did you have time to hire somebody to take care of the yard?"

"I inherited him and a maid with the house."

"Gee, it seems the old lady took care of everything, didn't she?"

"I'll say."

"Did you get a chance to start her book yet?" Michael asked.

"I started it and finished it last night." I answered.

"What did you do, stay awake all night?"

"No just till three."

"What did you think of the book?,

"The book or the idea of time travel?" I asked.

"Both!" he said.

"I really liked the book after she entered the picture."

"Jennifer, she entered the picture on page one."

"Not really, all she was doing there was telling the reader who the story teller was. And time travel, I don't know; I honestly don't know. Logic tells me it's impossible but my logic is beginning to fail me in certain areas."

"What do you mean?"Michael asked.

"Well for one thing the little Hot Wheels cars and trucks on the shelf in Joey's room are dated from 1968 to 1990. And at the bank today I found a letter in the safety deposit box dated the 2nd in which Mrs. White not only tells me when she and Joey died, before the fact mind you, but she also gives the cause of death and she invites me to check with a Dr. Holbrook for verification."

"Did you check with him?"

"Check with whom?"

"Dr. Holbrook, Silly."

"No, I figured he had been bought and paid for like the banker."

"What's the banker got to do with this; is he dated too?"

"No. of course not; but I'm sure he would tell me the truth if he knew it. Mrs. White commanded a lot of loyalty. Why, poor Trey was still worried about the old lady getting upset if we scratched the car up. I wouldn't trust anybody that knew her to be completely honest with me; after all I'm a stranger."

"You won't always be a stranger; perhaps in time."

"There's that word again. Tell me, Michael, you read *A Place in Time* long before I did. What do you think? Is the story a real one or did she have a very vivid imagination?"

"Jennifer, nobody could have imagination enough to name wars before they happened."

"Are you talking about Vietnam?" I asked.

"Yes, and World War I and II, and Korea; in one chapter, Uncle Morgan talks about wars he has lived to see and he mentions Korea; we are now fighting that war. She wrote this in 1910 or to my way of thinking it would really have been 1993. The next to the last chapter just before the time change is dated 1991, so I figure that if they went back in 1991 to 1910 and the book came out two years later in 1912, then it would really have been 1993, and Vietnam should be in the 1960's and early 1970's."

"How do you figure that?"

"In the chapter where she makes a trip to see Morgan and they plant the trees, she says she is forty six; that was 1989 according to the book. She says she went to school with this boy Philip, that she grew up with him and he went to Vietnam straight out of high school, which would have made him about eighteen at the time. So backing a forty six year old woman up to the age of eighteen would have made her eighteen in 1961. And her friend might have been younger than her by a year or two because she says he is also her brother, Jimmy's friend and Jimmy is younger than her. Philip would have been in Vietnam in 1963 or 64. I think the war went on for many years because Uncle Morgan's grandson is about sixteen or seventeen in 1991 meaning he was born in 1974."

"You devil, you've been studying this thing for years and you let me stumble around in the dark. You believe she did the time travel thing, don't you, Michael?"

"Yes I do, and I think her motive was her son. The only thing I don't know is how, but I bet you are where you are to find this out."

"Why do you say that?"

"Because your motive is in that dedication; have you forgotten it?"

"Not for one minute. But the three years difference in the date and my birth is not enough for me to go off half cocked looking for a time machine."

"There is no machine. I don't think a machine is necessary. I think it's done in the mind or with the mind. Remember the last night Morgan spent in the library before Happy and Beth and Joey came to visit. She said he stayed later than usual. He goes over that night with Merlin again and again, and he leaves late. Up to this time he did not have the answer but the very next night, he and his niece Beth (Elizabeth Windom White) are having their late night chat on the porch when he demonstrates time travel to her. I believe it is done with the mind."

"How real could it be if it's done with the mind? How could it include others? How could it last after the person whose mind it is done in dies? Remember he did die first. And explain the dated cars in Joey's room. How did he do that in his mind?"

"Okay, Jennifer, let's say I am wrong. It didn't happen. Explain to me how she knew things were going to happen before they happened? Many books she wrote were futuristic and not just futuristic but 99% accurate. Events, architecture, fashions, ships, people she refers to, movies. She wrote about things before they happened. Even to generals in battle as yet unfought, and names for mental conditions thirty some odd years early. Tell me how she knew."

"Deaths and causes of deaths before the fact; you forgot that?"

"Whose side are you on anyway?"

"I don't know. You're pretty convincing. The dedication is my biggest question."

"You said a minute ago it was no big deal."

"It is and it isn't. I've been trying to think of why any writer would dedicate every book they ever wrote to the same person in one stroke of the pen and never change their mind. They would have to mean an awful lot to each other and I've only seen the lady one time. What if you are right?"

"Right about what Jennifer; you are not making a whole lot of sense?"

"What if I did find the answer in the house or I will find the answers; maybe I will know her between 1910 and 1912? Or maybe I did?"

"I think I understand what you're saying now, and I don't think you have, or you would know it and you were genuinely shocked by the dedication. The possibility that you will know her and that you would know her in time to be her inspiration or whatever in 1912 is an interesting one."

"Frightening is a better word."

"Ah come on, girl, where's your sense of adventure?" Michael teased as he pulled up to a big garage. I was wondering if we were ever going to eat when I spotted the little restaurant he had bragged about earlier. Penny's Truck Stop, the sign said boasting the best coffee and steaks on the highway.

As we walked in I could hear a woman singing to the jukebox; she was bent over the counter washing dishes by the sound of things and she didn't see us at first. When she did, she looked up and called out, "Hello."

She was a beautiful woman with short curly coal black hair and big brown eyes. Her complexion was smooth and tanned. The only makeup she wore was deep red lipstick. When she finished drying her hands I could see her nails were the same deep red. She was a little shorter than me, probably five foot two or three, and well built. The thing that I was most taken with about her was that she didn't seem to know how pretty she was; she was so natural acting that she seemed unaware of her good looks. She remembered Michael and began teasing him right away about being a Yankee. When I ordered and she noticed my accent she burst out laughing.

"Another Yankee", she said.

"I was, I told her, but now I'm a Kentuckian. I just moved to Glendale."

"You're the lady I've been hearing so much about; Mrs. White's niece or something."

"Yes, I am; did you know her?"

"Everybody in the area knew about her but few people could say they really knew her; she was a very private person. But around here you'll learn if people don't know your business, they guess it."

When Peggy, as Michael had called her, went to cook our steaks, I tried to talk him into continuing our earlier conversation about the time theory, but he was too busy talking back and forth with her. I was hurt and was seeing a side of Michael I had not seen before; the flirt, I was to later learn, was the public side of him. The haunting laugh I had loved earlier was going strong now and I wondered if someone had told him; probably more than one someone had told him how much they liked it and that he had learned how to use it. I heard him ask her about her children and lost myself in the roar of the big trucks driving up and down the highway in front of the restaurant not hearing her answers.

When she brought our steaks a few minutes later she bumped my arm and winked at me, kidding Michael about ignoring me. I knew then she was as uncomfortable with his behavior as I was. He turned red with embarrassment and managed to include me in further conversations with Peggy.

The steaks were every bit as good as Michael said they would be and we ate and talked back and forth with Peggy until a couple of truckers came in and she got busy. I watched Michael watch Peggy and wondered what he was thinking.

We drove home in silence. When he let me out at the house I didn't invite him in; I was tired and angry with him and I was in no mood for apologies. Once inside I went to my room for a robe and slippers and to the bathroom for a hot bath. I did my best thinking in the tub or on walks. It was too late to go exploring around Glendale, so I went for the hot bath.

I settled in to the hot, hot water and watched my legs turn beet red from the heat. It felt wonderful and I laid my head back on the big claw foot tub's high back to relax and unwind. I thought of Michael almost immediately and a wave of anger swept through me. I spent a minute or two telling him what a cad he was, in my mind, then turned my thoughts to some of his arguments in support of time travel. I looked around the room for some sign that he might be right but laughed and admitted to myself that a bathroom was not the most ideal place to ponder such a possibility.

A claw foot tub and a pedestal sink were standard fixtures in old buildings. The toilet with its high oak tank suspended up the wall was less common but still not unheard of. There was nothing unusual about the room at all. There was nothing to tell its age as being anything but the roughly eighty odd years of this house and the surrounding houses in Glendale.

After awhile the phone rang and I knew it was Michael so I didn't answer. It rang on and on and finally on about the twentieth ring I couldn't stand the noise any longer and got out of the tub. I stood dripping water all over the hall floor and freezing to death while I gave him only yes and no answers to his questions. He let me go only after I promised I would see him again before he left to go back to New York.

On the way back to the tub I stubbed my toe on the door and bending over to see how bad it was hurt I saw a magazine tucked between the shelves of the little table by the tub that held the soap and bath oil. I took it out and found it was another Victoria magazine. I smiled and settled back in the tub with my new find.

I took my glasses out of my purse in the floor by the tub where I had put it when I hurried to the bathroom when I first got home. I put them on and read, *A Toast to the Spirit of Katherine Hepburn*, on the cover. Her movie, The African Queen, was one I looked forward to seeing. Then I saw the date across the top above the word Victoria; it was August 1991. Overjoyed I wasn't, but I opened the magazine and began to scan the pages for proof that the date was not a hoax. Everything seemed to point to a joke. All the pictures were of Victorian clothing, houses, gardens and furniture. I began enjoying the magazine and soon found the promised Katherine Hepburn article. I read on and it was not until page forty-five that I was once again reminded of the date. It said, "She recalled in her 1987 memoir, *The Making of the African Queen*.

I seemed to be in 1951; there was no disputing this, but was the house? Of course it was; it had to be. The real question was not what year it was but whether Elizabeth Windom White had indeed traveled back from 1991. I put the magazine down on the floor and laid back. The water was cooling now and I concentrated on bathing and getting out of the tub.

It was nine thirty when I climbed the attic steps. I walked over to the chiffarobe for a gown and back to the bed where I threw off my robe and put the gown on. With my hairbrush in my hand I walked over to the beautifully ornate floor to ceiling mirror on the wall beside the stairs. I had hardly given it a thought until now; it was so out of the way. There was little light to see by in this part of the room and I thought it a very strange place for a mirror.

Turning away from the mirror I stepped on the hem of my gown and fell against the mirror. My elbow hit hard against it. I rubbed it checking for blood and then looked to the mirror.

I expected it to be broken but instead found that it had moved a little. I stood up and touched the edge of the mirror and pushed gently. Nothing happened. It seemed to be braced against something solid but there was a certain give to it and it had clearly moved some with my fall; the shadows on the wall indicated this quite clearly. I pushed again, harder this time, determined to solve the mystery. The mirror moved a little more so I pushed harder. This time it opened wide and I could see a room on the other side. I stepped across the threshold half expecting the lights to come on but for some reason the attic was not included in the light game and I wondered why.

I turned the lights on and looking around I saw I was a small room with a desk and some bookshelves, though I knew it wasn't the missing library because it was too small. On the desk was a lamp which I also turned on, a small television and a few bits of paper, and a folder full of more paper. I scanned through the papers and found what I believed to be pages of an unfinished book. This was Mrs. White's study, I believed, and now I hoped I would have my answers.

I sat down in her chair and started opening the drawers. There were the usual pencils, pens, and paper. The long low drawer in the middle had several ribbons for the typewriter. The only thing odd was the paper said "recycled" on the many packages. I wondered what recycled paper was and took a few sheets from an open package. It was ordinary paper to me. The long low drawer in the middle of the desk had a keyboard from a typewriter and a cord that hung doing nothing; I wondered where the rest of the typewriter was. There was also a small box that read, "Ink Cartridge," and several flat black things called diskettes. I picked up one, read the label, and put it back. The only other thing in the drawer was a small red and white book that looked to be an instruction booklet for the television. I thought that strange but put it away with the other stuff. There were no answers in the desk drawers so I turned to the shelves and began reading titles. Mrs. White's books, all twenty-nine of them, were in dated order from 1915 to 1950.

My copy of *A Place in Time* was from this group, I was sure, as there was a small empty place on the shelf. Beside her books was a bigger bare spot where several books had been removed, and then all of Louisa May Alcott's books, one particular book 'Under the Lilacs' looking especially worn. There were also several books of poetry with authors' names I didn't recognize, like Yevtushenko, Cummings, Patchen, Ferlinghetti, and McKuen. I opened the Yevtushenko book, a small brown paperback called *Selected Poems of Yevengy Aleksandrovich Yevtushenko* copyrighted 1962. I sat down and looked through it for something interesting *"I want to congratulate you mother on the birthday of your son,"* it said. I loved the poem and looked for something else soon came upon a long piece called Babi Yar. I recognized the name as the sight of a horrible crime against the Jewish nation during World War II. I liked Yevtushenko and I was glad I had chosen this book to read. The others I would read another time; for now I would snoop around the room a bit more.

Near the desk was a small table with a blue rocking chair pulled up to it. There were several worn National Geographic magazines, some with covers missing, a stack of tablets, also worn looking and a small red box. Inside the box were dozens of broken pieces of pencils and crayons. These must have been Joey's, I decided, and I opened a tablet to find out more about him. The pages were filled with a childish print of names Mom, Dad, Frances, Morgan, Blanche, and Joseph; faces of people he knew; faces rich in detail. I recognized a younger Mrs. White and Blanche, and there were several of Trey and one of Lawyer P. On other pages trees were crudely drawn with what I believed to be attempted stars on top. Christmas trees I guessed. How strange it all seemed. I picked up more tablets and found the same thing in all of them.

The rest of the room was pretty open and across the   r o o m I   noticed for the first time a floor length window which on closer inspection turned out to be a door. I opened it and stood amazed. Before me was a brick terrace full of huge flowerpots with small trees and bushes in them. There were two chairs and a single table. It was a private garden spot for her and Joey. How beautiful. I walked to the edge and looked out at the grounds smooth and dark below. The garage in the distance hid a glass-roofed building I hadn't known about till now, probably a greenhouse.

Many of the trees near the house were beginning to bud and would shade this spot from the hot summer sun. I wondered how often Mrs. White had sat here in the evening and looked down over the property and up at her beloved stars. She had said that stars called to her, that she felt she was from the heavens not the earth. She had also said that man knew more about the heavens than the planet he lived on because she believed it was in the far memory of all people that we had really come from out there. I looked up at the stars and thought of her, wondering if her theories of spiritual development that she had recorded in a series of books entitled "The Genealogy of a Soul" were real. I felt very old now, as old as the stars, and wondered if I had known her before and if this might explain her gift to me.

It grew late and I went inside. I looked around the room feeling very close to her almost as if she were here. I wondered how many of her books had been written here and how many hours her son had sat with her while she wrote, sketching her. I took the clipboard and turned off the lamp on the desk and left the room propping the mirror door open, something I seemed to forever be doing in this house.

Dreams of Broken Promises

1947

Morgan married his childhood friend Rebecca Hays in October 1945 at the end of the war. She kept him grounded; he told people who asked about their relationship. She was practical and he was a dreamer. She was a good listener, she was warm, and she was quiet and practical. Theirs was a marriage between two friends.

He hadn't been close to a woman since Happy married. He was twenty-one then and away in England where her letters had come less and less often, finally dwindling to an occasional card. Uncle Edward kept him so busy there was hardly time for women. They had gone along working, studying, and enjoying each other's company and the years had gotten away from them. When he had come home and found he had to stay, he had been bitterly disappointed. He felt trapped by the responsibility of his mother's care and the house he never wanted. Without Old Ned the town seemed empty; the house, his refuge as a child, now closed in around him.

He had been teaching at the University since his return to America when his father died. He worked long hours and traveled as much as he could to escape the void created by the absence of the old man and Happy, the core of his childhood eaten away by the years.

With Becky to keep his mother company, he again spent summers in England with his Uncle Edward. The bombings of the recent war had badly damaged great portions of the grounds and they spent a lot of time overseeing the restoration of it to its original beauty. The house itself remained intact and Morgan placed incredible importance on that. Butler House would always be there for him, though for now he was living in the Williams house in Glendale, driving his father's car; and Becky and he were expecting their first child.

Morgan prayed this baby would be a girl. He could not bear the thought of a son for him to betray as his father had betrayed him. He would have preferred no children. He felt himself too old at thirty-three and too set in his ways to be bringing a child into the world. He questioned the sanity of any new life being introduced into a world that had barely escaped destroying itself in a global war. The ashes of Hiroshima and Nagasaki were barely cooled; how could people go on living and making babies, he wondered?

Life was hard enough for him. He wondered how different things would have been for him if he had not met Merlin and become consumed with the how of that meeting. Would he have been a farmer like the boys he grew up with? Would he ever have lived in England and come to love his Uncle Edward like a father? Would he have read anything more than the newspaper and the *Farmer's Almanac* his neighbors took such stock in? Would his father have called him a liar over something else in life or would they have had the regular father-son relationship he saw in those around him? Strangers yes, but strangers on good terms with no forgotten dreams between them.

He could, he reasoned, give that day in May credit for altering his entire world and he wondered if it had been meant to do just that. His Uncle had the same encounter and had done almost nothing about it. They had discussed this and still it seemed unresolved in his mind. Was his Uncle Edward so steeped in the legends of Merlin's powers that he had met him as he would meet a woodcutter in those same woods with no second thought? They had talked about it and, they had covered every argument possible. It all came around to the fact that meeting Merlin had drastically altered one life and barely made an imprint on the other.

Morgan, American born and raised on Old Ned's magic, had been so open to the possibility of meeting more men of magic that he had been changed forever, at every point not only of the map of the woods where the encounter took place, but at every point where Morgan Williams' life had taken a different turn. He was not a farmer tilling the soil like his neighbors; he was a professor following in his Uncle Edward's footsteps. Why remained the key question.

Everything went back to his meeting with Merlin. History was a study of time. History repeated itself. It was the possible repetition of that night and the meeting that he wanted most out of life. Everything else took a back seat to that; his uncle, his father, his teaching, his wife, his future.

The thought of living that future out here in Glendale frightened him. He wanted more. He had always wanted more. He wanted a land where boys could dream and never know the hurt of being different. Yesterday was where his heart was, and it was in yesterday that he put all of his faith, all of his prayers, all the energy of his being,

He felt smothered by the prospect of becoming a father. If the child was a boy he would have to stop searching for answers to ancient questions. He would never want his son to look back and think him a failure as his father had done. He would never want to stand in judgment of his son's career choice as his father had stood in judgment of his. He would never want a son to spend a lifetime trying to erase the pain of loving a father as desperately as he loved his own, never able to say so -- running head long away from that love into friendships with other men, searching for the male role model his father couldn't provide with his long absences and his stern manner.

He wouldn't know how to keep things from going wrong in his relationship with a son. Had his own father been hell bent on making them strangers or had fate had a hand in that? Had the very lucrative job with the railroad been too good to pass up for a man used to having money? Had the money been more to him than the family he left behind?

His Mother had done it all. Father was a household word like pitcher or bowl. Hadn't he done a great job replacing his father with Ned and Uncle Edward? Hadn't he ultimately pursued male friends to the exclusion of female ones till he could relate no better to his mother and his wife than if they were household servants? Didn't he like it that way? Hadn't he married a woman much like his mother, who could be kept busy with cooking and cleaning, babies and town gossip? He knew so little about women he would not have dared to marry any one at all if Becky had not filled the bill so well. She could have her babies and he would provide for her, as long, that is, as they were daughters. Sons would rock his world as surely as Merlin had and he would be lost.

His job kept him busy through the school year and he planned to join Uncle Edward on an archaeological dig in Peru during summer break. Gone like his father; gone off in history trying desperately to find the answers to questions that had plagued him all his life. The baby would be born before school was out and he would be packed and on his way, away from the house that still smelled of his father's pipe and reeked of his serious nature.

His Mother had lived with that seriousness until it had become her, the way it had been absorbed by the walls, the furnishings, the draperies, and the air. Would it ever be different? Would laughter ever be welcomed within the walls of the old Williams house or would they crack and crumble under the strain?

His father's study had become his and it was the one room he kept sealed against fresh air. As for the rest of the house, he raised the windows and opened the doors on pleasant days almost as fast as his mother closed them. He wanted new life in the old house; she wanted sameness.

And as much as he wanted change in the house, he wanted sameness in the study. There he kept the windows closed and the draperies pulled tight against the winds of change. He lit pipes filled with the tobacco his father had used though he himself had never acquired a taste for pipes. He polished the trains his father had sitting around the study to preserve that strange mixture of tobacco and sweetly scented oil he remembered from his childhood. When he entered this shrine it was to think about his father, to remember back, to call forth the picture of a man too serious and too busy for him whom he had loved dearly.

He was sitting in his classroom in the early light of a January morning when word reached him of his daughter's birth and he wept.

He had been granted a reprieve; he would be able to continue his search; there was still so much to do, things he had been torn between doing and giving up on as an impossible dream. Morgan thought this more than a chance happening; it bore more significance to him than just the birth of a girl. It was a sign to him that his search was valid.

He vowed there would be no more children, no more risk of a son. He was torn enough between America and England. England could win out at the drop of a hat and if Becky wanted the boy with her, and he was sure she would. He stood no chance of doing any better by a son than the worst of fathers. There was no Old Ned in Glendale anymore and Uncle Edward was off with him all the time. Where would a son get male guidance?

Becky and he had separate bedrooms since the discomforts of pregnancy had kept her up half the night and she had grown concerned for him and his work. They had not been a passionate couple. The sleeping arrangement was a good one, and he felt she would welcome its continuance as much as he.

He planned to finish the day before going home to see his new daughter, believing there was a lifetime ahead of him for that. But at ten o'clock another message was delivered to him; this one told him his sister Bea was dead, Bea the eternal child.

The drive home was pressed full of thoughts of the beautiful simple Bea, Bea at her graduation, Bea getting married, Bea on birthdays being rolled in the snow by the other children and her crying out to stop them. Bea sitting with her mending by the fire, hiding the fact that she could barely sew by holding the needle and thread in readiness until Happy got finished with her mending and then slipped it on to Bea's lap and took Bea's for her own, something their parents seemed not to see. Bea struggling to maintain some semblance of understanding the schoolwork Happy quietly did for her, and then exchanged papers with her doing the work again for herself. Bea struggled to keep up with what they all took for granted. Bea, the sister they all loved for her unassuming gentle ways; Bea pregnant and aglow with happiness, Bea broken hearted at the grave of her newborn daughter four months ago, and now Bea herself dead. Morgan could not believe it. He could not believe life went on in his house where he took it for granted and life ended at his sister's where it was valued for the simple beauty to be found every day in everything as Bea had done.

Happy, Julia, Sarah, Theresa, and Kay were all at his house when he drove up. Happy and Sarah were in Guy's old truck pulling out of the driveway. He stopped and so did Happy. They got out and stood hugging each other in the driveway crying over their loss. Sarah laid her sleeping daughter down on the front seat of the truck and joined them. "We were going over to get the body ready when you came up," Happy said. "Carol, Carl, and little Lee are inside. Theresa is taking them home with her. Sarah and I will stay at Bea's until the services tomorrow; then I will take the two older children and Kay will take the baby."

"Who is with Bea now?" Morgan asked Happy.

"Deborah, and of course him," Happy said. Morgan took him to mean Bea's husband and shook his head.

Sarah's young daughter screamed and stood up in the front seat of the truck. Morgan went to her and lifted her out. She laid against his chest clinging to him and quieted down, her eyes drooping with sleep. "Let me take her inside with me, Sarah, she doesn't need to be there when you're taking care of Bea."

"Don't I know it, Morgan, but she screamed and hung on me inside no matter who tried to hold her. She always did like you. I know she'll be okay now." Sarah said, as she kissed her daughter's and then her brother's cheek.

Happy leaned out the truck window where she sat ready to go and called to Morgan, "Your new daughter is beautiful Morgan." He waved and blew her a kiss as she drove off to Bea's and he went in to the mad house of chattering women.

Bea was buried beside her infant daughter the next day and within a few weeks her three-year-old son Lee followed her to the grave.

Morgan spent spring break watching his new daughter, Melanie, pink and soft against the white lace of her cradle. Life truly did go on.

In late April the family get together went off as scheduled. All the sisters, their husbands, and children had come to celebrate Mother Williams' sixty-eighth birthday. Happy's five children and Bea's two chased in and out of the house like they had always been a family. Morgan could hardly tell which two were Bea's they were so interwoven with each other, with four brunettes, one blonde, and two redheads, all Williams' and here to say just that.

He wandered down the worn path to the orchard to escape the laughter and squealing of thirty some odd children and the adult conversations of Bea's having mourned herself to death over the death of her baby daughter and the irony of the second baby following her to its grave so soon, as if he had mourned the loss of his mother.

Morgan sat on a low hanging branch and watched the festivities from afar, his natural position. He had always been on the outside looking in on this thing called family and yet their deaths tied him in knots. He couldn't seem to shake the feeling death was teasing him, taking from him, leaving him to mourn and to question the feeling he would live to the end but only after having watched them all go before him.

Happy came up on him from behind and tapped him on the shoulder. Frightened out of his wits he turned around expecting to meet the hooded form with the scythe. Breathless, wet with perspiration, and staring into the face of his sister, "God you scared me," he said after he got his breath back.

"I'm sorry. I was looking for you. I needed to talk and I thought you'd be out here." Happy said, sitting down beside her brother. "Morgan," Happy began, "I was having this recurring dream in which Bea said to me, 'You didn't do what you promised me.' It is about to drive me crazy. I can't sleep."

"You sound like you already have your answers." Morgan interrupted Happy. "What's the matter; are the kids too much for you?"

"No, quite the contrary; they're wonderful. You know I always wanted nine like Mother and I thought, God willing, I was two closer to my goal."

"Happy, what are you trying to say?"

"I told my neighbor, Honey, about the dreams and she told me to tell myself before falling to sleep each night that I would ask Bea what I promised her. It took three nights of trying but it finally did work. Bea said I promised I would make her husband take care of the children; I had enough responsibility with my five. I haven't had the dream since.

Am I going crazy? I don't want to give the children up. What can I do?"

"Happy, I know you loved Bea. I know over the years you did things for her she couldn't do for herself, but this time I think she's telling you not to. She's telling you you've done enough."

"But I want them, Morgan."

"Yes, Happy, but Bea is still their mother and she wants you to keep your promise. I'm sure after you think about it you will do what is right."

Morgan was glad that some of life's problems were so easily settled; his certainly hadn't been. He had dreamed of his encounter with Merlin so often, in the many years since it happened, that he could no longer separate the dream from the waking, it occupied so much of his thought. Why? It was no longer a matter of proving things to his father. It was an obsession by which all of man's problems could be solved and most especially, the one man, Morgan Edward Williams. The perfect cure was time, time to go back and correct the wrongs.

The Greenhouse

1951

The chirping of birds woke me early the next day. I went down for coffee and hugged Blanche who was busy at her work in the kitchen, then went back upstairs with my coffee, gathered up the folder from the night before, and went out on the terrace and stood against the railing looking out across the yard. It was a beautiful morning for soaking up the sounds and colors of awakening nature. I loved spring so much and yet, like Mrs. White, I was more partial to the fall. I looked at the folder with the unfinished work in it and thought of my own writing. Admittedly I had only dabbled with it and I could not do justice to an Elizabeth Windom White book. Would I even dare to try? I put the thought out of my mind for now and stood leaning from the terrace. Trey shouted, "Hello," and I waved to him. I watched him go into the greenhouse wondering how many mornings he had waved to Mrs. White and Joey when they stood here as I did now. How many things was I doing exactly as she had done? She knew I would find the mirror entrance and her notes; this I was sure of.

I decided to let Michael see some of my writing and go on from there. I hurried back downstairs and brushed past Blanche out to the yard to talk to Trey. There was so much to know, especially about Joey.

I ran across the yard to the garage and past the car. The greenhouse was a few feet beyond.

It was very Victorian looking with white metal trim intricately woven into patterns of flowers and birds. Inside were a couple of tables surrounded by chairs. A small pool with a young boy pouring water from a vase sat almost in the center of the front half of the house. The fountain was turned off and the pool was empty. Beyond the fountain were rows and rows of flowers in raised beds. There were huge fans overhead to cool the plants under the hot glass in summer.

Trey was bent over a bucket of some liquid mixture and didn't hear me come in. I watched him for a while. His love for his work was written on his face and in his every gesture. When he saw me he took off his work gloves and held out his hand to me. "Hello, Ms. Stone," he said.

"Call me Jennifer, Trey."

"Okay, Jennifer. Did you want something?"

"Yes, I wanted you to tell me about Joey."

"That could take a while; is there something in particular you want to know?" he asked looking very intense.

"Did he spend much time with you?"

"Yes, in nice weather he spent a lot of time out here. He loved to splash in the water. That's why she had the pool and the fountain put in. He loved water, but he didn't really swim. "How old was he?" I found myself asking.

"He turned sixty-two twelve days before he died."

I was flabbergasted; "Sixty-two. I didn't realize he was that old."

"He was but he was also very young. Every year we had to have a cake and candles and they all had to be lit. He would count them with her help and then she would light them and we all had to help blow them out. He would clap and cheer and ask for his presbents. That's what he called them; I think he could have said presents if she had told him how. He could say a lot harder words than that; he was always asking people if they were comfortable. I think she liked some of the funny little things he said and did and she didn't want them corrected. She doted on him; that's for sure, and he was one spoiled kid, though he was not mean spoiled."

"Did you ever pose for him?"

"You must have found one of his tablets. He was always drawing people. No, I never posed for him; he just drew while we talked or I worked. You know he carried his magazines and tablets with him everywhere. She even had them put in his hand in the casket and a little car or two in his pocket. She said he didn't like to have his hands empty, and she was right about that; If you took him somewhere in the yard or the house without reminding him to bring something with him, he would pick at lint or his own fingernails or the buttons on his shirt."

"What was he like?"

"He was very easy going unless you crossed him."

"Crossed him how?"

"He had trouble with language. I don't mean he couldn't talk because he could and did but he didn't always understand what was said to him. If you told him you were counting on him he would count on, two, three and if he felt threatened by what he thought you were saying he would become sullen and pull away from you. You couldn't reach him for hours sometimes after this. Mrs. White always made it a point to explain things over and over to be sure he knew exactly what was going on. I would get so tired of listening to her say the same thing again and again, but I knew it was the best way, and I learned in time to do the same thing to keep him calm."

"Did she ever leave him with people when she went on tours?"

"Never; he was always at arm's length, except for the time he spent out in the yard and here in the pool. Sometimes he would come without her but if he stayed very long she could always be counted on to show up. She worried a lot about him. She never really trusted anyone to look after him. And with her money she could have hired anybody she wanted to."

"Did he ever talk about things that you didn't know anything about?"

"Like what?"

"I don't know Trey. I don't know."

"Well he would say he was going to warm his coffee up in the microwave."

"Is there anything else, anything at all?"

"Yeah, now that I think about it, he would talk about a man on the moon. He would say man on the moon, over and over. Is that the kind of thing you mean?"

"Yes, Trey; by the way, do you know where the key to the library is kept? I've searched the house and can't find it."

"No, I don't, but Blanche might know."

"Speaking of Blanche, can you teach me how to talk to her with my hands the way you do?"

"Yes, but it would be better if you asked her; I'm not very good at it."

"Wouldn't she be offended?"

"No, I think she would be flattered. She taught Mrs. White or Mrs. White taught her; I can't remember which. Anyhow it's a lot faster than note writing."

"Thanks Trey; one more question before I go. Have you read Mrs. White's book *"A Place in Time?"*"

"No, I've never heard of it but I would like to read it. I've read all of her other books."

"If you'll come to the house, I'll lend you a copy, but you must promise me you will be very careful with it and return it as soon as you finish reading it."

Trey nodded a hearty yes and we started out of the greenhouse together. A big white ball of fur pushed past us as Trey closed the door. "Hello Kahlil," he said, walking on while I stood staring in disbelief.

"Trey, who does that cat belong to?"

"That's a good question. Mrs. White always said a cat didn't belong to anyone, and with Kahlil I have to agree. She comes and goes as she pleases and allows no one to touch her except Mrs. White, though she will brush up against other people's legs sometimes. She tried to make friends with Joey but he always ignored her unless his mother asked him to pet the cat. Then he would twist his face up to show how uncomfortable the whole thing was for him and touch Kahlil for a moment, and go back to what he had been doing before Kahlil appeared. She sleeps in Mrs. White's bed with her, sometimes on the pillow in her hair. She said she would wake up from a bad dream sometimes feeling like she was being crushed by some great weight and the cat would be sleeping on her chest, or in the small of her back. To my knowledge no one else has ever touched her; she's almost wild."

"Or very selective," I said, as we entered the house. "I wonder where she's been sleeping since the old lady died; it sure hasn't been in her bed, because I sleep there; she requested it."

"There's all kinds of beds in the house. I'm sure she's fine, Jennifer."

"Of course," I mumbled but I wasn't so sure. The poor cat had lost her family, and no one had or could comfort her. I loved cats myself and would love to have the company.

When we entered the house Trey was still in the lead as he had been since I had stood transfixed by the cat's sudden appearance. We climbed the stairs and he stopped at Joey's room and went in. I was puzzled but followed him past the shelves of tiny cars and trucks. He opened a door that I had mistook for a closet and started up a small flight of steps. At the top of the steps he opened another door and I followed him. We were in Mrs. White's study right beside the terrace door. I laughed out loud and Trey turned to me puzzled.

"What's so funny?" he asked.

"I didn't know her study connected to Joey's room like that," I said.

"Well, how do you get in here?" I said nothing but led Trey through the open mirror door into the attic bedroom. Then I closed the mirror. He stared and scratched his head in wonder.

"You know I have come here for years. I played with Joey in his room when I was young and I thought I knew everything there was to know about this house."

"How did you come to know the White's?" I asked, as I led the way back through the mirrored door and into the study for the book.

"Blanche is my aunt; she raised me. My parents were killed in a car accident when I was about three and she started bringing me here with her."

"Trey," I said, as I handed him the book, "I'm curious about how Mrs. White got up and down the steps at her age." He smiled from ear to ear and led me to the door leading down to Joey's room. We walked through it and he closed it to reveal another door behind it. He pushed a button on the wall and the door opened to a tiny elevator barely big enough for two people. He stepped in and I followed him.

When we stepped out again on the first floor we were in the dining room. The door here was not visible it simply faded into wood paneling on either side of the giant china cabinet.

Trey took the book and went back to the greenhouse while I looked for Blanche. Back upstairs in the hall in front of Joey's room. I stood staring at the door we had left open. Should I continue to leave it open, I was wondering as I approached it, and then I saw the long white fur all over Joey's bed, and knew this was where Kahlil was sleeping. I left the door open and hurried to the pantry as fast as I could, to look for something to leave as a trail for the cat from Joeys' room to mine.

Blanche interrupted me in my search, handing me a tablet with a note on it; "The phone is ringing," it said. I hurried to answer it and wondered why I hadn't heard it and more importantly how she had. It was Michael and he said he was about ready to hang up when I finally answered. I invited him over. He seemed surprised but agreed and said he would come right on.

I hurried back to the kitchen to find Blanche and grabbed up the tablet from the table as soon as I saw it. "How did you know the phone was ringing?" I wrote, and handed her the tablet. She pointed to a light over the kitchen door. It was unlit now, but I guessed that it flashed when the phone rang. I wrote, 'Why?' on the notebook that Blanche now held.

"Mrs. White did not always hear the phone so I would tell her when it rang. Also she spent a lot of time walking in the yard. She loved the outdoors so much." Blanche pointed to several benches scattered under trees in the huge yard and wrote that Mrs. White would sit on them to write sometimes.

I took the notepad and wrote asking her to teach me her language; tears came to her eyes. "Yes, Mrs. White said you would ask," she wrote back. I hugged her and went to my room.

I took my briefcase to the study and laid it on top of Joey's things; I searched through it looking for some of my better writing to show Michael. If my purpose here was to finish "The Caretaker," she either had a lot of faith in me or she knew something I didn't know; either way my writing was involved, so I needed an honest opinion. Michael was not the kind of person to beat around the bush and he would be a good judge of ability since he wrote professionally himself.

I took the stack of papers and went to the terrace to read and wait for him. I had hardly sat down when I heard him calling me from the bottom of the steps. I told him to come on up and we faced each other a moment later in the study. We embraced and he kissed me. We stood for a long time holding each other forgetting time and the room and everything about last night as he took my hand and led me towards the big bed.

The phone rang and I pulled away from him to answer it; it was for him. He took it and I heard him say, "yes," and, "two o'clock." He hung up and turned to me. "I have to leave at one; a private plane will be ready at two, and I still need to pick up my bags at the hotel and check out." He smiled and tried to kiss me again but I pulled away.

I had other things on my mind now, like my writing, the unfinished work, and his leaving. I got up and walked to the study; I didn't want him to see me cry. I hardly knew him. Why should I care if he was going back to New York today? Everything was moving too fast. I needed time to think.

"You didn't say a thing about the study," I said.

"I was too busy." he said walking towards me.

"I want to show you something," I said, changing the subject and I walked to the desk chair. The desk now stood between us and I picked up the folder and handed it to him. "It's an unfinished work of Mrs. White's," I said. "Do you think she might have wanted me to finish it?"

He took it and leaned against the doorframe, reading it. I offered him Joey's rocker. He didn't hear me; he was lost in the story. I watched him as he stood turning the pages. He seemed to always be leaning against something as if he couldn't stand alone. It is the way I remember him best; his tall slim body outlined by a doorframe.

"Do you write?" He asked when he was about half way through the notes.

"I was hoping you could tell me," I said, walking to the terrace to pick up the writing I had left there when he had come upstairs.

He took the second pile of papers and I took Mrs. White's notes holding them to my breast and biting at my lower lip. I was always miserable when anyone read my work. I stared at him watching for any sign of disapproval.

He had read only a couple of pages when he looked up shocked. "Jennifer, my God, you write a lot like her. I swear it's hard to see the difference. Maybe she did want you to finish the book. Maybe she hoped to give you a leg up with this book. She might have been trying to give you a starting point. Did you find a letter telling you what to do?"

"I didn't find a letter and, as of yet, no journal which I hope for the most. The study is pretty bare; just a few books, the television, and a keyboard to a missing typewriter," I said, as I opened the desk drawer to show him.

He studied the keyboard flipping it over and upright again. He looked puzzled as he sat down in her chair, swiveling from side to side. I watched him intently hoping he would make more of the bits and pieces than I had.

After awhile he sat up with a big smile and plugged the loose end of the keyboard cord in to a small hole in the television and pushed a button that said power. The television lit up and identified itself as a Videowriter asking that we insert a Videowriter diskette. We both laughed excited by our discovery.

I remembered the diskettes in the drawer and got one. Following the machine's on screen instructions, we found ourselves reading from *Helena*. Michael selected chapter nine and the screen changed to reveal the first page of the last chapter. We read along together amazed.

"There may be an instruction book; have you run across one?" Michael asked. I reached around him to the red and white booklet from the drawer and handed it to him. He sat for some time reading through the book looking up only once to ask for coffee.

I went downstairs for the pot figuring this could take awhile. I had run down the steps in my hurry but with my hands full and the hot coffee pot I stood at the bottom of the steps looking up. The elevator would reduce my chances of falling and being burned so I turned back to the paneled wall looking for the button.

I know I must have looked pretty funny standing there with my hands full searching the wall, but Blanche rescued me by reaching around me and pushing the button -- a knight standing on the shelf beside the crystal glasses. I would never have found it, and I told her so and thanked her as I hurried into the elevator. As the door closed behind me I could see her laughing.

In my absence Michael had begun typing and the words were appearing on the screen. It was a letter to me giving me a breakdown of the book's contents, so I could use the machine instead of a typewriter. When he finished he asked for a piece of paper, and I got it for him, and the machine printed the page out. I was amazed and the look on my face must have shown it. He smiled and spoke softly as if speaking to a child as he came to my side and put an arm around me. "Welcome to the 1990s," he said.

Pipes Books and Castles

1955

Morgan and Uncle Edward were in Peru together; it was early morning and neither of them had slept well the night before. They were tired and anxious to wrap up some last minute details before going down the mountain for supplies. Uncle Edward always supervised the trips down to make the best use of them and to keep people on the dig as much as possible instead of on the roads; barely narrow paths at some points, they were not always that safe.

Both men were hard working enthusiastic archaeologists and this day, with or without sleep, was like all the others, except for a nagging feeling Morgan had that he could not shake off. They had eaten a light breakfast, and gone out to begin the day's work, the first to arrive on the scene. A couple of others were just coming up, Morgan remembered, when the earth gave way under his uncle's weight and he plunged into the pit below. Morgan himself had barely escaped the same fall.

Dust and rock sprayed through the air blinding him and the others. He clamored to another descent carved in the earth and hurried to get to Uncle Edward who lay face down, nearly buried in the dirt. Morgan, choking on the still unsettled dust that filled the air, covered his mouth and nose with a handkerchief and ran over to his uncle. He knelt and began clearing the debris from in front of his face to ease his breathing and then quickly set to work clearing the rest.

He screamed out for help and soon everybody was in the pit helping though he was unaware of the others, working frantically to free his uncle. Feeling as if they were in a time warp or something and they were the only two people there, he believed the whole weight of the dirt and stones covering his uncle were his to move and he worked on exhausted. Sweat poured from him. A slight breeze passed over him and he felt a terrible chill, an omen to him that he would not be able to save his Uncle. He drove himself harder seeming near hysteria.

The others who watched Morgan as he clawed at the dirt were ready to haul him out of harm's way and to continue to dig on their own when they spotted his uncle's shirt. A cry of joy rang out and Morgan paused to look around him.

When everything was cleared away someone began to feel for broken bones and someone else pulled the still frenzied Morgan away from the body. He heard someone ask if any bones were broken and came to his senses. He had never witnessed such an accident on a dig before and the others had, being more seasoned. They knew what to do.

He thanked the man who had pulled him away and still held him by the arms. Freeing himself he bent to speak to his uncle. "Are you alright?" he asked.

"Yes, I am, except for a terrible pain in my chest. I'm not sure I can move."

"There are no broken bones as far as I can tell," the woman who had been examining him said.

"Morgan, lad, turn me over please and for god's sake get me out of this hole so the others can get back to work."

Several people laughed and mumbled among themselves that the old slave driver was quite himself, no need to worry. A litter was sent for and Uncle Edward was placed on it. His nephew held his hand as the four carriers, all strong sure-footed natives, used to the treacherous mountain paths, began the climb up the side of the pit. Morgan could hear some of the workers talking among themselves about how lucky Edward was to be alive.

There were no doctors anywhere on the mountain; no one knew or could say what the damage was. Without this information a trip down the mountain by jeep with the injured man was out of the question. A doctor and a helicopter were called for by radio over the long distance between the dig and the city at the foot of the mountain. Uncle Edward died before help arrived.

Morgan accompanied the body home to the London countryside and he now stood in his uncle's study with tears streaming down his face. He had no one left. His uncle, his brother, his friend, all the one man, Edward Morgan Butler, age fifty-five, was dead.

He was tired of loving and losing. He was tired of life. He was tired of dreaming and searching. The old familiar vision of death taunting him and leaving him to mourn the loss of everyone before his end came to mind. In the top desk drawer he had found a letter addressed to him in his uncle's handwriting.

Dear Morgan, my son,

When you read this I will be gone. Do not mourn for me. Do not weep for the old fool who coasted through life riding on your coattail for these many years. I'd have long ago given up. Only the picture you held of me in your mind has kept me going.

I hope, when you are reading this that I have died a young man, not ancient like our old Grandfather Jim. In the end the poor old soul was forgetful to the point of being unable most days to remember the names of his children. The night before his death I recall that he had been married to our Grandmother Butler for some twenty years plus, and he called out most plainly the name of his first wife, Millie, who had been dead thirty years, and he said that she was in the kitchen getting supper.

Now that is old and that is forgetful and that is not what I would wish for myself, and I hope it is not what others would wish for me. Youth is a far better time to die, though now being past fifty, I would not be considered young to many. Still, compared to Grandfather Jim, I have a decided edge.

Young Morgan, I have enjoyed life more since meeting you than I ever had before. I have searched with you for the answers to life. I have loved you like a son and yet with the little difference in our ages I have been able to be with you as a brother, and more importantly, as a friend.

I beg you to continue with your dream and I bequeath to you Butler House and its grounds in the hopes that you will find Merlin and his time portal or time machine or at least his secret. I have stood many evenings in the north tower searching the woods for the light you spoke of. I had hoped to be the one to give you what you desired most in life thereby showing you the depth of my feelings for you.

You are more than my sister's son. You are more than family; you are the reason I have accomplished what I have in life. I have strived above all else to live up to the image you held of me in your heart and mind. Never having been a hero to anyone before, I may have erred, though I pray not.

I wish you success in all that you do and I cherish the many good times we shared. I wait for you at Butler House with love. Uncle Edward.

Morgan stood with the letter in his hand. He had loved his Uncle Edward and he was glad to have been with him when he died. He was glad that he had faced death head on though admittedly he had lost. He knew he had done everything possible to save his uncle's life. Morgan felt that he and death knew each other firsthand now and he challenged the hooded figure to take him before he found the secret of time and stole away all opportunity for him to do so.

The dig had been one he had almost missed. He was glad now that he hadn't. He was glad that the thought of a boring summer in Glendale quarreling with himself and with Becky over his daughter had been motive enough to bring him back to the Peruvian mountains, though he hated the frigid nights and the high altitude. Something had pulled at him and he wondered now if it was a knowing that his Uncle Edward would die.

They had been writing to each other about the dig and the area and its history for months but it was not the history of the place that had come to interest Uncle Edward. No, for once the present happenings of a place meant more to him. His letters had taken on a whole new subject as they continued, and Morgan's curiosity was aroused. He had referred back to books on metaphysics and sent copies of text to his uncle in answer to questions asked. He had become engrossed in the change in his uncle and the almost mystical quality of his letters. He had to join him in the mountains and now he was glad he had. He would always be glad he had. He felt strongly that the letter he had just found in the desk drawer and now held in his hand had little to do with the man he had just buried. That uncle was brand new and had died in his infancy.

The mountains had changed him completely. They had brought out the best in him and still more. The mountains and their secrets of today, not the secrets of the past, had changed the man he had loved into a spiritual mystical being.

The mountains had held answers for him too; they had sustained him, and they had made him stronger.

The Indians told wonderful stories of meetings with beings of other worlds; beings with secrets not unlike the ones he was searching for. If his uncle had learned anything he could use, if he had met any of these beings himself, Morgan felt sure that he would have left that information for him. Or he would have wanted them to get together immediately so that he might take Morgan to the source and let him hear for himself.

Their years together had made the question of time one they were both asking, so he could only assume that his uncle had not been able to answer the question, or possibly he had found a way around, and this possibility intrigued him too. He was happy for the change, the alternate answers, if that is what his uncle had found, and he hoped with new zeal for the end to his own search, either through time or an early death, to end the mystery and the misery he felt life held for him.

Two small boxes of pipes lay open but undisturbed on the desk before him. He lifted the lid and took them out again one by one. He looked at them and tried to remember what he could of them and of the times he had seen each particular pipe in the hands of its late owner. He himself had never smoked though he had tried hard to acquire the habit upon inheriting his father's pipes; like Uncle Edward his father had never been without his pipe. Morgan guessed after years of watching them both and now with his second set of pipes that he just wasn't British enough.

Yes, he loved the country and its castles, its land, its writers, its legends, and its digs; when he was fortunate enough to find one. But the most he could get out of the British pipe was to enjoy the wonderful smell of the tobacco with its many different aromas when someone else was smoking it. He looked at each pipe as he packed them away in the boxes again and closed each box.

Then he went out into the sun his uncle had always told him would cheer him up in time of crisis. It had seldom worked but he did it anyway, out of habit he guessed, half expecting to hear the old familiar prodding and an invitation to walk in the garden -- the beloved English gardens which he had learned to respect and love almost as much as the people that planted them.

"Yes, I will join you on one last walk through the garden and the fields," he felt himself saying to someone, but to whom? Was Uncle Edward here with him? Was he here to see his affairs settled? Was he here to tell Morgan something he had not told him in his many letters or in their recent weeks together? Was such a thing possible? Morgan believed so and he walked outside.

He felt a presence at his side as he walked around the outer circle of the garden. He waited for directions, something to tell him which path to take, which flowers to stop at in remembrance of another walk on another day. It was not to be though, for while the presence still seemed to be at his side it offered no hint of a particular path or patch of flowers.

Finally a very frustrated Morgan took a nearby exit from the garden and walked to the front of the house. He walked a few hundred feet in front of it and still further away and turned. He stood but not alone, he felt, and admired the grand old building. It was as if he were seeing it for the first time. Oh God, he grew depressed with his next thought, the prospect of it being the last time he would stand here in the yard, and tears came to his eyes.

He burst through the heavy giant front door pushing it aside as if it were made of paper, almost knocking poor old Bentley, the butler, down in the process. "Are you alright?" he asked, stopping to help the old man regain his composure.

"Quite so, quite so," Bentley replied with dignity. "Just a bit shaken, Sir," he added.

Morgan excused himself and hurried to the door leading to the north tower, looking briefly at the narrow circling flight of stone stairs before beginning his climb. Driven, he ran as fast as he could, pushed along. His tears stopped and a smile stole across his face. He understood or thought he did. He understood where Uncle Edward was leading him.

He felt clearly that the answer was in the tower and he hurried up the steps climbing them in twos and threes. The presence seemed to be right in step with him. He arrived at the top breathless and took a moment to catch his breath before going to the window to look out. The countryside green and beautifully manicured lay about the house like a velvet blanket. The woods' edge was off to his right and the deeper woods beyond, forming a half circle. Everything was clearly visible on this beautiful late summer's day.

He searched for the reason for his climb to the tower. He felt the presence beside him perhaps looking out as he was but nothing out of the ordinary happened. He waited and continued to search the countryside and then the clear blue sky for some hint of what his uncle might be trying to tell him. He stood for over an hour, tiring and yet anxious to know something. It grew late and he remained in the tower with the presence.

At dusk as he finally started down the stairs, he felt he understood. He laughed out loud and turned back to the windows along the walls of the tower. The message was plain to him now; Uncle Edward was telling him to keep on searching, not to give up. He laughed and laughed.

He had spent the past seven summers and years before his marriage to Becky with his uncle. They had studied side by side and they understood each other. He would stay here; he knew the answer was here. Perhaps some night when he least expected it the light would appear in the night sky, low over the woods, and he would beat feet to the spot where Merlin was and get his answers.

Throw Away Age

1987

Morgan left the university president's office with papers in his hands with words to the effect that he was no longer needed, no longer wanted. This forced retirement, though it was expected, hit him hard. He still lived, he still breathed, he still thought, and yet somehow he felt like the life had been kicked out of him.

Once out of the administrative building he stood on the wide circular steps looking down on the crowd of people; they looked as small as he felt. He thought of the media's name for him, "history giant," and laughed to himself.

He was living in a throw away age where everything was used and tossed, and he was just one more of those disposable things he saw thrown in the trash every day. People were just beginning to become interested in the throwing away of the elderly, and only because of growing health care cost. The elderly were bankrupting a system. It wasn't their personal worth in terms of their knowledge and the love they offered, that had science and government interested; it was dollars and cents. Leave it to man, Morgan thought, to prolong life only to confine that life to the lowest income bracket and an old folks' home.

No one listened, not Becky, not Chris Lee, not the University, not the kids on the back rows in the halls where he spoke. Today's kids didn't care about kings and generals long ago dead, or their fights, or the lands they fought for. All they cared about was using things and tossing them aside, forgetting the old in their excitement for the newer, shinier model.

His students weren't that different from Chris Lee and his friends, only older. If it wasn't shiny, or neon, or deafeningly loud, they didn't give it a second look. He pictured a future generation of these people and saw hearing aids as the hottest selling item in their old age, every man and woman having at least one. Their music today was turned up so loud they were deaf to all else, especially the value of life, of age. He was sure they would go down in history as the most hearing impaired of all recorded generations.

Now that the seriousness of man's daily garbage dumping had become a subject for study, he wondered when age would receive the same priority? At first this had amused him but when some of the better colleges had begun studies on the problem of trash, he knew it was no joke. This today was no joke either. He was not ready to shuck everything for a rocking chair on the side porch. He had a teenager to raise, although God knew he was bungling that terribly. He and the boy hadn't had a conversation that hadn't ended in an argument in months. Still he did have the job to do and he had other jobs to do too. He had speaking engagements scheduled but he stopped himself with this thought. He had seen those cancelled and no new ones scheduled for more than one retiring colleague. They would put him and his ideas on history, and all of his carefully written and oftentimes awarded papers on periods of history, in the same archives he had researched them in.

But he had a sudden idea, and he rolled the idea around in his mind before descending the steps, walking with a new purpose. There would be time for one more paper before word spread of his retirement and that paper would be on the throw away age he was living and dying in. The thoroughly modern practice of throwing away the elderly should be stopped, he felt.

He headed to his office. His things had to be packed which would take a few days. His replacement, a middle age nerd, a term he had borrowed from his grandson Chris Lee's crowd, would rush him to get the job done. But he did have the summer, and in the mood he was in now he might full well take the summer. After all it took years to bring it all in; weeks might be a conservative estimate of the time needed to clear everything away -- the nerd be hanged.

He walked across the beautifully manicured lawn toward the history building. It was some distance but he loved to walk; he did his best thinking then. The day was sunny; the skies clear, at least as clear as skies got anymore. He could remember the bluest blue skies of his boyhood and wondered how man had botched up something so beautiful and so far away. This took him back to his thoughts of the paper on the throw away age and he considered calling it *The Care of the Aged Through the Ages* and laughed to himself. He felt far from aged; seventy-three wasn't old. He would tell anybody that wanted to argue different how he felt about that.

Arriving at the front lawn of the history building he noted the expression on the face of the statue of The Thinker. That poor dumb Joe may be aged, he thought, and god knew he'd been sitting there rain or shine for as almost as many years as Morgan himself had taught here. Still thinking about the same question, Morgan guessed and wondered when or if the sculptor had ever found the answer to the question that had prompted the carving of the statue.

Suddenly he heard his named being called. Turning towards the sound he saw Zack, his best friend and head of the English department, standing on the walkway below the statue he had just been studying. Zack waited till Morgan caught up with him before going into the history building. "I was looking for you, Morgan."

"You've found me, my friend; I was just dumped formally and I was on my way to my office to begin the task of erasing me from the memory banks of the university," he said, handing Zack the formal notice telling him his contract for the coming year would not be renewed.

"What is this and how did it get so wrinkled?" Zack asked unfolding the crumpled paper.

"I believe, today it is what's called a pink slip though as you can see it is white; and it is wrinkled or rather wadded up because I felt that a far better choice of things to wad than Dr. Burroughs head, when the urge overtook me.

Zack laughed and straightened the letter as they walked on. The big double doors were open to welcome the warm day and a little fresh air. Morgan had told them often enough that just because it was the history department did not mean it had to smell like his grandmother's musty cellar. He didn't see 'the Nerd' as a lover of fresh ideas or fresh air and figured the practice of recirculating the Museum's air, as he fondly called the building, would fall by the way side. The Nerd would want to revamp everything, put his mark on the department, so to speak. When he'd been here a few years he would probably find, as all professors before him had, that the mark was quickly erased when you were gone.

Morgan considered the possibility of his having been a nerd once and asked his friend Zack. "Tell me, Zack, do you think I was ever a nerd or that possibly I am one today?"

"No, Morgan, not today, and after knowing you all these years I will honestly have to say I doubt you could have ever been one. Why do you ask?"

"I was just thinking about my replacement but never mind him. Tell me what do you think of my doing one last paper before they throw me out? I want to call it *The Throw Away Age*, but I feel I would probably stand a better chance of getting it published if I called it something like *The Treatment of the Aged Through the Ages*.

Zack laughed at Morgan's titles; "You've picked a strange time to go crazy on me. You were supposed to do that while you were teaching here, not when you are leaving."

"Delayed am I? Well you're just picking on my titles because you have a few years to go before the pink slip ends up in your mailbox," Morgan teased.

"Maybe not as long as you think," Zack said to him as he stopped and laid his hand upon his friend's arm.

"What's wrong?" Morgan asked, concerned by Zack's unusual behavior.

"I have cancer and it's inoperable."

Morgan's face turned ashen and his hands trembled; he looked hard at Zack unable to believe what he had just heard.

"Don't worry; I have time enough left to write a paper or two. I'm thinking of doing my first one on the rewriting of the English Language.

It's been done you know. Take the word nerd you used earlier; it has replaced dope, which is now something you do, not something you are. Wheels has replaced automobile; awesome has replaced great. My friend has been replaced by my main man, though I don't know if the same phrase is used in reference to female best friends."

He stared at Zack in disbelief. "You'll go out making a joke, won't you?" Morgan said as they stood in the hall outside his office.

"I hope so, but they say I'll have a lot of pain in the end, so maybe I'll disappoint you."

I hope I'm there to know Morgan thought, remembering he had not been present at the death of many people he had loved in the past. He'd been in England when Ned and his father died. He had a knack for being in the wrong place when he was most needed and vowed to himself that this time would be different, as they entered the door of his office, walking past Missy Spencer, his secretary, and on into his private office.

"You know, Morgan, summer break is not a good time to get news of this kind. I have nothing to do but think and my thoughts are fearful ugly things. I don't want to die, not just yet, never to be honest. I don't want somebody digging me up in a few hundred years and taking my tired old bones apart in some college lab. They might reconstruct this old relic and actually make me handsomer than I am today."

"How much pain are you in?" Morgan asked Zack trying to get some details, between the bad jokes of a man who always had covered the worst of life's problems by wisecracking. It belied his sensitivity. People only thought they knew him. He guessed Zack wanted it that way and he didn't answer Morgan.

They both sat down onto the leather sofa in Morgan's office tired from the day's bad news and their long walk up two flights of stairs. Zack rested his head on the back of it staring at the ceiling, his breathing labored. Morgan looked at the old man beside him; realizing he had noticed changes in him the last few months though he never dreamed it to be anything more than getting older.

They were both white haired, their faces lined with age; battle scars, Morgan called them, and God knew he had done his share of fighting, especially lately. Everything about today irked him; he laughed realizing he had another word for Zack's revision of the English language and turned to him to give him the word, braced a little against the news of his cancer. Zack was asleep.

Sitting quietly beside him, Morgan stared at a patch of sunlight streaming in through the open window, remembering back to that day in May so many years ago. He would love to be able to take his friend Zack back with him away from the painful ugly death ahead of him, and vowed to work harder for the answers to the wonder of time, answers that had eluded him for over sixty-four years.

The morning passed with Zack sleeping and Morgan daydreaming. A steady breeze blew in through open windows carrying the smells of late spring, smells of the rebirth of nature. A lone bird sang and whistled, occasionally leaving one branch to fly to another. Morgan wondered why. Was the bird celebrating the season or was he too flying around looking for answers?

Morgan had traveled, studied, and read all his life and ended up flying from here to there only marking the seasons. Had it really been sixty-four years? My god! He gasped sitting up suddenly. Zack is sixty-two, have I really been searching longer than he has been alive? And he sits here beside me old, worn, and poisoned by cancer.

It can't be so Morgan argued with himself and sat back weeping. He wept for the time gone by and for the unfruitful search that had consumed him and the years. He wept for loved ones that had died without him and for death gaining time on his sleeping friend. He wept because he would know death first hand again, and in a little while he would experience it himself

Missy knocked lightly on the door at 11:45. Morgan walked to the door and opened it shushing her. He left the room and was about to close the door behind him when Zack stirred and called out to him, "is it lunchtime?'

"Yes, Zack, are you hungry?"

"No, but I need to get some work done; I'll walk out with you two."

"Irked,' Morgan said as they parted beneath the statue of The Thinker. Zack looked at him puzzled. "It's another word for your paper," Morgan explained.

"So it is. So it is," Zack said laughing as he turned toward the English building.

Morgan stood staring after him until he was out of sight. Missy had walked on, missed him beside her, and turned back. "Are you okay, Professor Williams?" she asked.

"No, no I'm not," he replied, his eyes once again filling with tears. Searching for words and unsure he should tell her about Zack's cancer, he said instead, "I've been let go."

"You've been what?" she shouted surprised.

"I've been forced to retire. Don't look so surprised," he snapped. "This is a disposable age; the younger, newer model will be taking over in the fall."

"I'm sorry and I'll really miss you, Professor Williams."

"I know, Missy, and I'm sorry I snapped at you; it's an era I'm angry with, not you."

"I understand, sir."

"No, I don't think you do, but in time you will. I promise you that, in time, you will. I'm taking the afternoon off; I'll see you tomorrow." Morgan said as he turned away from her and began the long walk back to his car parked at the Administration Building.

The car's shiny black body, large and square, stood out in the parking lot among rows and rows of little red sports cars. Was it a law, he'd often wondered, that college students and personnel had to drive red sports cars? And if so, why had he never been told?

He approached the car from the rear noting the license plate, something he always did. His grandson Chris Lee consumed by the 1935 Ford and its mint condition, had urged Morgan to get a license plate with an antique car on it. "Register it," the boy urged repeatedly and since he wouldn't, his worse fear was that the boy would do it without telling him.

Morgan argued that the regular license was more suitable. The car was not an antique; it was younger than he was and he was not an antique. Antiques were things put aside in attics or cellars for years and drug out again with the settling of estates. The Ford had been driven almost continuously all of its fifty-one years; therefore it didn't qualify anymore than he himself did. "Old yes, antique no," he always ended up telling Chris Lee.

The windows were open as they almost always were. Morgan liked fresh air. He opened the front door to get in and stopped short. There was an empty soft drink can lying on the seat; the last few drops of cola spilled out. He picked the can up and reached in his pocket for his handkerchief, furious at the can, its owner, and society in general for producing both. He realized the incident had brought him back around full circle to no longer being needed or wanted by today's world and like the can, he was disposable.

He wiped the seat, put the handkerchief back in his pocket, got in the car, and began the long drive home lost in thought. He was not ready to be shelved and he had no intention of being tossed aside. He would think this thing through until he had a plan for the years ahead or Merlin's secret of time, which would allow him a most welcome relief from them.

An Appointment Kept

1951

I was alone now in the big house but I was no longer afraid. It was more like an old friend than I would ever have thought a building could be. Michael had flown back to New York. I missed him but it also gave me a courage I would not have thought possible, for now I knew I had to go it alone. My questions were for me to answer and the key was for me to find.

I spent most of my time on the upstairs terrace often eating supper there enjoying the setting sun, and welcoming it again the next morning as it retraced its journey across the sky.

Slowly words began to come to me. Words that might be written later but for now they danced across my mind as the sun did across the sky. I had played with the machine in the study and knew it well, but I had not toyed with the idea of writing a book long enough to feel comfortable with the thought.

I went through the house talking to myself and to the cat whenever she put in an appearance, which she was doing more and more frequently. At night I put out small bowls of sardines leading from Joey's old room up the back stairs to my own. Sometimes finding the smell of fish so strong the next day I could hardly stand to sit in the study and always finding the bowls empty.

Kahlil's fur stopped appearing on Joey's bed and began appearing on the cushion in the desk chair. On the morning I found her hair in the chair under the dormer in my room, I was thrilled. She was probably watching me sleep and I held out hope that she would join me in the big bed one night. It had been weeks and I had bought enough sardines to raise eyebrows at the grocery; even Trey and Blanche had asked why I ate so many of them.

Michael and I had exchanged letters since he left. He had written me from so many places I gave up trying to keep up with him. I just prayed he would not go to Korea as so many of his friends at other newspapers had done. He talked a lot about the possibility and seemed happy with the thought! But it worried me; I had an uneasy feeling we had lost each other to a war before, though I couldn't explain where the feeling came from. I put it off as worry plain and simple, the influence of Mrs. White being accountable for the direction the worry had taken. Still I couldn't shake the very real feeling of having known Michael all my life; his face was as familiar to me as my own, and so were his moods. I loved him and that too made no sense in light of how little time we had spent together. It could be explained only in Mrs. White's terms and I turned more and more to her writings, looking for the words that would set feelings and thoughts of Michael in order.

I had taken the two big pictures of Mrs. White and Joey from the wall in the living room and brought them up here to the study. I stared at her picture a lot and found myself talking to her after awhile, not just about Michael but about everything.

I sat outside many nights past the sun's setting. Tonight darkness came on slowly and it was warm for a May night. I dozed for a moment and I thought I heard her call my name. I awoke startled, stood up, and hurried into the house. As I entered the study she was sitting in the desk chair. In a moment the image faded but for that moment it was so real I could have reached out and touched her.

I reasoned that I was spending too much time in the study and thinking too much about the woman. I needed some fresh air, a funny thing to think after all the time I was spending on the terrace; nevertheless I felt a need to get outside and walk on solid ground. I hurried downstairs and outside.

The grounds stood before me half hidden in shadows as I stepped off the side porch. The moon was big and lopsided, not quite full but big enough to light my way across the yard. I walked not really caring where I went; I just needed to feel the grass, and the earth beneath my feet; kicking my shoes off I carried them along.

Before I realized it I was at the cemetery gate. I was here with her again; it seemed that I could not escape her no matter what. I thought of *A Place in Time* where Morgan is pulled along by the spirit of his Uncle Edward and wondered if Mrs. White and I were acting out this same scene.

At the cemetery gate I could see that the earth had settled some; the flowers remained here at her request to melt into the ground and become a part of her and Joey. I knew now as I had not known the day of her farewell party that the two thousand forty-one roses were in commemoration of her return to life here on earth in 2041. I remembered a scene from one of her books where she talked of burying one of her many cats at the base of a tree so that, as she had put it, they would become one with each other, a strange thought then, but now I felt I understood.

Hers and Joey's stones stood with only their names and the single date March 4th and March 6th respectively. Their dates of birth nobody would have believed. This too was at her request, one of many requests, which made no sense at all and seemed to paint a picture of a very eccentric old woman until you knew her secret and then they made perfect sense.

I walked away after awhile to the formal flower garden strolling among the scattering of white blooms glowing in the moonlight. I agreed totally with Morgan's Uncle Edward; they were mysterious and ghostly looking and they brought and added a dimension of light to the night.

I sat down near a fountain where another stone child stood with a vase of water spilling out over his shoulder into the pool at his feet. I pulled my skirt in a bunch and dipped my feet into the pool. The water was cold as it whirled about me and splashed occasionally on my face and arms. The garden was the most magnificent place on the grounds; and Trey and I had made plans together to expand it, and he had hired extra people to help with the task. I wondered now if Mrs. White had made the paths appear to be non ending for just this reason.

That she knew me, and how I thought and felt, was the most undeniable and yet the most mysterious thing about all of this. I felt more and more that our souls were linked in some great bond that was unbreakable. I longed more and more to know how and why she knew me so completely; it was if she had spent a lifetime studying me. I wished to know her in the same way.

While it was true that I had her house, her grounds, and her books, she had a decided edge on me. She knew things about me I could only imagine about her; and I held stubbornly to the thought that I would not be writing the end to any book of hers until I had the same answers to her being that she seemed to have to mine.

I tried to quiet my mind and to enjoy the night and the garden. The smells were wonderfully relaxing and I used them to peel away the layers of questions and the fatigue of the day. After awhile I saw a shadow of a woman coming towards me and I sat hoping it was the woman from the study chair. I lost the image and sighed heavy with grief. I tried again to retrieve it and found I could not. I went back to the smell of the flowers and the relaxation they filled me with; almost immediately the woman stood again in the same spot. I fought to keep the image this time dwelling on her dress, her hair, and her walk. She was caressing a single white flower. I fought trying to identify her until she was close enough to speak, if indeed she got that close and had any intention of speaking. She came to me slowly though we were still quite some distance from each other. She reached a point in the garden where she stood in direct moonlight as the tall flowers behind her had given way to much shorter ones; she looked like me and I screamed in fright as the image faded into the night.

I got up quickly to leave the garden and there in front of me was Mrs. White. She smiled and reached out a hand to me. I took it as if it were the most natural thing in the world. We walked around the outer circle of the garden together saying nothing and then she was gone. I was no longer afraid; I was certain that she was real and had come to me from some other time, and not the other side of life that we know as death. I hurried across the lawn to the house and up the stairs at a run.

I sat down at the desk and turned on the power to the machine. I was glad now for the time I had spent getting acquainted with its workings. Words raced through my mind and I found myself typing faster than I ever had, trying to put it all down before any bit of it got away. I didn't stop for corrections but went blindly on; driven by feelings and ideas I had never given voice to before.

I began with the vision of Mrs. White in the garden and her reaching out to me. I too would be a time traveler. For now I would do it on paper and perhaps as Mrs. White had written about Morgan, given enough time to study and explore it, I would do it for real.

Elizabeth Windom White had been in her eighties, I would have supposed, when I saw her tonight and she had kept an appointment with me here in the garden on a warm May night in 1951, several weeks after her death. She was not dead when she traveled therefore she had been able to pass up the date of her physical death. Was time real I asked myself? And then I answered in the same words she had said Morgan, the boy in 1910, had used; "I had forgotten the fell of time at its best, flexible, moldable time."

I thought back over Michael's arguments that it was done in the mind. How real this would make it I could only imagine. But Mrs. White had said we are the sole creator of our reality, responsible for every skeleton in our closet, every monster under our bed, and every angel on our shoulder. If she was right, and I have no reason to believe she wasn't, then could this reality be a creation born over many lifetimes? Could my being here at White House be because of other lifetimes spent knowing her? I had until now tried to fix the explanation on my current life. For the moment I needed also to consider having met myself in the garden; as vague and as misty as the woman appeared to be, she looked unmistakably like an older me. Was it an attempt to time travel either through my own power or Mrs. White's? What was I doing in the garden with me? Was the answer in *A Place in Time* where Morgan, the boy climbed down the trellis while Morgan the man sat on the porch?

I listed the known facts: There are many things in this house that are from 1968 through 1991, magazines and books, toy cars and trucks, dishes, appliances, this machine. I knew I had a book to write about White House; I would get to The Caretaker later I hoped.

Birds were chirping in the half light of early morning when I stopped typing. I stretched, turned off the machine, and left the diskette sitting in its slot in readiness. I dragged myself off to bed and slept until the sun shining through the ceiling windows made the room so hot I woke up, covered with perspiration; then I put on a robe and headed to the bathroom.

Smelling coffee as I came down the attic stairs I knew Blanche was in the house somewhere. We needed to talk but first I had to sneak up on the day. I was in the tub when I heard a gentle tapping at the door. I felt a slight breeze and looked around to see a steaming cup of coffee sitting on the little table and Blanche going out the door. I wanted to thank her but I knew she'd never hear me so I picked up a bar of soap and threw it against the door. She turned startled by the vibration and I slowly mimed, "Thank you." She understood and mimed, "You're welcome," in return.

I lay back in the tub nursing the cup of coffee in my hands thinking about last night and wondering if I would ever see Mrs. White again. I thought of my writing and wondered if the sixty plus pages would grow to become a complete novel. I wondered if the title *White House* said all I wanted it to say. I didn't just want to imply Mrs. White's house but to convey all of the mystery of the place with its hidden elevator, mirrored study, and locked library with its missing key, and to tell of the love that lived here for a man-child and of his mother, who had brought him from another time that he might be safe, as she had said in *A Place in Time*.

That she had moved them back years was certain, at least in my mind. That she moved forward and backward at will was becoming almost as much of a certainty. How else had she kept her appointment in the garden with me last night? How else had I met an older me only moments before her visit? When the water began to cool I got out of the tub and went to my room to dress. Blanche was dusting in the dining room when I ran down the stairs excited and ready to begin my first sign language lesson with her. She had to know more than Trey about the house because she was always in it and I wanted to know everything there was to know.

At first she was thrilled to be sharing with me but she soon became very frustrated by my inability to readily grasp the hand movements she was so adept at. The question of who taught who was now apparent to me; Blanche was much too impatient to teach anybody anything. Finally she took me by the hand and led me to the peach bedroom, motioned for me to sit down on the bed, and opened what I thought was the chiffarobe to reveal a television set.

Then she searched through a vast assortment of oblong white things that looked like books with the word Polaroid written on them. She kept taking them from the shelves beside the television, reading their labels and then putting them back and getting the next one out. After a few minutes of this she found the one she wanted, turned on the set, took a black box from the white Polaroid cover and put it into a slot below the television. The whole thing seemed a lot like the machine in the study except that there was no keyboard, when suddenly the room was filled with the sound of a woman s voice explaining sign language.

I watched and tried to repeat what I saw while Blanche went back to her dusting. I would be a long time learning this very difficult language, not because I was stupid but because I had a habit of rushing into things at breakneck speed making it twice as hard to learn. Also I had been born left handed at a time when teachers and parents forced children into right-handedness leaving me extremely awkward with my hands.

I watched the woman and was looking for a way to turn the machine off when Blanche returned and pushed a button that made the woman go backwards and I sat awed. When the woman was back to her original greeting and introduction, Blanche turned her back around and the whole thing began again. I know I looked ridiculous sitting in the middle of the bed trying to understand what Blanche was doing because she stared at me hard for a minute on her way out of the room, paused and pulled a small tablet she often carried out of her apron pocket, walked back to the television and wrote as she looked at it. After a while she came back to where I was setting, patted me on the arm and tore the sheet from the tablet and handed it to me. It reminded me of Michael and the machine upstairs. Thank goodness for people that understood machines; it made life a lot easier for people like me.

I found I was too impatient to sit through the whole lesson again. Words were coming and going in my head like leaves in a fall wind. I had to stop this and go upstairs to write. I picked a phrase form the early part of the thing Blanche had called a tape and memorized it to show my good intentions then I turned off the machine and went to Blanche to show her I was trying.

She was in the hall coming out of the living room with her dust rag and polish in one hand and a small weird looking thing that said broom on its top in the other. Try as I did I could not see any bristles but Blanche was getting used to me by now and sensed my problem. Handing me the rag and polish she turned the broom thing upside down and there hidden away under it were two long cylinders with brush bristles on them. Not your everyday ordinary broom to be sure, but then there wasn't much around here that was ordinary and I handed her a note signed, "I'm hungry", repeating the words aloud for myself so I could keep my mind on what I was doing. She smiled in approval and led the way to the kitchen. We fixed sandwiches, poured ice tea, and sat down together to eat lunch. She slowly repeated some of the simpler signs and wrote them down for me when my memory failed me. I promised to remember next time and sat off for the study with my tea.

Sitting down at the desk I powered up the machine but then decided I would reread last night's material first to be sure of where I was in my story. I took the stack of papers out of the long middle drawer and picked the last three pages to read; it would take too long to read the whole thing and I was afraid my writing mood would pass. With the mood reset I began to type. I found it to be like a fever that would not break but went on and on. After several hours I looked up to see the sun at eye level behind the house, even with the terrace railing. Where had the day gone? Was this a sort of time travel too, day fading into night as I had sat engrossed in my writing?

The ice in the glass had melted and sat on top of the warm tea like oil on water. I stirred it with my finger, drank it down, and returned to the machine.

It was eight thirty when I went down stairs for something to eat and for more tea. I opened the microwave oven door for my dinner, which I knew Blanche had left for me. Across the top of the plate was a paper napkin with the words microwave on 2 to warm your food. I had not used this machine before but I had watched Blanche when she cooked bacon for our bacon and tomato sandwiches I took the plate over to the oven hidden under a roll top on the counter. I put the plate in and turned the timer to 2, closed the door and pushed the start button. While it was warming the plate of food I fixed myself a glass of fresh tea and stood in the doorway looking out.

Out of the corner of my eye I saw a woman walking at the edge of the garden, she was looking to the house and waved as I saw her. I recognized her as Mrs. White and ran out to see her, forgetting the food until I heard the bell ring signally that it was hot as the door closed behind me. I could eat later; for now I had an appointment and this time I prayed I would have sense enough to ask some questions.

When I reached the garden she was gone. She was teasing me and I realized that the mystery was mine alone to decode. She had no intentions of answering questions; she planned only to whet my appetite. I laughed as I sat down by the pool and put my feet in the water.

It was a warm night and I stripped down to my slip and stood under the vase of pouring water and wet myself down. It felt wonderful; I hadn't realized I was so tired. My back ached from hours at the machine and my eyes were burning. I shuffled my feet around in the pool thinking of how Joey might have succumbed to the magic of this water on a warm night.

Feeling sleepy I lay down on my back using my arms for a pillow and stared up; I shared Mrs. White's fascination for the night sky. I remembered trying to count stars on a summer night when I was a little girl. I had lain on a blanket with some friends and one of them had said that if you counted all the stars you would die. I can't remember if I counted them to see if she was right or if I hoped I might die. I was a terribly lonely girl, never very close to anyone.

At home my parents had argued and slammed doors in each other's faces all my life. Sundays were the worst day of the week for it was the one day my father was sure to be home from work and the day they argued most. I hid in my room when I was small burying my head under a pillow to shut out their voices. When I was older and could get outside I did, going anywhere and everywhere to get away from them. By the time I was ten years old I knew every museum, library, and park in our town. But I had always gone there alone keeping to myself, to avoid explaining or having to bring kids home to hear the shouting.

I came away from them fearing relationships. I had always satisfied my longings to be with people by watching others. It would probably serve me well now that I would be writing, though it had been a hollow empty part of me for many years. It was funny to think of that kind of anger and hate on a night like tonight here in this garden where peace abounded.

I thought of Michael and wondered if I loved him most because he was not here? This need to belong was best handled by me at a safe distance; Denver to Glendale was distance enough, if he was still in Denver; the closest he had been since he left was St. Louis.

My father had been gone a lot with his work and I wondered now if the fighting weren't so intense because mother hated being alone with a child. Perhaps I was as responsible for their fights as Daddy's absence. She might have felt trapped, as trapped as I had when I hid in my room with my head under the pillow. I wanted to ask her now but then as a little girl I could only see my side of things. Would I be the same kind of wife and mother? Did I fear this most of all? Was this the reason I was still unmarried at thirty-five?

I turned my thoughts back to the stars unwilling to count them now that life offered so much, but looking hard for the dippers and the bear, none of which I had ever been sure of finding. Always as I was just zeroing in on a completed sign I would have second thoughts about my accuracy and end up playing a game of follow the dots to make patterns of my own.

I was sitting by the pool with my legs drawn up and my arms around them when a car drove up in the driveway; the car stopped and a man got out. I recognized Michael as soon as he stood erect and I hurried to my feet calling his name as I ran.

We talked away the night and went up to bed about two; Kahlil was in the desk chair when we came upstairs and had run at the sound of his voice. When I woke up she was in the chair across the room staring at us. I was glad to see her back and I told her so. Michael opened his eyes, smiled and pulled me back down beside him. I fell back to sleep in the safety of his arms not waking again till almost ten; wiggling free I went to make coffee.

Downstairs I emptied his ashtray and put our dishes in the sink while waiting for the coffee; then I went upstairs for a hot bath. In the hall I passed one of many phones in the house and took it off the receiver, putting a pillow from Joey's bed on it to muffle any sounds it might give off. I hoped Michael slept at least till I got out of the tub because I was terrible company in the mornings and liked to spend this time alone.

On the terrace the brick floor glistened after an earlier summer shower; everything felt fresh and new. The sun shone through a scattering of clouds with patches of a brilliant blue wrapped around them. I had moved the machine outside on the table and sat writing; when I looked up, Michael stood in the doorway smiling at me His feet and his chest were bare, his long blond hair smoothed back with a stroke of his hand, sleep written on his face. "How long have you been standing there?" I asked.

"Long enough; have you got any coffee left?" He asked pointing to the small pot on the table. "How's the book coming along?"

"Terrible," I answered.

"You need a break, a diversion. Let's do something. Let's go somewhere."

"Don't you get enough of going, Michael?"

"Yes, but I was trying to think of you; I bet you haven't been off the property since I saw you last."

"Except for grocery shopping, you are so right. But I don't feel the need. There's a healing about this place."

"Healing? I didn't know you were sick."

"I'm not sick. I mean it more like a healing of the spirit or the soul."

"That I could use some of, so let's stay here. What do you want to do?"

"Nothing really."

"Great we'll sit around and look at each other or how about a walk in the garden by moonlight?"

"It's the middle of the day, Michael."

"Yes and its too hot for a walk now. I was just thinking of how to spend the evening."

"Let's get through the day first."

"Okay, I'll read the paper and you can fix breakfast."

"I don't eat breakfast and I'm not exactly the domestic type."

"Okay, Jennifer, you read the paper and I'll cook."

"That's fine with me; come on." I said picking up the machine to carry inside. Michael gathered up the extension cord and followed me to the desk.

As I led the way to the tiny elevator he asked, "Where do these steps go?"

"To Joey's room; would you rather walk down that way?"

"Sure; maybe I'll find a 1957 Chevy I could drive."

"Michael," I said looking surprised. "It's only 1951."

"Yes, but the fifty-two is out."

"What's that got to do with a fifty-seven? Besides you probably wouldn't know one if you saw it."

"Oh yes I would, Jennifer; I have dreams."

He seemed so serious I abandoned the idea of using the elevator, closed its door, and turned towards the steps. The landing was small i looked like the steps and the elevator had been made out of an existing closet. We were standing very close on the semi-dark landing when Michael teasingly suggested dancing. I laughed at his antics.

Suddenly there was a loud rattle and I realized he had probably stepped in one of the small bowls of sardines I had put out for Kahlil. His face drew up in the most grotesque expression as he lifted his foot to look at it. In the close quarters he lost his balance fell flat on his butt. I burst out laughing; the crushed sardines looked bad. I hurried off to the bathroom for a washcloth laughing. Michael was still sitting cradling his foot when I turned on the overhead light. It looked worse in the light but it was still funny to me; I couldn't stop laughing.

"Would you care to explain?" he said gruffly.

"I was trying to make friends with the cat." I said.

"I don't think she likes the menu." he said still a little mad at me.

"She likes it okay or rather she did; I think she may be getting tired of it. I've been putting it out for her for weeks."

"Why for God's sake?"

"I wanted her to sleep in my room with me like she did Mrs. White."

"Oh, and has it worked?"

"She slept in the chair last night. When I woke up she was staring at us."

"Does that mean you won't need this?" he asked as he handed me the small bowl with the squashed sardine he had cleared off his foot.

"I guess not," I said taking the bowl and leading the way down the steps.

Once in Joey's room Michael was like a little boy in a toy store. Every car he saw fascinated him more than the one before. His eyes were huge and his mouth hung open. When he saw the little black and white car, he froze and turned pale.

I called his name but he didn't seem to hear me. I called his name again, this time touching his arm genuinely concerned by his actions and a little afraid. I realized that though I loved him he was a stranger to me; never had this been as apparent to me as it was now. He finally came back from wherever he had been and picked the car up. Turning he handed it to me and asked me to read the bottom. I read 1957 Chevy."

"Jennifer, I have dreamed of that car, that exact car for years." he said.

"But how Michael; it's five years off."

"I don't know," was all he said and he put the car back on the shelf; and we left the room he was visibly shaken by the little car and I wanted to know why.

"The dream is never finished," he began; "I am in the car and I am driving along a mountain road. That's really all there is. It's no stranger, Jennifer, than some of the things that happen around here; it just feels so different happening to me."

"I know that feeling well enough; I have been in a state of shock for weeks. Just when I think I'm getting used to the mystery of this timeless house something happens to shake me up again."

We had a leisurely day and later we went in to Elizabethtown for an early showing of *The African Queen*. The whole time I was watching the movie I was thinking about the article in the 1991 Victoria magazine and picturing Katherine Hepburn forty years older. I thought too of how knowing the future is not always the best way because I couldn't enjoy the now for thinking about the future. I wondered if Mrs. White had shared that feeling and I thought of the hundreds and hundreds of times future happenings would pop up. In a single day it would begin with the morning newspaper and end with the evening news. Much of it like a well rehearsed play you had seen so long ago but had forgotten some of the lines to.

We left the Grand theatre, a tiny little place tucked snugly in the corner where two rows of stores and office buildings met and walked along the quiet almost deserted streets of the tiny town. I thought of how unlike Jackson Boulevard it was here; no delicatessen smells, no rows of baby carriages at the entrances to the many stores, no wall-to-wall people in the terrible hurry they always seemed to be in. I was still amazed by the people here in this beautiful part of the country; their waves as they drove past the yard and saw me standing there, their smiles and the time they took with me in stores, as if they had all day. I loved it here. I loved the openness of the big house and the yard so unlike my tiny apartment on the fourth floor of a building that smelled like everybody's supper.

I longed for fall; Trey had told me so much about it. I longed to see the park like yards of the many houses covered in fallen leaves and whole families raking the leaves into big piles and the children playing in them and spreading them all over the yard again. I longed to smell the leaves burning on a frosty day and to be standing in the warmth of the fire.

"Jennifer," Michael called my name and I turned to him startled.

"What?" I snapped.

"Where can we get a bottle of wine? I've been looking for a liquor store and I don't see one anywhere."

"There are no liquor stores; it's a dry county."

"It's a what county?" he asked looking at me as if I were crazy.

"A dry county," I repeated, though I knew he had heard me and he knew exactly what I meant "There is a wine cellar at the house so you won't go without your wine," I added.

"Thank god, I mean, where's the romance without wine?"

I laughed knowing he was just kidding. Neither of us drank enough to matter. He was just full of romantic ideas about courting or had read too many old romances and thought this was what women wanted. He was a thoughtful gentle man, rare enough today and I wondered how he would have fared during the women's liberation Mrs. White had written about; I wondered how I would have fared?

We passed the Taylor Hotel having parked at least two blocks north of the theatre. I had chosen the parking spot for the walk, something we both loved to do.

We drove to White House in silence each of us lost in our own thoughts. At the house I closed the gate behind us, something I had not done in weeks except when Trey and I went shopping together. I realized too late what a chance I had taken with my swim last night and I decided in the future to close the gate at night.

Michael had mentioned a moonlight walk in the garden and we might end it with a dip in the pool. It wasn't deep enough for any serious swimming but it was still nice.

We got out of the car at the house and went inside and immediately Michael asked where the wine cellar was so I took him to the basement to show him. As we walked past the pool table he grabbed me and pulled me close. We kissed and laid against the table, "Have you ever made love on a pool table?" he whispered.

"No, and with a half dozen bedrooms in the house I don't plan to. He looked hurt but I knew he was kidding; he was always kidding. There was always just enough passion in his kiss and his eyes to pull me to him and then somehow it always felt like he was laughing at me or at women in general. I never really could decide which, but that he was laughing was unmistakable.

I got the wine from a small refrigerator while he shot a few balls of pool at the table; then we started upstairs together. "The old lady thought of everything." he said.

"Everything," I echoed.

In the kitchen I got three red wine glasses from the pantry and we went on the porch to sit. It was warm so we moved to the steps and finally carrying the ice-cold bottle and the glasses we went to the garden pool. I sat the glasses and the bottle down beside me and Michael noticed for the first time that I had brought three glasses.

"Why?" He asked, "Are we expecting company?"

"We most definitely are and here she comes now," I said walking toward Mrs. White who was making her grand entrance into the night by way of the north end of the garden. We met mid way and hugged, and then we walked back to Michael and the wine. Michael did not yet realize who the woman was but had done his usual gentlemanly thing and gone for chairs from a nearby clearing in the yard.

"Hello", she said to him and he recognized her voice and that shocked me. Then she reached out her hand to him and placed something in his hand. I couldn't see what it was but Michael's shocked look turned to one of panic. "Do you remember this?" She asked him.

"Yes," Michael stammered.

"Michael, do you really remember it? The first time you saw it you were doing some research for me back in your college days. Joey had left it on the desk at the hotel we were staying at and you picked it up and looked it over. Do you remember now?"

"Yes, yes I do remember. I had forgotten where I saw it. I loved the look of the car so much. I started dreaming about it and forgot all about that day with you. Is that why you came here tonight, to set that straight in my mind?"

"No, Michael, I came here tonight to see the two of you and no more questions please; you'll spoil it for Jennifer," the old woman said.

I sat and watched her and Michael as I poured wine for the three of us. He was flirting with her like he did with all women regardless of their age. I enjoyed her way of handling him and reminded myself that she had lived through the women's liberation movement and she could probably handle an army of Michaels. He seemed to become very young with her like a boy with his grandmother and yet she too seemed young, ageless.

I watched her for some secret to her personality, some truth that would explain who she was and how she had become that person. She loved to laugh and talked as softly as the whisper of the wind on this quiet summer night. She was so feminine, so pale, that I found myself feeling my own face for its roughness from too much time in the sun.

Perhaps one of her old hats could be found around the house to protect me from the sun; maybe that and a lot of cold cream could give me the smooth pale look she had. I found myself wanting to copy her every move. She smiled at me about this time and apologized for having ignored me.

"That's okay, Elizabeth; I'm use to being ignored when Michael has another woman to talk to. She smiled and Michael looked embarrassed much like a small boy caught with his hand in a cookie jar. I stopped short with the realization that I had called her Elizabeth for the first time and that it had seemed so natural. I felt like we had been friends for many years and I would come to know in a few short months the very real basis for that feeling.

We talked, enjoying the wine and each other's company late into the night and Elizabeth asked us if we would mind leaving her alone in the garden for a while. Both of us were taken aback by her question since we considered the garden to be hers and of course we agreed to give her this time alone. As we were about to leave she called to Michael, "Remember to put the car back on the shelf in Joey's room, or he will miss it."

Michael took off at a hard run. On his way to Joey's room I was sure. Elizabeth and I were alone together. I hated leaving her. I said goodnight and started toward the house reluctantly. She called me back and took my hand with great tenderness. "Are you happy here, Jennifer?" she asked.

Tears came to my eyes and we embraced. "I am ecstatic," I whispered and kissed her cheek.

"I know you are full of questions and they will all be answered in time." she said softly and laughed at her use of the word time knowing how the word affected me. "He will be gone tomorrow and we can talk again then. You do love him don't you, Jennifer?"

"Yes, Elizabeth, I do love him."

"Good night," we both said and I walked to the house and left her by the pool.

& Pull Weeds

1989

Beth stood in her mother's room in front of the mirror putting on her makeup. A wisp of auburn hair fell in her way again and again. She smiled remembering the time her niece Candy had come up behind her and tried to put some straggling hairs up in the barrette where she thought they belonged and Beth had turned startled, never liking anyone to fool with her hair. "It's part of the look," she told Candy. She knew she was running late and her mother hated to be kept waiting. Since she couldn't fix her hair under stress she had fixed her hair at home, grabbed her makeup bag and Joey and hurried over here, knowing that since she wasn't driving she could put her makeup on in the car if she had to.

"Elizabeth," her mother called from the kitchen. The ringing of the phone interrupted her reply to her mother and she breathed a sigh of relief. She had plenty of time now; her mother would be on the phone awhile, as she always was.

Beth lifted the lid to her mother's jewelry box to get a pair of earrings; in a hurry she had forgotten hers on the bathroom vanity at home. A folded piece of notepaper caught her eye. It bore her own handwriting so she opened it and read.

& pull weeds

We drove another time along a road we'd traveled since my beginning and before. Thirty summers' weeds and winters' snows have covered the earth covering the grave belonging to a man I've never known. Early though I remember Mama telling of his wisdom and her love never faltered or died through all the thirty & perhaps that is where I met the man, through Mama and her memories. Today as we turned up the narrow half gravel, weed road I got the feeling as always of entering a world of souls, of dead, good and bad alike, and too this man; she walked reverently to the spot and stood and wept for thirty years every time she'd place her flowers & pull weeds; and weep remembering things I couldn't know The spot, this hillside place was real only through her tears until its twenty-seventh winter as we put a grave beside his. Rain fell and tears and cries rang out; the whole place reeked of roses & the road encircling was lined in black cars now. I have memories too & I go with Mama to stand beside her and hear her muffled sobs in the wind. Today I stand here with her reverence & me, my eerie feeling kind of a fear; really I remember gods when I look around the countryside & fancy them dancing among the stones and dead over a spot; and weep & pull weeds. I look up the hill behind me at that gruesome trio of trees with heads together to shade a stone or two. Here in this place a cold chill goes through me and a fear grabs hold and hangs on; I cannot it seems shake the feeling. I must thank Mama for teaching respect for the dead and memories no one can take from me & love I can tell or wait for thirty years and stand as she does. Someday that's all I'll have of her and in turn my children of me.

Beth's mind flashed back to the last time she had seen her grandmother alive. She stood with her back to the fireplace trying to get warm and looking to her grandmother's bed. The old lady was especially talkative that morning and Beth was glad. Glad to be listening to something besides her private thoughts and worries. Maybe Grandma was not as bad off as they thought. This was her greatest hope for she loved her dearly and couldn't bear to think of her as gone. Granted she was eighty-seven and couldn't live forever but please let her live as long as possible, she had prayed.

She never heard her grandmother complain of pain and always found her to be in good spirits so why not forever she thought as she lost herself in some story from her family's past, stories she loved and never got tired of hearing told and embellished with her grandmother's wonderful brand of humor.

For months she had visited pretty regularly with her mother and had watched the old woman become more and more bedfast. Now she got out of bed for nothing. Now they were dealing with bedsores along with everything else. But one thing that left Beth determined not to believe the reports from the doctors about how bad things were was her Grandma's outlook. She was so alive, more alive than many people her age.

When her grandmother died a few days later she was devastated. The funeral two cold wet days later prompted the writing of the poem about the ordeal as a tribute to her grandparents, one she had not known because he had died before she was born, and the other she had known and loved so well.

Her mother and Aunt Kay were by her grandmother's side and she had called out to Kay just before she died. Eight months later Aunt Kay had died on her birthday and on the anniversary of her father's death. They had died at the same age of the same thing. Beth remembered later hearing family members attribute Aunt Kay's death to the old belief that the next person to die would be the last name said by the dying person.

Years later with her son Joseph she had come to know and understand the passing of generations and on Memorial Day she had given a copy of the poem to her mother.

She thought it strange to be reading the poem today; she had just been to Zack's funeral a few days before. She thought of his long suffering and the change to her beloved Uncle Morgan, who seemed suddenly older, his face sadder, and his hair whiter.

Her mother had that same beautiful white hair, their mother's hair. She hoped she would have it when she grew older but doubted it would be so since she had the auburn hair of her father's family and they tended to gray and to gray late. She remembered her Grandmother Windom had died in her seventies and her hair, so long it touched the floor when she unfurled it, was barely streaked with gray.

Auburn hair, her father's good health, and too, her mother told her once, hiding her face with her hands in some peculiar way when she was embarrassed was all she got from her father's family The rest of her she thought was a Williams through and through and she was proud of this. White hair or not, she was a Williams.

"Elizabeth," her mother called again as she entered the bedroom. "That was Aunt Becky; she wants us to come visit and try to cheer Morgan up. Do you think you can?"

"Sure mother if it's okay if I take Joey."

"Why do you always say that? You know Joey is welcome everywhere you are. People haven't seen you without him for so many years they would think you had lost your head if you showed up alone."

"You didn't answer my question," Beth insisted.

"Elizabeth Windom White, stop it. You worry too much about that boy. Aunt Becky invited all three of us; so are you going or not?"

"Yes, of course, Mother," Beth said. "And you are right I do worry too much but..." Beth didn't finish; Joey was at the door of the room having come when he heard his name. Beth knew she worried but this dear sweet beautiful boy that stood before her, getting taller every day, was something to worry about. It had never been any other way. When he was little she had worried about his future when the problems of the day were enough to keep her awake nights and strung out days. Today worry was a habit, a way of life, she thought as she followed her mother and Joey out of the room and down the hall.

They spent the morning shopping for wallpaper for Fergie's room, which is what her mother called her peach colored guest room. Beth had been unusually quiet and so had Joey while her mother had talked nonstop. It was usually the other way around but Beth was thinking about Uncle Morgan and poor Zack.

Today she felt old and she worried about her mother who was past seventy though she neither looked it nor acted it. She could remember Joey when he was small and how she held him and rocked him. Now Joey was taller than she was though he would, she knew, remain small like the Windoms. It seemed natural to her that he would take after her since he was so much a part of her that she could not remember not having him, loving him.

She realized now that she had one more of her father's habits that was pure Windom. This quietness she and Joey were enjoying to think things through was exactly like her father. While her mother was being a Williams now, talking long and hard to keep from worrying.

Back home Beth spent most of the afternoon with Joey sitting on the stone bench under the big maple tree. It was their favorite spot in their tiny little yard where Joey sat quietly flipping through the pages of his National Geographic and left her to her thoughts.

She stared at her reflection in the window of the house. People she guessed would think her vain if they saw her do this and she realized she did it often. She always seemed to be looking for herself. At times like this when death and old age claimed someone she knew and loved it was worse. She wondered what more would happen to her with aging. She already had a stiff right knee which kept her awake nights. She had endured years of hot flashes, was in terrible shape and out of breath after climbing a flight of steps. She already stared at young people wondering where the years had gone. She would sit sometimes with pictures of Joey when he was little, or his baby clothes, that she had saved.

Today she felt every one of her forty-six years. Today she wondered more than ever what tomorrow would bring. Today a middle-aged woman stared back at her from the window. She looked away from the stranger to her beloved nature, shuffling her feet through the orange and brown leaves falling everywhere about her with the slightest breeze. The warm bright sun on her face as she looked up felt wonderful. The afternoon was hers and Joey's and they sat till the dying sun's warmth was gone and went in to supper.

They were up early the next morning for the drive to Glendale though the thirty plus miles seemed longer. Perhaps it was the going backwards from Brooks to the sleepy little town of her roots but it seemed to be an all day affair even when the visit was cut short for some reason.

Beth loved the town and looked for familiar buildings once they left the interstate. The modern brick bank on the right, the tiny log houses, now an antiques shop, also on the right and the old train depot, which hadn't served as such since the thirties.

As they crossed the tracks, roads running along both sides of it could be followed all the way to the loop which circled around joining Main Street at both the east and west ends of the tiny town.

They were on Main Street now where the new of the bank and the hotel and a couple of service stations were separated from the old.

Across the railroad tracks on the left was an old general store with its bench out front, inviting the weary to rest. Three more antique stores and the quaint little restaurant, the Whistle Stop, were on the right. The rest of Main Street was lined with tall old trees and white houses of all sizes and shapes.

Straight ahead at the end of Main Street stood the old blacksmith shop with its sign hanging by one end; the letters faded to the color of the wood and barely legible read, BLACKSMITH. The wood fence all around the shop was as dark with age as the shop itself. The hitching post stood ready for a horse. Behind the shop and to the right the big white Christian Church sat circled in roads leading out of town west and south. A wide green lawn separated it from the roads with a cemetery behind the church and to the left. At the old Blacksmith shop they turned right and immediately into the Williams driveway on the left. Theirs was the biggest house in Glendale, added on to over the years as more children were born, now with three stories and a wing with wrap around porches on the ground floor and an all white flower garden. A few late roses still bloomed.

The house sat back off the road with the usual rows of trees lining the driveway on both sides; a tradition, Beth guessed, for it seemed to her that all old houses in the country had the same trees. These were maples of some sort and not too tall. She remembered her mother saying they had all been replaced over the years as the originals had diseased and died. The trees in the orchard, her mother's most favorite place in the world, had also been replanted, many of the new trees too young to bear fruit.

Beth planned to walk there today; the weather was perfect for a stroll down memory lane. She would see the place where her mother jumped out and scared the devil out of the Jenkins boys after they had teased Uncle Morgan. She would ask about the tree that begged to be climbed and hoped that somehow it still stood despite the years. She would walk the orchard path perhaps as far as the old school.

They were out of the car now; Joey was getting his book bag; he was also pale and agitated, Beth noticed. "Joey," she said softly, "this is Uncle Morgan's and Aunt Becky's house; we've been here before. We will visit for a while and then, Joey, we'll go home. Do you understand?"

"Yes ma'am."

"We're going to eat lunch and maybe go for a walk, Joey; this was where Grandma lived when she was a little girl; perhaps she'll show you her room," Beth explained as they walked across the yard toward the side porch.

"Not my room."

"No Grandma's room."

"Does Grandma have toys in her room?"

"She might, Joey; we'll see. Are you ready to go inside and see?"

"Yes ma'am."

"Okay, Son, follow Grandma. I'm right behind you."

Morgan came hurrying out the side door to greet them. Happy and Morgan embraced; Beth held Joey's arm keeping him at a safe distance. After a short while she hugged Uncle Morgan too and Joey shook his hand; never looking up he said, "Where are Grandma's toys?"

"Not yet, Joey; we need to visit for awhile first. Can you wait?"

"Yes ma'am," he said, as he followed his Grandmother and Uncle Morgan, walking arm in arm, into the house, Beth behind him. The house was dark and strange even to Beth. She knew Joey missed the big windows and the sunlight of theirs and Grandma's house. As inviting as the house was to her, it was like stepping back in time a hundred years. Her mother had told her everything was exactly as it was when she was a child living here, and indeed it might be, for Beth now near fifty had seen no changes in her own lifetime. She would watch Joey closely and be prepared to take him outside if he became too upset.

Again and again Joey kept insisting on seeing Grandma's toys and Beth regretted having mentioned them. Finally her mother tired of his interruptions, took him to her old room, introduced him to a half dozen dolls, and brought him back to Beth. Things were not well between them when they returned so Beth suggested a walk for herself and Joey; the mention of coffee cancelled the boy's fears and brightened his mood, and the walk was put off.

They talked the morning away over coffee, Aunt Becky preparing lunch, Beth helping when she could and keeping a watchful eye on Joey, sitting quietly with his magazines, Happy and Morgan remembering friends and happenings from their childhood frequently drew Becky into the conversation. Beth loved these sessions; she had always loved them. Her mother's memories told over and over in answer to her countless questions. She loved the faraway look in her mother's eyes, who never looked more like Uncle Morgan than at these times. Written on their faces was the joy of their youth, erasing the years, the lines, the white of their hair. They became young again, children stepping out of the time worn pages of the family album.

The stories and the laughter continued through lunch and cleanup. Joey relaxed now, Beth ecstatic, and the three white haired children teasing, laughing. They had come here to cheer Uncle Morgan up and she considered the day a success. The walk around Glendale was the icing on the cake for her.

Once back at the house, a faded blue pickup truck arrived moments behind them. Morgan crossed the streets and hurried to sign for the delivery of three good size pine trees. They were unloaded and the truck gone before Beth could convince Joey that it was not his Uncle David's truck, though she admitted to Joey that the truck did look like her big brother's. Joey always saw sameness; he loved repetition, sought out the familiar to reassure himself that all was well in his world.

They crossed the street and approached Uncle Morgan, aglow with excitement. "I have lots of help today," he said.

"Yes," Happy chimed in, "now where do they go?"

"Over there along the property line, Happy," Morgan answered pointing north across an open beautiful green lawn.

"My God, Morgan, I never noticed that row of pines before. How long have they been there?"

"Since our neighbor got his new truck, right Morgan?" Becky teased as Morgan picked up a tree in each hand and struggled to carry them. Beth motioned for Joey to help with one while she grabbed the other.

Becky and Happy laughing, picked up the third tree and followed. The holes were dug and waiting and Beth sent Joey back to the porch for the shovel they had forgotten.

Becky elbowed Beth and pointed to the driveway on the other side of the row of pines, the three new trees would be joining. "Your Uncle Morgan is doing his civic duty."

"What do you mean, Aunt Becky?" Beth asked trying to understand what pine trees and empty driveways had to do with civic duty.

"The man who lives in that house," Aunt Becky said, pointing to an unpretentious looking white house next door, "drives a fire eating dragon that your Uncle Morgan has been unsuccessfully trying to hide for two years now. Morgan plants trees on behalf of Glendale's historic image, and the man keeps parking the dragon further and further out his driveway so it can be seen."

"He's actually proud of the damned thing," Morgan shouted between shovels full of dirt.

"What dragon?" Beth insisted.

"See for yourself, Beth, here it come now." Morgan said dropping his shovel and walking toward Beth.

Joey covered his ears and gritted his teeth. Beth rushed to him. The noise, loud even to her, would set Joey off; she had to distract him. "Son, run and get your books; they're on the porch. I'll join you in a minute." she said, as she gently took his hands from his ears so he could hear her.

Morgan was tapping her on the shoulder now, trying to get her to turn towards the roar of the dragon. She watched Joey move safely to the quiet of the porch then turned apologizing to her uncle who seemed unaware of anything but making his point. Beth turned in the direction of the roar; a bright green 4 by 4 pickup truck, with wheels so big you could walk under the truck, and orange and red flames painted all over the body.

Beth burst out laughing; "My God," she shouted, trying to be heard above the roar of the motor, "it does look like a dragon."

The driver waved as he pulled in his driveway, turned off the truck, and the tree planting continued.

"Morgan, he's out of driveway; if he wants to be seen now he'll have to park on the street." Happy observed.

"When he does, I'm going to rent a tank and ram the damn thing." Morgan said and all the women burst out laughing at the thought of a tank and the dragon doing battle.

Their visit a total success, they started home about three in the afternoon tired and happy. Uncle Morgan seemed radiant as he and

Aunt Becky waved from the driveway; they pulled out on to the street. Beth looked to Joey contented in the back seat of the car with a Seven-up, his magazines, and a black 4 by 4, like the dragon; he had just taken from his pocket for the first time. It had been there all day, she knew, despite her having told him countless times to leave his Hot Wheels at home

Merlin Long Ago

1991

Finishing his business at the pipe shop in Louisville's Jefferson Mall, he gathered up his assorted packages from the glass counter top in front of him, thanked the clerk, and left the store.

He walked to his car deep in thought; thinking about the slow thick traffic brought on by a really thick fog; a fog that for once was somewhere besides in his mind. He drove on not noticing anything until a loud horn's honking brought him to his senses and he found he was on I 65 on the long drive home with no idea how he had gotten there.

He drove on thinking of Happy and remembering her hanging from the branch of an apple tree in the orchard where they had spent so many childhood hours, or upside down hanging from the old hitching post that still stood in front of the abandoned blacksmith shop, which he now owned and kept carefully preserved just as Old Ned had left it. He could still see her face upside down and red with her dress and petticoats down around her head, with her pulling them aside so she could see him better while he read After a while she would gather the skirt of her dress and the petticoats in to a bunch and tuck them between her legs and hold them there swinging and humming or staring off as he read.

Happy had been a close friend then and now they saw each other every few months and at the yearly family reunion in late summer.

Rarely did they return to the orchard to walk the path worn there long ago by two children that had died and given birth to two aging white haired strangers. When this had happened he couldn't be sure. He had gone to college in England and Happy had moved to Elizabethtown soon after she had married Guy Windom in 1936. The death of their childhood had happened about then he guessed, and the white haired strangers had grown from the ashes.

He thought back to the days before he had left and their last few walks in the orchard. Happy was still Happy then and she still sang all the time and she still loved poetry but never better she said than when he read to her.

Her husband Guy never called her Happy; to him she was Frances or Franny. Maybe that was why she had changed or maybe it was the babies that began coming right away. Her first daughter she had named for Shelley and then she seemed to forget. She forgot to be happy and to read and to sketch. She forgot to be the girl he had grown up with and loved. To be sure she was busy with the babies; five of them in eight years, some natural born and some adopted, were a lot of work and responsibility. Responsibility intensified by Guy being gone all the time with his work. He had seen them cool to one another over the years. Perhaps that was another reason for her to become Franny and to leave the childhood nickname their father had given her behind.

He had seen a change in his own wife Becky after their daughter was born, the child taking more and more of her time as his work had taken more and more of his own.

He finished the long drive home thinking of yesterdays he wished desperately he could relive and of his childhood when he had been more at peace with himself. It never mattered he told himself that he had not been accepted by any of the other children he knew; his memories of Happy and Old Ned had been enough for him.

He drove into Glendale remembering the time Happy had dared him to put down his book and join her in the top of a tree where she was eating an apple, which she swore was the juiciest one she had ever tasted. When he had climbed very near her, shaking terribly, she had reached out her hand to help him the rest of the way up and he had fallen. His concussion had kept him away from his books and the orchard for awhile.

He laughed at the realization that she had never read to him at any other time and she hadn't liked it one little bit then. She had always been happier on a horse or in a tree or in a fight with some boy knowing she was as rough as any of them -- probably the one reason they hadn't teased him anymore than they did; they would have had her to deal with. What a crazy world, he thought, when girls are boyish and boys are dreamers.

He pulled in his driveway and drove around the house. Becky's van was not there and then he remembered having seen it at the Depot when he had come into town. He gathered up his packages and started toward the house, the sound of rock music blaring in his ears. He saw his grandson Chris Lee in the den as he came in the back door. Walking over to him he tapped him on the shoulder. Startled the boy shot up off the couch and reached for the dial of the radio beside him. "Hi Grandpa, I didn't expect you home so early," he said.

"That's obvious from the volume of that damn radio and your feet being on the table. Are you trying to go completely deaf with that damn thing?" He asked, as he reached past him and turned the radio off. Chris Lee mumbled something under his breath, grabbed up the radio, and started upstairs to his room.

"Christopher Lee," Morgan shouted. The boy stopped dead in his tracks at the sound of his grandfather's voice. "Don't ever call me that again; do you hear me, boy? Do you hear me?" Morgan shouted.

Chris Lee mumbled "Yes Sir" and stomped away reminding himself that he should be more careful around his grandfather; he had forgotten about the old man's bionic ears. Reaching for his earphones around his neck as he walked up the steps he reminded himself to stay out of the way for awhile or risk having to listen to another lecture. If there was one thing he knew his grandfather to be good at it was long boring lectures; after all that was how he made his living.

Entering his room he closed the door behind him and flopped down on his stomach on the bed. Setting the radio on the bed in front of him he put the earphones on and turned the radio back on as loud as it would go. To hell with the old man he thought; who needs ears like Superman?

Morgan was at the table reading when Becky came in. "Hello, dear, when did you get home? I thought you were going to be late."She said.

"So did a certain young man. Becky, when I got home he had his shoes on the table and I could hear his damn radio before I crossed the yard. Don't you care if he goes deaf?"

"Don't get started on the radio. You know he plays it too loud and I know he plays it too loud, but he's seventeen and I can't be with him every minute. I'll talk to him about it again if it'll make you feel any better," Becky said and made a mental note to remind Chris Lee of the age and value of the table he insisted on using for a footstool.

"You better before I take the damn thing away from him." Morgan said.

Becky had a headache and wasn't in the mood to discuss the radio Chris Lee insisted on drowning out the rest of the world with. "The new wicker chair came in," she said, in an attempt to change the subject.

"You mean the old wicker chair came in; you know the Depot only sells antiques," he teased her.

"Okay, Morgan, the new to me, old wicker chair came in", she said laughing. One of the things she loved best about him was how easy it was to get him off any unpleasant subject. Being a gentle man he had always hated arguing. She knew too this was the main reason Chris Lee was such a sore spot with him; they had done nothing but argue about the boy or with the boy since he had come to live with them when he was a baby.

At first she had wondered what there was about the baby that kept Morgan on edge, but soon she realized it was the responsibility of the infant when he had hoped they would be free to be alone together for the first time in their life and be able to go to England to live.

"We have raised our daughter; why do we have to start over again with our grandson?" he had asked her once in desperation. The boy had proved to be more difficult to cope with for her too. He hadn't slept as well as his mother, or eaten as well either, and he was a far less affectionate child than she had been. While she knew all of this to be true she often wondered if they weren't the ones that were different.

They were older and didn't have the energy to keep up with Chris Lee and his friends. They didn't volunteer their time or their house for gatherings. Morgan, a teacher himself, seldom went to P.T.A. meetings and when he did he never took an active role. Chris Lee had responded in kind she felt. They were not a family the way they had been when their daughter was a child. Sometimes she hated Melanie for abandoning her baby and her responsibility to them. But she hated Melanie for Chris Lee most of all; he deserved better she felt; they all deserved better.

Often she wondered what Chris Lee himself thought about being brought up by two crotchety old people when his friends had parents young enough to enjoy them or at least if they weren't enjoying their children's loud music and fresh mouths they were better able to cope.

She put her purse in the pantry behind some things and reached for an apron. That was another thing she knew that had changed; she never had to hide her purse from her daughter when she was growing up. If she wanted money for something she came to her or her father.

But today though they were considered to be well off, they found they could not or would not give Chris Lee the outrageous amount of money he thought he should have. And then she had found all too often when they had refused him he would take it out of her purse. She had taken to hiding her purse when she realized this but without confronting Chris Lee about her suspicions. Somehow she just couldn't bring herself to call her grandson a thief, at least not to his face. This was something she had also thought was better kept from Morgan.

She busied herself around the kitchen getting dinner ready for them, dreading the meal, which, she knew, would be like so many others before, with Chris Lee sitting sullenly picking at his food and asking to be excused before he'd hardly eaten a bite. Later she was sure he would wind up at McDonald's with his friends. She didn't blame McDonald's for enticing young people; she thanked them. She knew there were other dinner tables around the area where the air was just as strained as the air at their own. She had talked with other children's mothers. With her family however the generation gap was stretched tighter over a wider span of years.

She would hold out the one happy bit of information she had for Morgan for when the scene was played out at dinner and he was left feeling drained with the fight between old and new that he fought daily in his mind and more recently out right with his grandson. Fran had called to say she was coming for a weekend visit and she was bringing Beth and Joey. The news would please him and help him through one more uncomfortable evening.

Later Becky and Morgan were arguing about Chris Lee when she remembered to tell him about Fran's call. He was shouting from the bathroom and she sat on the edge of her bed brushing her hair as hard as she could to try to shut out his words. He drove her crazy sometimes arguing about Chris Lee. What had happened to the gentle pleasant easy going man she had married. She could only vaguely remember him; it had been years since they had been able to talk civilly about the child, she thought, and then corrected herself. "I'm so sick of this bickering. You have no idea how it makes me feel to be caught in the middle between two people I love as much as I love the two of you." she shouted tearfully flinging herself across the bed and burying her face in the pillow.

Morgan dried his face and threw the towel aside hurrying after her. Sitting down on the bed beside her he rubbed her back gently and waited till she calmed down. This was not the time or the way to reason with his wife; he knew that. Night after night it was always the same. They would start to talk over the day's events and inevitably they would come around to Chris Lee; He stood between them splitting them apart.

Since the day he was born Melanie had ignored him and Becky had taken over for her. She had allowed Melanie her period of mourning for her dead husband by helping out with the baby and had wound up with the full time job. Melanie had run like a scared rabbit as soon as she was on her feet and they hardly ever heard from her.

These Vietnam statistics, Morgan felt sure, were not in the records. A wife loses her husband to enemy fire, a baby loses its Mother, and the Grandparents lose their privacy, their peace of mind. War was a very effective weapon; with countless people dead, dying, and going through the motions; a ripple effect with no water's edge to stop it.

When would we ever be able to close the books on Vietnam, he wondered? Would the pain ever stop? Hurt built upon hurt and when things were almost pieced together, America goes to war again, trading a jungle for a desert for variety's sake. Were they afraid our history books would get boring or our young men grow old?

He often dreamed of Chris Lee diapered and wrapped in the American flag from his father's casket. He saw the uniformed soldiers present, take the draped flag off the casket, lay the baby in it, wrap him, and hand him over to his mother. Melanie refused the baby and the flag and he was then handed to Becky who accepted him awkwardly and with great pity.

He was named Christopher Jr. when Christopher Sr. was being buried. That had been the only thing Melanie had done for the boy. She had raged over that one point. He was never to be a senior. Chris was dead and no baby could take his place. No baby could be him.

Chris Lee was three days old the day of the funeral. He knew that moment haunted Becky and clouded her judgment when it came to Chris Lee.

Morgan remembered the hate and anger in Melanie's eyes almost as clearly as the pity in Becky's. He felt his heart sink then. Maybe he knew his daughter better than he thought he did. Maybe he knew the moment of placing the baby in its grandmother's arms had more significance than anyone else realized at the time.

The look on Melanie's face, the hate, the anger, and the obstinacy was what he had seen on Chris Lee's face over and over as they had repeatedly locked horns with each other. It was more than a generation gap between them; it was all out war. He resented like hell what this child had done to him.

Becky was right about one thing; he had changed, they had changed, the world had changed, and it all came together in his mind in the personification of this boy with Melanie's eyes. The thing that ate at him the most was that though he knew it was as much his fault as it was Chris Lee's that they didn't get along, he couldn't stop himself. He remembered reading something once about a similar relationship between two people, 'It's not what you find out about the child; it's what you find out about yourself.' And he had found the ugly side of himself. The anger and bitterness of a lifetime side of himself and the boy had bore the brunt of it almost from the beginning.

What had happened to him? What had become of him? How had he let this happen? The alarm on his wristwatch sounded and woke him from his reverie. He stood and walked out of the room. Becky's deep breathing told him she had fallen asleep. He closed the door gently so as not to wake her and turned around bumping into Chris Lee.

"Hello, Gramps," the boy said startled.

"Hello, Chris Lee," he answered without mentioning the beer he was sure he smelled on the boy's breath. It wasn't worth it, he decided. His friend Zack had long ago told him to pick his battles and if he hadn't listened and tried over the last few months they'd have killed each other by now.

He heard hate in the boy's voice, and saw it in his face. It was what separated them and hurt Morgan the most. He felt the hate was a living thing. A thing Melanie had planted and left in his care. The hate and the child had grown and he was not sure which was which anymore.

He walked downstairs feeling tired. Catching sight of himself in the big mirror that hung above the steps he noticed an aged worn white haired man that frightened him almost as much as his relationship with the boy did.

He was not growing old gracefully as was expected of a man of his station in life. He was an educated man, a man who had traveled the world, and a man who had talked with and spoken before some of the most learned men in the world. Morgan Edward Butler Williams, noted historian; an expert on the past, yearning for the past, but stuck in the present.

At the bottom of the stairs he turned toward the library and unlocked the door before him, entered a small alcove, and relocked the door, then turned and opened another door and entered the library. He stood for a moment to let the feel of the room fill his senses. The smell of musty books, of pipe smoke long settled on the curtains and carpet, and the oil from his father's antique trains all melded together into a unique and wonderful smell of the long ago. This was his study and his father's study before him.

His father's trains were still placed about the room the way they had been left in August 1939 when he died. Morgan oiled them and fussed over them as he had seen his father do, and talked to them as if they were living things; something he had never seen him do to be sure. His father had been a practical man, a businessman without a frivolous thought in his head. He had loathed the dreamer in Morgan and had tried to make a railroad man out of him, finally giving up.

Morgan had sensed from the moment of his decision to be a teacher to the day in August when his father died that he was disappointed in his only son. He had heard arguments between his parents about his decision to teach and his father had raved at the idea of his son doing woman's work. Morgan never forgot those words; they haunted him, as did the look of disappointment and the thought of the gasping figure of his father dying on the street on that hot August day of a heart attack. He was still a young man, only fifty-eight, and until that day in the best of health.

Morgan had wished hard for many years to meet the same fate, to die when he could still think clearly, to die when he was still allowed the dignity of making his own decisions. And here he was at seventy-seven forced to retire though he had the greatest number of history students sign up for his classes than anyone in the history of the university. He made history come alive for them they all said. He was not flattered by their words; he accepted this as truth. He made history come alive for them because he believed it was alive. He believed that all things past were still there somewhere out of sight, at the beck and call of anyone with the secret handshake, access code, or whatever. The only thing stopping him from going back was the how.

He had devoted his life to history believing it was alive. He had tried to pass his belief in the past on to his students and this had done what for him? Had it prolonged or postponed his retirement? Yes, but only for a couple of years. Had he found a protégé in all those years of teaching? Had he found someone that believed in the hidden implications he had made year after year?

Had any of them understood? Had any of them come to him after class wanting to know more? No they had not. They had taken their required credits in history and had made good grades because his enthusiasm had been contagious. Then they had graduated and moved on. He had never heard from any of them again. Wait there had been one young man, he remembered. What was his name? Never mind he told himself; that was a false alarm. The boy had no enthusiasm for history; he had only come back, he said, because teaching history had seemed easy and he was looking for an easy job with security.

Morgan could have told him a few things about security but he didn't. He had heard enough stories to fill a book, about teachers trying to stay on at the university when there were budget cuts or there was some new teacher that showed more promise. He had Merlin to thank for the fact that this had never been his problem. His search for the code had lit a fire under him, a fire that had kept his position open with no serious competition for the nearly forty years he had taught, both here in America and in England.

Now what did he have to show for all those years of search? He had nothing but a vast collection of books on the past, on time, on Merlin, on meditation, and on the metaphysical.

Now his books blended on the shelves with his father's books on Eastern thought and trains. What a curious combination of interest, trains and religion, he had thought when he discovered the first small book on Buddhism hidden in a far corner of the very top shelf. If he hadn't got the library ladder fixed all those years after his father's death, he might never have found it. After that he had read the titles of the books more carefully. He learned a good deal about Eastern religions through the small library his father had started and he had added considerably to over the years.

He had also come to love the trains and had read every one of his father's books on them, even the technical books. It had something to do with that look of disappointment on his father's face and to do with recovering the past. If he could, he would meet his father again and they would talk trains and he would erase the memory of that look from his mind.

He studied the room from the door where he still stood, for how long, he wondered looking to his watch. Only a short while he noticed relieved. He had always needed time to unwind, to quiet his thoughts, and to separate himself from the happenings of the day, before he began his meditation.

The room was his refuge. He had added insulation to the floor, ceiling, and walls to sound proof it against the noises of the house.

No ringing phones, no doorbells, no television, or microwaves to distract him. He had never experienced the side effects of unexpected interruptions he had read about. He hoped he never would.

The only thing he had not been able to do was make the door disappear when he came inside and so he did run the risk of someone knocking. He had tried to offset that possibility with the addition of the small alcove and the second door to muffle the sound if someone ever did knock. He had told them often enough not to and in the end he had to trust them not to disturb him. This was one of the reasons he kept to a schedule.

A timer set for 8:45 turned on the desk lamp. He wanted to be able to see the old familiar trains and books as soon as he entered the room. He wanted to be able to focus on his painting of Merlin that hung above the fireplace, as soon as he made the adjustment to the quiet and inviting solitude of the room.

On the desk there was always an open book waiting; he loved books so much he had trouble putting them away. Some nights he would read all night and no matter how late it was when he left the room, he always sought out a book to open and have ready to read when he returned the next time. When there was no unread book he would open an old familiar one and read it again.

He walked to the deep red leather couch and touched its cool back as he had always done when his father sat there. They would talk or rather his father would talk and he would stand with bowed head cringing at his words. Upon leaving the room after each of their times together as a way of saying he loved his father and he forgave him his unrealistic expectations, he would touch the sofa's back; though he could never bring himself to touch the man who sat there, his shoulder within easy reach. The ritual had continued as a remembrance of the past, as a tribute to his father.

Every night at this time he would come here, pour himself a glass of wine, and sit down in his father's place on the sofa quietly absorbing the room and its treasures. Sometimes his eyes might settle on a favorite object and he would remember the time and place of its acquisition, going over every detail of this event as an exercise in remembering the past.

At other times he would focus on the ever familiar picture of Merlin and that night so long ago. Every day of his life he relived the vision going over the scene again and again thinking the answer to time lay in the meeting itself, determined one day to find it.

He would begin with tea on that day and recall moment by moment the happenings leading up to the meeting in the woods. He would draw forth all the emotions, the fear of being lost, the cold of the wind and the rain, the fatigue at the end of the day, the hunger of having missed supper, The image of his Grandparents' well lit dining room with his family sitting down to a table full of wonderfully delicious foods; the smell of puddings hot from the oven and fresh brewed coffee; his place at the table empty.

He would draw forth the image of the gnarled trees and stumps of this untended part of the woods, the sounds of the night animals stirring as darkness fell. He would remember wishing for shelter from the rain and a warm fire to dry himself by and then magically... Merlin had stood stirring a fire and adding a log. The crackle, the smoke both unseen and unheard before, were suddenly there in what had been a bare spot in the woods moments ago.

With the mood set, the emotions, the smells, the wonder of the meeting would unfold and be played out and time would be spent trying to bring forth the real Merlin again. Now an old man he was very familiar with every facet of that evening so long ago and had a question for every time he had recalled "the grand adventure" as Uncle Morgan had called it.

Merlin would not get off so easy this time; the magic of the dancing light would not appease the old Morgan the way it had Morgan the boy. Morgan stayed in the woods a little longer than usual tonight; he needed the time, he needed Merlin and his magic.

He left his study at half past one and climbed the stairs to his room. He could not sleep and sat in the window seat staring out at the autumn night thinking about his sister's visit.

He was up at daybreak to get ready and then he had nothing but time on his hands until she arrived. He went to old Ned's grave and stood and talked to him, telling him everything he would share with Happy when she arrived.

When Morgan told Old Ned about his meeting with Merlin on his first trip to England, he was eight years old and he had asked if Merlin could come to him and talk to him and tell him about his future could there then be no real death; Old Ned had told Morgan about other lives and how sometimes love between two people spanned countless lifetimes. Because he came to believe in reincarnation he felt he and Happy had probably known each other over the ages.

Old Ned had been the wisest man he knew when he was a boy so it was to Old Ned he had taken his questions. Old Ned didn't laugh like most grown-ups did when a boy went to him with dreams and make believe; in fact Old Ned was the king of make believe and fantasy, though when he told his stories to the wide eyed Morgan and Happy they swore it was true. Then Old Ned would do some magic around them all to protect them from the evil eye or whatever else Old Ned thought they might be in danger from.

Old Ned's family had come from Jamaica when he was a small boy and he had brought with him all the legends and magic of his forebears. He had practiced good magic on Morgan and Happy and others of his friends usually without them knowing anything about it until it was all over.

Morgan remembered when he had been in love as only a boy can be that first time. It had been with the new schoolteacher who Morgan swore was the only person he had ever known that was blonder than he was himself. That was the only time in his life he had gone without his hat without being made to. He had been so proud of his hair then and when the other boys had teased him about his curls he had held his temper and had made Happy do the same. "First love," Old Ned had said chuckling, "it makes a fool out of boy or man,"

That Valentine's Day he was sure Old Ned had used his magic because the teacher had kissed his cheek when he had given her his hand made valentine card, and she hadn't kissed any of the other boys. Later Old Ned had given him a magic potion to help him fall out of love with the teacher when she married the minister and darn near broke his heart. If it hadn't been for Old Ned's magic he might still be pining away for the pretty blond teacher that he talked Becky into naming their daughter after. He might still be sitting in the Baptist Church on Sundays too.

Well tomorrow would be Sunday and if he could talk Happy and her family into staying over he would sit in the Baptist Church once more for her. He knew she still went though he had given up church going long ago.

He sat for a while longer by Old Ned's grave talked out but sitting just the same. He had often come here over the fifty years the old man had been gone and talked out his troubles, shared his triumphs, and yes, even his quiet thoughts.

Old Ned was as real to him now as he had ever been and he was another thing from the past that called to him. He had no one today to talk to like he had when he was a boy when both Old Ned and Happy had been his confidantes.

He got up after awhile and took his watch out of his vest pocket to check the time. It was past time for Happy to arrive and he started across the field behind the blacksmith shop towards his house; as he did he looked up to see Happy's white hair in the sunlight with her big smile and open arms ready to greet him. He practically ran to her swooped her up and spun her around. "I was beginning to wonder if you were coming?" he said to her kissing her on the cheek.

"Why, Morgan, I'm not late, you are. I've been standing here for quite some time watching you talk to Old Ned. I didn't know you still did that after all these years, but then I should have figured it; you always did live in the past.

"In the long ago," he corrected her and they both laughed as they headed across the yard to the back door with their arms around each other.

He could hear Beth's voice as they rounded the corner of the house and a strange deep voice he didn't know. Joey stood with his hand outstretched to his great Uncle Morgan. Morgan shook the boy's hand and said "Hello" while Beth stood behind Joey prompting him to say hello too. When he finally did, Morgan recognized Joey's voice as the one he had heard earlier. "Joey, have you grown up when I wasn't looking." He said teasingly.

Joey smiled and dropped his head. Morgan knew he spoke very little and shushed Beth's efforts to get the boy to answer him. "Beth, let him be himself around here; we understand and we respect his differences.

Don't we Becky?" Becky nodded in agreement and asked if anyone wanted something cold to drink?

"Would you like a coke?" Morgan asked turning to Joey.

"I'm allergic," Joey said.

"Okay, Joey, what would you like to drink?"

"Coffee," the boy replied without raising his head.

"Now there's a man who speaks up when he wants something," Morgan said laughing. "Beth, you said he didn't talk much but I think he does pretty well. Now come on boy and let's make that pot of coffee."

Joey followed him to the coffee pot mumbling something he thought no one could hear; when his uncle answered him he perked up. Morgan liked the slow methodical, quiet boy. He liked his manners best of all and thought he might teach Chris Lee a thing or two if he stayed around for a while. He took the lead in fixing the coffee, bending down to smell it before he dipped it into the filter. Morgan stood watching half amazed as Joey leveled out the second scoop full, put the basket into place, and turned on the pot. Joey woke him from his reverie with a request for cups. Morgan scratched his head in wonder and turned to Beth with his mouth half open. "There's nothing the matter with that kid; I can tell you that right now," he said

Beth who had watched the whole thing hugged her uncle and whispered, "He can do a lot of things for himself; coffee is very important to him so he has learned to make it when I wouldn't. He drinks too much of it but it's our fault for giving it to him when he was little. His doctor said we could use black coffee as an alternative to Ritalin and we did. Now I'm afraid he's as hooked on coffee as I am, maybe more so."

"Coffee won't hurt him, believe me it won't, if it did I'd have been a goner a long time ago," Morgan said. "Beth, you should be very proud of yourself for the job you've done with Joey. I remember him as a little boy; he has sure changed; he is a fine young man."

Beth squeezed Uncle Morgan again and leaned her cheek on his chest with tears in her eyes. They stood quietly together watching Joey who was watching the coffee.

Joey poured and served the coffee, then sat down with the magazines he had brought while the adults caught up on news of each other's lives,

Joey occasionally showing a favorite picture to anyone that would look, while they talked away the day.

Dinner was a long casual one interrupted only by Chris Lee's continual shifting in his chair hinting at being excused. Morgan ignored him and made him sit out the meal with the family hoping some of Joey's good manners would rub off on him. Becky had finally tired of it and sent Chris Lee on an errand asking Joey if he would like to go along.

Joey looked to his mother frightened at the idea of leaving her. Morgan thought it might be Joey had better taste in companions than Chris Lee and he got him off the hook by asking him to make another pot of coffee. Joey seemed relieved and sprang up and around the table to the coffee as fast as he could, knocking over a glass of water as he did.

"Never mind the mess, Joey; I'll wipe it up; you go on," Morgan said,

"I don't want to go," Joey said again, frightened by the prospect of being separated from his mother.

Beth got up and went to Joey, "Son, your Uncle Morgan didn't mean for you to go anywhere. He meant for you to go on and make the coffee. Okay?"

"Okay," Joey said, still shaken.

Morgan cleaned up the water with a paper towel and went to Joey. Patting him on the shoulder he felt the boy pull away. He remembered then that Joey didn't like being touched and looked for some other way to reassure him as he reached around him to toss the wet paper towel in the trash can.

"You got a basket," Joey said

"What sort of things do you like to do?" Morgan asked, handing Joey the coffee canister.

Joey seemed confused by the question and once again Beth rescued Morgan by coming up and whispering for him to be more specific, "Give him choices", she said.

"Choices?" Morgan questioned looking as confused as Joey.

"Yeah, you know, like do you like to watch TV or play pool? You know, choices."

Joey interrupted them, "I like to swim," he said, and they both laughed. Beth hugged her son, and he laughed with them.

"He almost always chooses something you haven't offered," Beth explained.

"I like to swim," Joey repeated two or three times.

"We don't have a swimming pool, Joey; besides it's too late in the year to swim," Morgan added.

"It's not bedtime?" Joey asked nervously.

'No,' it's not bedtime; Uncle Morgan means it's too late in the year. It's too cold."

"When it warms up, I go swimming," Joey reassured himself.

"Yes, when it warms up," Beth repeated.

Morgan had listened and was beginning to realize Joey dealt only in absolutes. You had to be very specific with him in order to be understood by him. No taking anything for granted. He wasn't sure that wasn't the best way to talk to everyone. The English language had become much too informal for him. He thought about the crazy ways people had of referring to each other, "you old son of a gun." He'd never been comfortable with that kind of talk and decided Joey, autistic or not, was on the right track. He was brief, exact, and didn't talk much. Most people today were afraid of silence and talked on and on about nothing and everything; when young people weren't doing that they had a radio or a TV blaring away.

He wondered what there was about silence that frightened people. Was it their thoughts? He had heard Becky say often enough, "I'm uneasy around quiet people, because I never know what they're thinking." He himself thought it was the other way around; people talked without thinking, so he worried what they were really thinking or if they were thinking at all.

Morgan began clearing the table and Beth who was still standing joined in. Becky resentfully got up from the table and started to put things away. Morgan was loading the dishwasher and Becky bumped against him angrily. He knew it was her way of reminding him she resented him helping with household chores. She had called him "Susie Homemaker" more than once to drive her point home. It made no sense to him for her to get angry with him for pitching in so he continued to help whenever he felt like it.

Becky stewed in silence as the table was cleared and the kitchen cleaned She had made her protest known to Morgan and as usual he had ignored her. She knew she should be happy he was considerate enough to help out. Her mother and other women she talked to about this had said so often enough. But she didn't think he was being considerate; if he was then he wouldn't do it when he knew it upset her. She thought what he was doing was being his usual perfectionist self, and this made her feel like she couldn't or didn't do the housecleaning good enough to suit him. It was her job, not his; she didn't go to his classroom and she didn't want him in her kitchen.

A breeze blowing in through an open window filled the room with the smell of fresh brewed coffee. Becky breathed deeply forgetting her anger. She was tired; it had been a long day, just how tired she hadn't realized until now. "Let's take our coffee out on the porch; it's a beautiful night," she said aloud.

"That's a great idea," Happy said and turning to Morgan she added excitedly, "Remember evenings on the porch with Mama and Papa when we were little?"

"Remember! Happy, how could you remember any of it; you were always asleep?" he teased.

"Oh Morgan I was not; not more than a couple of times anyway and then only after a long day of hard playing."

"Playing hell, you mean fighting."

"Fighting?" Happy questioned.

"Yes, fighting. You always did love a good fight." He continued teasing his sister until they both laughed out loud walking to the porch with their coffee cups in hand, their voices trailing off into the night.

Beth smiling watched them walk off. "You know, Aunt Becky, Mama always seems so young when we are here; it's as if the years disappear or somehow they never happened. It makes me feel so funny, good but funny. As if I'm not real or if I am real where did I come from? Because the years don't seem to have happened, so when was I born? And where is my childhood and where is Joey's? I know I must sound crazy but I love to come here. I love to be where all of the stories from her childhood happened and I half expect to see the Jenkins boys or some other childhood villain pop out from behind a bush and see Mama chase off after them with her petticoats and her hair flying."

"My God, Beth, you sound just like Morgan!" Aunt Becky said sharply.

Beth's face felt hot and turned red with embarrassment. She had gotten lost in the moment and gone on so she probably did sound crazy, she thought, following her aunt to the porch. She was glad for one thing; her aunt's back had been turned to her so she had not seen the hurt or the embarrassment caused by her remark. Beth remembered her mother saying many times that Aunt Becky could be very short with people. Her mother liked Aunt Becky, she knew, and she understood that her main shortcoming was that she was too practical. "Not an ounce of the dreamer in her," her mother had said more than once.

The screen slammed hard in Beth's face. She bit her upper lip till tears came to her eyes as she reopened the screen for Joey and herself. When she got outside Aunt Becky stood with her back to everyone rubbing her hands back and forth along the porch railing. She was upset and Beth felt responsible and dammed uncomfortable as she found a chair for Joey and patted the seat to indicate to him where to sit.

He reached in his jean's pocket and pulled out a couple of small cars, sat down, and patted the empty chair beside him for Beth. Smiling at him she whispered that she would rather stand and tousled his hair. He reached for her hand and pulled at it. She walked a few feet in front of him and her hand slipped out of his grasp.

She faced him standing with her back to the railing beside Aunt Becky. She breathed deep rhythmical breaths trying to compose her thoughts. She watched Aunt Becky, who suddenly looked very old to her. Admittedly the moonlight cast shadows and perhaps the lines of age she saw were only in those shadows. She felt old so often after a long day she tried not to think about age or aging though she knew she was fast approaching the big five o. Her mother was twenty-six years older than her, so Aunt Becky was somewhere in her late seventies. Certainly not too old to dream though many people she knew had stopped dreaming while they were still young.

She felt sorry for such people; to her life was a dream; a dream of tomorrow, of rainbows, of climbing new heights, of meeting new people.

Some people stopped dreaming early; some like her aunt had never dared to dream. She moved closer to Aunt Becky, "Thank you for a wonderful day and a great supper."

"You're welcome, child," the old woman answered smiling slightly and moving away. Then she asked if anybody wanted more coffee and went in the house for the pot.

Beth gave up and turned her attention to Joey who was showing Uncle Morgan one of the Hot Wheel cars from his pocket while her mother Happy slapped at her ankles chasing away a mosquito.

Morgan jumped up suddenly having forgotten something. "Come on kids," he yelled, "I've got something to show you."

Beth ushered Joey into the house and followed him calling back to her mother. "Beth, I'm not a kid so he can't be talking to me. You two go on; I'll be fine here." Happy answered.

They went down a long hall to an unfamiliar part of the old house's first floor. Uncle Morgan stopped in front of them and fumbled in his pocket pulling out a key. He unlocked the door and they entered another short hallway. It was dark and Joey frightened mumbled something Beth could not make out. Uncle Morgan answered him promising him light aplenty as soon as he opened one more door. Joey quieted down and Beth patted his shoulder to reassure him of her presence while they waited for the promised relief.

The door opened and the smells of the room in front of them reached Beth almost before she realized there was light. "My God this place smells wonderful! Where are we?" she asked.

"Look around, girl, look around."

Beth turned around and around. The smell seemed to be coming from everywhere, unlike the light, which came from an ancient tiffany lamp on the desk. It's a library Beth realized after scanning the walls of the room and seeing rows upon rows of books masked in half darkness. "Is this Grandfather's study, Uncle Morgan?" she asked.

"It was and now it's mine."

"I've never seen this room before; I had no idea. My God, the books, there must be thousands. I have better than a thousand myself, and there are so many more," Beth said as she rushed over and began reading titles. Hesse, a favorite, caught her eye immediately as did dozens of other authors familiar to her. Turning to another wall she saw Joey out of the corner of her eye; she had forgotten him in her excitement. He was holding something in his hands and Uncle Morgan stood by him smiling. She walked toward them to see what they were doing "Joey, what have you got?" she asked as she neared them.

"A car," he answered.

"May I see it, Son?"

"It's mine!" he answered as he pulled his hands away.

"Where did you get it?" Beth asked.

"He gave it to me," Joey said, pointing to Uncle Morgan.

"You got him a car; how sweet but how did you know he liked Hot Wheels?" Beth said.

"He always has them in his pockets; how could anybody not know? That by the way is not just any Hot Wheel; it is a 1935 Ford, just like mine." Uncle Morgan said proudly.

"It's mine, it's not yours," Joey insisted.

"Yes, Joey, it's yours." Beth patted him and explained that Uncle Morgan meant the little car he held was just like the big car outside in the driveway.

Joey gave the car one last look and put it in his pocket. Beth shuddered at the clinking sound of the car hitting other cars in his pocket. "I'm sorry, Uncle Morgan, I know you must have gone to a lot of trouble to get the car for him, but all of his treasures seem to end up beating each other up in a pocket or a favorite box." Beth said apologizing.

"Beth, forget it, and don't worry. The car belongs to him now; he should be allowed to enjoy it his way," Uncle Morgan said smiling.

"It may be one of a couple of hundred cars in his collection but he will remember where he got it and he'll miss it if it disappears." Beth told her uncle, still feeling bad about Joey's lack of enthusiasm for the car. She knew he was happy about his new toy; he just didn't know how to show it.

"He can tell you if one of them is missing?" Morgan questioned Beth.

"Usually, yes, though I do admit to having tricked him a time or two," Beth replied.

"Naughty girl," her uncle teased.

"Thank you, Uncle Morgan," Beth said, then turning to Joey she urged him to say thank you too.

"I did," the boy said and went back to his magazine.

"What do you think of my library?" Morgan asked his face aglow with pride.

"I think it's beautiful and I'm so glad I got to see it." Beth answered looking around once again at the shelves full of books.

"You told me at the homecoming last year that you did some writing, so I thought you might enjoy seeing what we have in common and maybe telling me what I don't have that I should."

"I collect classics, poetry, and new age. One of the books I recommend most is one nobody has ever heard of, and the writers I like best are Dostoyevsky, and most especially Thomas Hardy, Hesse, and Hemingway."

"I have all of them; now what is this favorite book no one has ever heard about?"

"*Le Grand Meaulnes* by Alain Fournier," Beth answered.

Her uncle smiled smugly and walked to the shelves in front of where she stood, reached up and pulled a tall dark blue hardback book from the shelf. "Is this the book you mean?" he asked as he handed her the book.

"Honestly, Uncle Morgan, you're the first person ever." Beth said, as she opened the book and flipped through the familiar pages.

"He has another book but he died in the war before he finished it," Uncle Morgan said.

"I knew he had written another book, yes, but I've never seen it. I didn't know it was available." Beth answered as her uncle placed another volume on top of the open book in her hands. She squealed with excitement, "Where did you get this?"

"My Uncle Edward knew Alain Fournier and his family briefly during World War I," he answered.

"Wow," was all Beth could say.

They left the library after awhile to rejoin Happy and Becky on the porch only to find the women had gone to bed. Beth excused herself and took Joey upstairs. It was past ten and Morgan had missed his nine o'clock appointment with Merlin for the first time in a long time.

He didn't mind though he told himself as he sat in the warm autumn night.

Beth came back down after about an hour, saying she couldn't sleep. They talked about the night and the family and then their talk turned to Joey, Beth's favorite subject. "Someday I'm going to find a place, perhaps a place in time, where I can know the peace I know here now and I am going to go there with Joey that he might be safe," she said.

Morgan stared dumbstruck at his niece. He had no idea that anyone else in the entire world had these kinds of thoughts. "Beth, tell me more," he said clearing his throat and pulling his chair closer so he would not miss a word. After all, this was a conversation he had played out in his mind countless times in his life, almost daily in the last few years. And while he had never lost hope that he would hear these words someday somehow, he had never dreamed it would be Beth. Then again why not, he thought; she is Happy's daughter and my niece; perhaps she got something of her tired old uncle that has escaped me all these years.

He remembered other things over the years watching his daughter grow up that had reminded him of his sisters when they were girls; still this was too much to hope for. He knew he could not have Happy with him in his dreams; she had sobered up considerably over the years; though he loved his sister he knew that love was for the young Happy, the one in the orchard, not the dear lady sleeping upstairs in Happy's old room; they were not the same people, not the same people at all.

"Uncle Morgan, I know you won't think I'm crazy when I tell you these things; Mama has told me so much about you. She misses the old days as much as you do, she says. I have listened to her talk about her childhood and her family and the people she grew up with till I've come to expect them to step out of the tapestry she has woven and resume life as it was then; as if all the years had not happened. I wish to be a part of this thing when and if it happens and to have Joey with me. If I am crazy then tell me now and I'll stop."

"Beth, you are the sanest person I know and I would not tell you or anyone else to stop dreaming if that's what you call it. I myself believe it's possible. I have read and studied almost nothing else since I was eight years old," Morgan said with a look that seemed to melt the years away.

"How did you become interested at such a young age?" Beth asked and then began to answer her question for herself almost before she had finished asking it. "When I was about that age I began having dreams about a soldier. I learned that he was fighting in World War I by looking in history books for pictures of his uniforms. His name always seemed to escape me but other details of his thinking and his feelings were as clear to me as if they were my own. Sometimes his fear occupied most of the dream and I would wake up scared and wet with perspiration, afraid to go back to sleep. I was afraid that whatever he was so afraid of would overtake him and through him, me; often he would be in this huge old stone house with twin towers. He would climb the steps of one of the towers and look around, seemingly for hours. I don't know what he was looking for but he seemed to know the land and to love it,"

"What was he afraid of; was it dying?" Morgan asked.

"No, I don't think it was dying, Uncle Morgan. He seemed comfortable with the fact that he would die from the beginning. No, it was something else and like his name I never learned what it was; perhaps I was afraid to know. I think my fear of losing him is what kept me from finding out. I know that probably sounds strange, my saying in one breath that I was terrified by the dreams, and in the next saying I didn't want to lose them. But I somehow felt from early on that this young soldier was a part of me."

"Beth, you're my kind of girl. I had no idea that we thought so much alike. Of course this is the only time we have ever really talked. I think that's a big part of what's wrong with people today; nobody has time to talk anymore. They're too busy running around trying to make a name for themselves, or make a fast buck."

"When I was a boy I must have been the loneliest person in the world; if it hadn't been for your mother I'd have probably never made it. Today we would put a kid like I was in therapy and talk the shit out of his dreams and leave a kid like Chris Lee in its wake. I understand what you mean by wanting to hold on to the dream. I too had a dream once; though I was awake at the time. I was eight years old and we had gone home to England. It was my first trip and the first time I had met my Grandparents and my many cousins and aunts and uncles. That and the long train ride to New York and the longer still voyage to England, was what everybody tried to tell me caused the dream, but I knew better.

"Granted I was excited; what young boy wouldn't have been; I wasn't that different. But I swear to you tonight as I did to my family then I did meet Merlin. He was as real as you are. He was as close to me then as you are to me now and his voice was as audible and his words changed my life forever. I have studied him and time and I know I can and will do what he told me." Tears fell on Morgan's face as he finished talking. He sighed and sat back in his chair as if an enormous weight had been lifted from his shoulders and his mind. "There, I have said aloud to you what I have uttered in my heart for sixty-nine years."

"Will you tell me what Merlin said, Uncle Morgan?" Beth asked softly as she reached out to him. He reached for her hand and held it for a long time deep in thought. She wondered after awhile if he had heard her question but waited quietly.

There was a picture of her Uncle Morgan, when he was a boy, on top of the bureau in the room where she and Joey were staying and she somehow saw the picture begin to come alive and the boy step down on to the floor as easily as if he had done it every day of his life since the picture had been taken. He held a book in his hand and his finger marked a place in the closed book that made the book extra fat and the white of the edge of the pages shine in the moonlight. It was a warm autumn night; the curtain stirring with a slight breeze through the open window drew the boy near. He leaned out and looked about and then with the book still in his hand he climbed out on the roof of the house down a trellis and on to the ground. A movement of the dazed elderly Morgan's hand brought Beth back to the moment and the boy and his book were gone. But gone where? Back to the picture on the bureau, Beth wondered? She jumped up and wanted to run up the stairs. She wanted to fling open the bedroom door and see if the picture was intact but her Uncle's Morgan's sudden grab for her hand to keep her brought her to her senses. She must have been dreaming or caught up in the magic of the dreams of her uncle she thought. "We're a bad influence on each other, Uncle Morgan," she said laughing.

"How so?" He asked her, shuffling a bit in his chair.

"Uncle Morgan, did you see the boy climb down the trellis just now?" Beth asked, half afraid he would either think her crazy or agree and they were both crazy, she decided; but she had never experienced anything so strange in her life and she wasn't about to forget it. She had to ask; she had to know.

"See the boy, my dear Beth; I was the boy," he said laughing.

She looked at him, her eyes widened, and her mouth flew open; then she too burst into laughter. They laughed for a long time muffling their voices with their hands for fear of waking up the rest of the household and spoiling the moment and the night. "How did you do that?" Beth asked after awhile. "I've got to know; how did you do that?"

"I answered your question," he said.

"What question?" Beth said seriously. "I want to know how you did that," she repeated.

"That's what Merlin told me I could do. You wanted to know and now you do." He sat back and his face softened; tears came to his eyes and he became quiet again.

"Oh no, you don't! You're not leaving me again! If you go, I go!" she insisted.

"Are you serious?" Morgan said looking her straight in the face. He sat erect and pulled her closer, his grip tightening on her arm and repeated his question, "Are you serious?"

"I have never been more serious," she replied.

"Then go you shall!" he told her," but first get a good night's sleep. We leave in the morning."

"Joey too?" she questioned.

"Joey too," he replied.

"Uncle Morgan, shouldn't we leave right now?" Beth said nervously, biting on her lower lip.

"Don't worry, child; tomorrow will be soon enough. There are things I must do tonight to ready the journey for the three of us." Morgan touched her chin softly and raised her head; their eyes met. "Beth, everything will be alright. Don't worry, there is nothing you have to do except sleep, and tomorrow when you awaken the journey will have begun. Good night," he told her kissing her gently on the cheek.

"Good night," she answered and turned toward the stairs.

He watched her go and then called softly after her. "What time do you want it to be?"

"A simpler, gentler time; the rest I'll leave to you. Good night." She said again. He watched in silence as she climbed the stairs and disappeared down the hail then he went to his study. It would be a long night. There was a lot for him to do.

Beth opened the bedroom door gently and stood listening for the sound of Joey's deep breathing. It was the first time she had thought of the possibility of his having awakened while she was downstairs talking to her uncle. She stood perfectly still for the few seconds it took her to adjust to the quiet of the room and focus on the hoped for sign that her child had slept in her absence and everything was okay. She smiled and sighed with relief leaning against the now closed door as she heard a soft snore.

She walked over to his bed and stood watching him for a long time before going to her own bed. She hoped she was doing the right thing. She hoped she was not risking her son's safety for a dream; a dream of what? She couldn't answer that question except in ways that applied to Joey. The world was too much for him, too noisy, too busy, too complicated, too competitive, too everything. She yearned for a quieter time, a time where she didn't have to hear every self appointed expert on the subject of parenting an autistic child tell her she needed to get away from him more. She did not need this! She wanted to tell the whole world they were crazy. She loved her son and she wanted her son with her. She did not want to leave him with others. She knew no one had ever told her own mother to get away from her kids; if mothers could be mothers in the fifties without a lot of expert advice, why not now in the nineties?

She stopped; now? Was now still 1991? Had her uncle begun his magic, whatever it was? What was she agreeing too? Agreeing hell, hoping desperately for? Did she believe there was a time for Joey, a time different from today; wherever today was? She was pretty confused about this house and its place in time after what she had witnessed downstairs. She remembered though that Uncle Morgan had said when she awakened the journey would begin so perhaps there was still time to stop this. She lay down on the bed with this thought, exhausted, and smiled softly with the knowing that everything would be better in the morning; it had always been so. Shelley had taught her that. She thought of her older sister, Shelley, and the times they had read and talked together, and dreamed of her and the night she had married and moved away.

The Year

1910

She cried and woke herself crying; the pillow was wet with tears. She sat up, ran her fingers through her hair, and reached for a tissue from the box on the night table. Joey's eyes met hers; I must have woke him up she thought and smiled at him, trying to brush the dream from her mind. She knew he would not ask her why she was crying and she was glad. That was part of the beauty of Joey; you didn't have to explain, and he wouldn't understand if you did; you're free to be yourself without a lot of pointless explanations.

Joey watched her quietly from his bed; neither of them liked to talk when they first woke up so both observed the silence. Beth looked about at the unfamiliar. She had never slept in her Grandparents house before. It seemed strange to her to refer to the house as belonging to her Grandparents; it was the first time she could ever remember doing so. Her grandfather had been dead all of her life and her grandmother had lived here with Uncle Morgan and Aunt Becky, and she had thought of the house as theirs. She had been told everything was exactly as it had always been -- no new furniture or modern draperies or carpeting, or for that matter anything modern beyond the household appliances, which had been ingeniously concealed in the kitchen, and they only showed when you wanted them to. The wood-burning stove had been electrified for convenience and everything else had been left as it always had been.

Beth loved the past her mother had told her about and she knew many of the oddities of the house and grounds from those same stories, stories from her mother's youth. She had formed a picture in her mind of the Jenkins boys her mother had fought with so often. She knew all the pranks played on the first old school marm that the kids hated till her retirement. Her mother had often said she thought the old teacher had held on as long as she did feeding on the hate of the kids; somehow it had nourished her and kept her teaching much longer than normally possible. Once this idea occurred to the children they had gone out of their way to be nice so she would weaken and quit, and quit she did.

She smiled remembering how different things had been with the new blond teacher. Every boy in school had fallen in love with her and every girl too, putting their jealousies aside. Things got noticeably boring after that unless you counted the dozens of embarrassing moments the boys had trying to court their newfound love. Her mother's childhood was so interwoven with her own that she couldn't separate the two and she had long ago given up trying.

This room she and Joey were in must have been the room her Aunts Teresa and Deborah had shared. The room was full of certificates of theirs and pictures too. Then she remembered the picture of her Uncle Morgan from the night before and looked to the bureau. The picture wasn't there. She got up, put on her slippers and robe, hurried to the bureau looking frantically about. Joey, sensing the excitement of the search, jumped out of bed to join her and the silence was broken by Joey as he asked Beth, "Whose room is this?"

"It was Aunt Deborah's and Aunt Teresa's," she told him still searching frantically for the picture of the young Morgan. "When they were children," she added, trying to get Joey's and her mind off the strange feeling she was having. She caught her reflection in the mirror and stood frozen. Why didn't I notice that before she thought to herself? She moved slowly toward the mirror for a closer look and spotted her clothes from the day before. Like the robe she was wearing they were the same color as before but they were different; they were somehow different. She picked up what she thought was her blouse and held it to her looking in the mirror as she did; the soft white cloth unfolded and fell to her ankles as she pulled away in shock.

Joey stepped around her and picked it up handing it to her with a smile. She took it and thanked him trying to control her fears, afraid for him. She was unhinged enough for the both of them; the last thing she needed now was to get him upset. They would have to dress in the clothes that were available for them and make the best of things. She explained to Joey that they were new clothes and went on about how nice they were; they were nice too, she noticed, as she finished buttoning the bodice. The shoes were quite an adjustment though after twenty years of sneakers. They were beautiful shiny leather with tiny buttons on the side and a small heel; she decided she liked them and hoped her feet would agree.

Joey looked so handsome when he was dressed. He was so pale with his dark hair combed with a part in the middle like always. She had combed his hair over again every morning for years but today the part looked so natural she just smiled. Was this a dream or were they really in the time period their clothes represented?

Little light shone through the big windows draped in yards of lace curtains. Maybe it was an optical illusion; maybe it was the old house playing tricks on her senses. Whatever it was she knew her questions would not be answered here in this room. She knew they had to go downstairs and face whatever they found and that, no matter what, she must remain calm and act as natural as possible for Joey's sake.

Taking one last look around the room she took a deep breath and opened the door. Joey stepped past her as he always did so as not to be the last one to leave a room. She ushered him by and told him she loved him. He smiled saying nothing and as he passed she noticed again how handsome he looked in the strange clothes he was wearing.

The smell of coffee filled the air almost as soon as they left their room and Joey was the first to comment on it. Beth nodded in agreement to what he was saying while trying to identify the other strange smell that blended with the coffee. Suddenly it came to her that it was the smell of wood burning. No that couldn't be she told herself, her mind racing with questions, hundreds of questions as to just how far reaching Uncle Morgan's magic would prove to be.

At the bottom of the stairs other wonderful breakfast smells occupied her senses and she forgot her questions. The lapse of memory lasted just long enough to throw her mind in neutral as she saw for the first time both the stove with its definite wood smell coming from it and the boy from the bureau picture standing in front of it. Her knees folded and her head spun around. She felt like she was going to faint and braced herself against the doorframe as she saw the young Morgan run to her.

His voice brought her back; it was the voice of a young boy, younger than her own Joey, and it was bidding her welcome to the year 1910. "Uncle Morgan, how did you do all of this?" she managed to ask.

"I think you better drop the uncle business, Beth," was his reply.

"Just how far reaching is this? Tell me everything," she insisted. "Be careful not to leave out a thing."

"We have enough money to last us several lifetimes at today's prices, meaning of course, October 1910," he said. "We are here and everything is as it was then. We have quiet and peace aplenty and we have years to get better acquainted. What else is there to say? For now we can eat a long leisurely breakfast without the telephone or television interrupting us. Then if you like we can go for a walk around town."

"Fine,' Beth said, "I would enjoy that very much and so would Joey. Wouldn't you, Joey?' she turned to her son who now stood with his coffee cup in his hand trying to figure out what had happened to the coffee pot of the night before. Morgan and Beth both laughed as they ran to help him.

"It's okay." Beth reassured Joey as she wrapped a small towel around the handle of the pot and poured them all a cup of coffee. "We've all got some adjustments to make."

'Indeed we have," Morgan said. "Indeed we have. Now let's eat while we sort out a few more facts.

Beth put a saucer under Joey's cup and turned to help Morgan with a big plate of hot sausage he was trying to balance with another equally big plate of scrambled eggs. "Did you cook all this for us?" Beth asked.

"For us and for Old Ned," Morgan beamed as he bent down to get a pan of biscuits out of the oven.

"Did I hear you right, Uncle, I mean Morgan? Did you say Old Ned?"

"Indeed I did. You will notice that I am twelve and you're still forty-seven and Joey is still twenty as you can see. I had no pictures of you to work with so I used the real you. I questioned having to do this at first and beat myself over the head for not having thought of this in time to ask you. Finally I decided on your current ages since you had mentioned that things had been best with Joey the last couple of years. Did I do the right thing? I hope so; in any case it is done."

"You most definitely did, and I thank you for bringing us along. I hope you won't regret it; I know I won't. There is one thing however that I didn't think of until just now. She looked to Joey thoroughly engrossed in blowing his steaming hot coffee to cool it. "What about Joey's care after. I hope you know the after I am referring to," Beth said.

"Yes, I think I do. It is the age-old question every parent asked regarding his or her special children, is it not? To begin with, we have not cheated death; we have only moved in time. I told you last night when we parted that I had a lot of work to do before we could do this. Part of that work had to do with a solution to this problem. I wouldn't and couldn't bring you with me if it meant leaving him to turn-of-the-century mental facilities. I had to know about your deaths. Do you want to know what I found?" he asked her.

"If you mean when we will die, no I don't believe I do. Please tell me there is some other way you can reassure me that we have done the right thing for him," Beth said sadly once again looking to Joey.

"I'm sorry, but I must tell you that you will be able to care for him to the end and he will not need the services of a private home or a public institution."

"Thank you, Thank you so much for telling me this, and thank you most especially for bringing us with you. Now tell me about yourself." Beth said

Morgan waited to answer her looking for the right way to tell her about his fate. Gathering his thoughts he spoke after a long silence. "Beth, I believe I am the soldier of your dreams," he said with bowed head.

"You are what?" Beth screamed jumping up from the table.

"I am the soldier of your dreams." Morgan said again. "Please believe me when I say to you that I don't mind. In fact I am glad.

Understand this, please; I had the same number of years left either way. This way I go doing something useful; the other way I die a slow boring frightening death, a day at a time. Old age, the golden years, they call it. Golden hell, leaden is more like it. You are forced to retire and then you sit home day after day watching your mind turn to lead. Don't you see, Beth, I had to do this? With or without you I had to do it. As it happens it is a lot easier with a built in caretaker. You will have to pose as my aunt or guardian or something. They don't let twelve year old boys run around living in big houses with plenty of money by themselves. Some well-meaning greedy town citizen would try to assume the post of caretaker and where would I wind up; probably in the poor house or worse yet an orphanage."

"But, Uncle Morgan, I hate war." Beth interrupted.

"Yes, Elizabeth, and so do I, but have you ever tried the alternative? Beth I was seventy-seven years old and losing control of my life, my time, my thoughts. Is that not worth fighting for?"

"Yes, I guess it is", she answered.

"When we finish eating I am going to go take a plate of food over to Old Ned while you get ready for a tour of the fair city of Glendale, circa 1910."

"Will you be long? Don't you want to hang around and talk to Old Ned? Catch up on old times so to speak?" Beth laughed at her own words. "Time, just exactly what is time anyway?"

"The answer to that will take some explaining. I've already had a long talk with Old Ned, which will do me for a while; I'll be right back." Morgan told her as he hurried to the back door with the plate of warm food for his friend. Beth stopped him at the door to cover the plate with a dishtowel from the table and watched him go shaking her head.

What had they done? How was it done? She wondered as she thought of the changes she would find in the town. The interstate would be gone, the new bank, the motel, the new depot all gone. David's of Glendale yesterday, full of antiques, today a bank full of money. And the antiques themselves; were they back in the homes of their original owners? No more wonderful meals at the Whistle Stop, no more long lines of tourists. And what about the dragon from next door? It wasn't even on the drawing board yet.

Morgan ran with the plate across the field. He stumbled and slowed his pace. Looking about him his eyes wandered over the old familiar landscape. He heard a horse whinny in the distance, looking toward the sound, and he saw the bluest sky he had ever seen. He had forgotten how beautiful the sky had been before pollution had become a household word. He had forgotten the silence of a fall day before machines.

He had forgotten the feel of time at its best; time, his beloved time, flexible moldable time. To experience again what you have already experienced; time to change and to be a better person, or perhaps a different person.

He entered the side door of the blacksmith shop. Sweat poured from Old Ned's arms and face as he stood by a roaring fire pounding a horse shoe into shape. The sound of the hammer on the shoe was music to Morgan's ears. He stood watching him trying to soak it all up. Hoping to recapture every move and gesture, even the smell of this man he had loved like a father and who this time would be his only male role model until he went to England and became close friends with his Uncle Edward as a young man like himself; perhaps to fight beside him in the war.

He would endeavor to be more like Old Ned, a man who had the respect of the city and the love of its children. He would let Old Ned have a stronger hand in the molding of his life. He would spend more time with him and less with Shelley. He had forgotten the power of the man but certainly not the love. He knew there would be emptiness in this boyhood he had not felt in the last; emptiness caused by the absence of Happy and he would let that place be filled by the big black man before him.

"I thought you would be chasin' roun' the apple trees with Miss Happy, boy." Old Ned shouted above the roar of the fire and the ringing of the hammer.

"What are you talking about, Ned?" Morgan shouted back so dumbstruck he dropped the plate of food.

The big man put down his hammer and came toward the shaking boy. "Miss Happy, she was in here not ten minutes ago on her way to the apple trees she said."

Morgan flew out the side door of the shop. Old Ned smiled at the fleeing boy shaking his head. "That boy acts like he done seen a ghost," he said aloud and laughed a big deep hearty laugh as he bent to recover his spilled breakfast. "Thank goodness Morgan think to cover it with a clean rag or Old Ned be eating dirt this morning," he said laughing again.

Morgan ran so fast he thought his heart would burst with the pounding in his ears. Happy cannot be here, she cannot; his thoughts raced with his feet slowing down only when he entered the small gate that led to the orchard. He stopped, his heart still pounding. The worn path of his childhood lay before him. The first step would take him back an eternity and he was afraid of that step; as afraid as if it were a living thing with the power to devour him.

"What are you doing in that silly apron?" he heard someone say. Staring in disbelief, he saw Happy dangling from the branch of a tree that had been cut down for thirty-six years. He knew this because he had kept count of the years; it meant that much to him. Once again Happy's voice pulled him from his thoughts. "What kept you?" she said. "I've been waiting for you."

"Never mind that, how did you get here?' he asked her.

"You brought me here silly." she answered.

"I did not!" he shouted, "I brought Joey and Beth, not you," he insisted.

"Silly boy, my picture was in the book. It's been there for years. Didn't you know that?" she asked climbing down from the tree. "Has it been that long since you've read Shelley? Did you ever read him after you moved away?"

"To tell you the truth, no; I never liked Shelley myself I only read him because you did. I've got to go. I've got to think this thing through. I've got to find out what's happened to Beth and Joey. I'll see you later," he told her, turning to walk away.

"Morgan, Beth and Joey are fine. I am here because of the picture in the book you carried with you Do you hear me Morgan? There is nothing wrong with your plan except that you will be reading Shelley again."

'Not this time Happy! Not this time!" he told her firmly mustering all the strength he had for the fight that he knew was about to break out. Happy's mouth opened and her look of surprise turned quickly to a smile. She was proud of her big brother; for the first time she was proud of him. Things might be more exciting this time she thought to herself as she turned back to her tree and once again climbed part way up and swung down head first from a branch.

Morgan shook his head in disbelief, waved goodbye and shouted that he would see her later. "I'm going to take Beth to meet Old Ned," he called back to her pulling off the forgotten apron and swinging it in wide circles at his side as he hurried proudly to the house.

"Elizabeth," he shouted as he ran in the door, "Are you ready?"

"Yes, Morgan, she called back from the kitchen; just let me figure out how to put on this silly hat."

"Here I'll help you," he said coming through the doorway. "Can we begin our tour of the town with a stop at the blacksmith shop?" he asked her." There is someone I want you to meet. Oh and Beth, don't look now but the girl in the orchard hanging from the tree is your mother."

Beth dropped her hat pen and bent down and to look for it as big tears filled her eyes. "I can't believe this has happened," she said, not knowing whether to laugh or to cry. She found the hat pen and braced herself for Joey's sake. Giving her new hat one last look in the tiny mirror over the kitchen sink; she led Joey past her and followed Morgan out the door closing it behind her.

Remembering the baseball diamond in the movie "Field of Dreams," she turned to the young boy on the porch beside her, "Morgan is the yard safe?"

"What do you mean safe?" Morgan said answering her question with a question.

"Let me put it another way. Is it really 1910?"

Morgan laughed, "Yes, it really is 1910."

"Is this the beginning or the end," Beth asked.

"You're the writer; suppose you tell me." The tall blond boy teased as he ran past her and out into the yard. "Let's take that walk now. I promise I'll tell you everything later."

The Library

1951/1910

Once again Michael was gone, this time before I woke up. I was not able to sleep and got up during the night to write, closing the door between the bedroom and the study; I wrote most of the night and crawled back into bed beside him just as the sun was coming up.

His note was on the bedside table, "You're beautiful and so is the book. Keep writing, love Michael..."

I kept as busy as I could each day and looked forward to the night and visits with Elizabeth, hoping she could answer more of my questions.

I knew things had not gotten better for Joey; she had written enough about that. The only thing she had gained for Joey by moving in time was that it was less of a rat race and those were her exact words. She had escaped the dreaded phrase 'age appropriate' and he had escaped to quieter times, but certainly not more understanding times. In the past people hid sons like Joey in attics, in backrooms, and in institutions; this she had stubbornly refused to do and according to Trey he was always with her. I hoped that other families had taken courage from her.

After supper I sat on the porch and waited for nightfall. I was restless and had been all day. I had written very little and yet I was tired.

Perhaps my talk with Elizabeth would quiet my many fears and I would get a good night's sleep.

At a few minutes to nine I crossed the yard to the garden. It was a very noisy night; insects and frogs were celebrating life while my mind made its own noises batting questions around in my head. I wondered why life got so troublesome just when it was most beautiful. Was it a game of chase between the two opposites, happy and sad, that we humans had to endure?

I sat by the pool and waited. It grew darker and no Elizabeth. I tried to shut out the night sounds and my worries with the wonderful fragrances of the flowers but tonight it didn't work. I lay down and made a pillow for my head with my arms and stared at the sky. It was very dark and cloudy. Few stars could be seen and no moon. Everything was clouded tonight by the threat of rain, even my mind. I stared at the clouds and tried to find faces in them, anything to pass the time. I was doing this when Elizabeth walked up and I didn't hear her. She stood over me and called my name. I sat up startled.

"You're very troubled tonight Jennifer; do you want to talk about it?" she asked. I fell into her arms crying.

She held me, stroked my hair and began to talk to me about her own youth, and her marriage to Joey's father. I listened enthralled. I had never read anything about her husband. He was not even mentioned in *A Place in Time*.

"Tell me about time." I said.

"Think of time as a series of rooms, each representative of an era or a lifetime if you will. You have only to quiet your mind to see the door between the rooms and to walk through. That is essentially all there is to it. I remember how furious Morgan was that it took him so many years to learn this.

"And that is what you do, quiet your mind?" I asked.

"And walk through," she added.

"And you can do this anytime you like?" I questioned.

"Anytime I like."

"And our other lives if indeed we have other lives?"

"Rooms"

"And the house itself?"

"Creation."

"What about White House?"

"Morgan never told me how he did it. To be honest I didn't ask. I wondered how the picture business was accomplished and at first I wondered about Old Ned, who was dead in 1991. But now that I can do it myself and it is past my death date it seems silly to have ever wondered."

"Actually it is before your death date by several years," I corrected her.

"Technically you are right, but there is still the matter of the fairly fresh grave with the body in it. What you have to know is when you will not be able to count on moving through the doorways anymore because you cease to live physically, and planning all of your travels before that time. Do you understand?"

"I'm not sure."

"Look, it's like this; I lived on earth eighty eight years; where I spent those years was as open to me as the heavens are to the stars. Now do you understand?"

"Yes I think I do. You're saying any room anywhere in the group of rooms during the allotted years of that lifetime, in your case eighty-eight years, years forward, or years backward, no matter."

"Yes. You know I never tried to explain this to anyone but Joey before and then only the part he needed to know to make the transition from the nineties to 1910."

"But Old Ned was dead in 1991 when you first traveled."

"Not in my heart," was always Morgan's answer to me when I asked."

"Did he ever meet his father again and talk trains with him?"

"No, Jennifer, he did not but he was happy. Perhaps they have done that on the other side by now but they did not do it here."

"Do you think he tried?"

"No, I think he was too unsure of his father's response to him. His father was his worst hang-up in life."

"His worse what?"

"Problem," she said. "He always knew they would meet again in another life to finish this quarrel, their differences to be ironed out perhaps with him the not so perfect father and T. the misunderstood son. He worried a lot about that."

"And you and Joey; do you think you will meet again in the next lifetime?"

"No I think our debts to each other are paid in full. Many of our lifetimes in the past had been lifetimes where there had been intense power struggles between us. Remember what I wrote about the session with the hypnotist when she had asked who Bronson Alcott was? My answer had been a woeful plea to him, "Joey, Joey, Joey why do you always have to be in control?"

"Then you do believe that you are a reincarnation of Louisa May Alcott and he is one of her father Bronson?"

"Yes I do."

"And the same death dates; did you arrange that to prove this to the world?"

"No I did not arrange that; fate did. But I have known it since Morgan told me the dates. You remember in *A Place in Time* I asked him not to tell me. He simply said that I would outlive Joey. For a while that was enough. When I believed that and was at peace with it, so much worry fell away. But I did eventually ask for the dates; when Morgan gave them to me I already knew that we had been Bronson and Louisa. The dates were only added verification."

"And then Morgan was killed in World War I as he had thought he would be."

"Yes, and it was what he really wanted, to die at Butler House. He had always said, 'I want to haunt Butler House in death as she had haunted me in life; it is only fair;" those were his exact words. He knew I had always been hung up on the word fair and he could win any argument with the word. Of course we missed him terribly. Poor Joey was the worst; he had grown so attached to Morgan. But by the time Morgan actually passed over, Joey had adjusted to his absence and I didn't tell him the rest. He wouldn't have understood anyway."

It was very late when Elizabeth and I left the garden. Exhausted I went straight to bed and slept till almost eleven when the sun once again made the room too hot to sleep in. I went to the terrace to sit for a few minutes to cool off before going downstairs for coffee. Trey was mowing the yard and the noise was impossible so I didn't sit long. I came in to the study and flopped down in the chair. Kahlil came into the room from somewhere and jumped up into it at almost at the moment I landed. Both of us were in shock for a while and she stared at me with her big blue eyes, and then sat down as if her being in my lap was the most natural thing in the world; for a long time I said nothing and made no move to touch her. While I was deciding whether to touch her or not she stood up in my lap and started rubbing against my hand which was hanging off the chair arm suspended in mid air. I scratched her behind her ear and she turned her head so I could reach the other one. I was talking softly to her telling her how beautiful she was and how glad I was to finally get to know her, when my hand hit against something cold on her collar. I looked to see what it was and there, buried amidst the long white fur, was a key fit into the collar in its own little case.

"A key," I screamed for joy, and Kahlil stared hatefully at me but remained in my lap. I had no idea how long she planned to sit here but I would not put her down, no matter what. I thought of the irony of the whole thing.

Elizabeth had planned this beautifully, probably including my current predicament. She knew how long it would take me to get this far with Kahlil. She also knew me well enough to know I would sit here waiting till the old cat jumped down on her own before I beat feet to the library. She was probably in one of her rooms somewhere laughing herself sick about this and it was funny. It reminded me of something I had heard a soldier say about the army once; "hurry up and wait." I had my key and I had my cat; I would wait and I would appreciate both in their season.

I spent the time with Kahlil rubbing her and tossing the hands full of loose fur into a nearby trashcan. She was enjoying this preening and would look up at me occasionally and then settle into my lap a little more comfortably. I waited continuing to rub her while in my mind I retraced the library as Elizabeth had described in it *A Place in Time*.

I followed Morgan through the library on his last night there before they moved in time. I pictured the double entrances and entered them. I saw the single lamp on the desk and the dark walls covered with shelves full of books. I smelled the wonderful blend of oil, pipe tobacco, and old books. I touched the back of the deep red couch in remembrance of his father, long since dead. I hurried to the shelves of books to find the authors Elizabeth had told Morgan about. I wanted to read Le Grand Meaulnes; it had been one of Elizabeth's favorite books and I wanted to read it too.

Kahlil slept while I dreamed and finally I dozed too. It was close to one when she jumped down. Startled I woke up and caught her out of the corner of my eyes running down the stairs to Joey's room. I got up and followed her down the front stairs hoping and praying I would be able to pick her up and get the key.

We met in the hall outside Joey's room and she meowed as she wrapped herself around my legs. I bent slowly not sure that she would allow it but hoping to at least be able to hold on to her long enough to get the key out of its holder. I looked at the long thin sleeves of the robe as I reached out for Kahlil wondering how much protection they would offer me if she decided to attack.

She settled into my arms before I could stand up and I took the key while I told her once again what a wonderful cat she was. I was slipping it into my robe pocket when we entered the kitchen. Blanche's mouth flew open in disbelief. She grabbed the notebook and wrote, "Nobody has ever held that cat except Mrs. White!"

I smiled with pride stroking the beautiful cat while trying to ask for a dish of milk. Blanche understood and got the milk. I sat Kahlil down in front of the bowl and she meowed her thanks. Blanche was standing near her still in shock when I left the room.

I didn't go straight to the library as I wanted to; instead I went upstairs for a quick bath and to get dressed. Something felt wrong to me about going to the library informally. The occasion was a special one and I felt I should look my best. Was I expecting to see Morgan there, I asked myself? No, I knew I wasn't, but I did feel there would be a wealth of information in the library about him and yes even about Elizabeth and Joseph White and it somehow seemed wrong to enter the room in my gown and robe.

I was just settling into the tub when Blanche brought me coffee, which I had forgotten because of Kahlil. I thanked her and sat back in the tub to drink it and to think. I realized for the first time that I was afraid, as afraid as I had been when I came here. Then it had been the whole house; now it was the library. But afraid of what I didn't know.

The library was the one unexplored area in the house left to me. Was I afraid the mystery of the place, a mystery I had come to love, would be lost? Or was it the fear of finding skeletons, monsters, or angels I had not met?

I got out of the tub as soon as I finished my coffee instead of waiting for the water to cool as I usually did. I went up to dress and took the time to put on makeup and put my hair up, even wearing the pearl combs I had worn to Elizabeth's farewell party. I felt a little foolish for all the trouble I had taken with my appearance as I walked down the front stairs, and I passed the same mirror Morgan had looked into to see the old man who was not growing old gracefully. I stopped and asked myself why? I honestly didn't know but at the back of my mind was the feeling that I would meet the real and future me in the library, and I wanted to face her with all the dignity I could muster.

At the library door I stood nervously fingering the key. I braced myself, put the key in the lock, turned it, and opened the first door. To my surprise the second door stood open. My heart was pounding in anticipation. My palms were sweaty; I felt as if my feet were lead and for a moment I was unable to step forward.

I heard the sound of voices and recognized one of them as Elizabeth's. I stepped into the room with a new courage and there before me stood a young Joey and the boy Morgan. Joey came up to me and took my hand leading me to a place on the couch beside his mother. He had done so after much prompting from her. Immediately he asked me to spell my name and settled down with his tablet and pencil to write it; I wondered if he would also sketch me as he did other people or if perhaps I were meeting him before he began to draw. Somewhere I could remember her having said that his interest in art had not happened till a certain age. He looked to be about twenty now and I found I couldn't remember what age she had said.

Morgan was a tall very blond boy and just the way I pictured him. He was the only person I knew who could say he had gone back to a young age and taken all the knowledge of his mature years with him. Most of us could only wish for such a thing. I wondered if he belonged in this time as he hoped to and then it hit me. I had traveled back to them and not them to me. I had not actually done it myself; it had been done for me. How I didn't know.

I was afraid to look down, afraid that my clothes and shoes would have mysteriously changed to an earlier era. Elizabeth took my hand and I could see she was young almost as young as I was. The years between us wiped out with the passing from one room to another just as she had told me they could be. "I see that you and Kahlil have become friends," she teased.

"Yes I said nervously. How did you do this?"

"Do you remember that when I traveled for the first time I was asleep?"

I thought back and she was right. Did it somehow make it easier to have it done to you or for you when you were not aware of it happening? I looked hard at my shoes. They hadn't changed. I felt a little safer. "I'm imagining this whole thing," I said aloud before I could stop myself.

"You wish," was her reply. I looked around the room; everyone was smiling at me, almost laughing really. As if it was all a big joke. I felt very uncomfortable. "Jennifer, go upstairs and change clothes so we can go for a walk. The only way you will ever know the wonder of what has happened is to see the town and the changes. Then you will be better able to write about it. No one will believe you if you don't actually experience it for yourself. They won't believe the women you saw in the garden or in the study chair."

I knew she was right and I turned to leave the room with a new courage. I would do it to be able to write about it. That was certainly reason enough. I had my hand on the doorknob when Elizabeth called out to me. "Jennifer, wait a minute, please." she said. I waited."Remember that the house will be very different when you step through the door. It will be the way it was when we first made our journey back, very dark and Victorian looking. I changed it a great deal for Joey. I want you to be prepared."

"Can you come with me, Elizabeth?" I asked.

"I can but I won't; I think as a writer you should experience your way, not mine." she said taking my hand. I patted her hand and let go of it. She opened the door and I walked through. She stood in the doorway smiling as I walked away and then I heard her close the door behind me.

The hall was so dark I could barely see though it was the middle of the day. Near the end of the hall at the dining room I saw more clearly by the light from nearby windows. The windows themselves were draped in yards of heavy burgundy velvet tied back to let in the little light possible with the thickly gathered lace curtains. The floors were carpeted instead of the bare wood I had grown use to. The wood paneling on the dining room wall was a deep brown as was the wood trim everywhere I looked. The furniture was the same deep brown, shiny and oily looking from polish. A cream colored lace prevailed everywhere from the curtains in the window to the spreads on the china cabinet to the long flowing tablecloth.

I walked to the kitchen and wanted to cry. Gone was the cheery air the white had brought and instead of white, everywhere I looked was the same dark wood of the dining room and the hall. Everything else about the kitchen was the same, the same stove, the same cabinets, the same sink but there was a single window now where before there had been a wall of glass. The side porch was now open to the weather except for its roof. The row of wicker chairs, were a natural wood color with pillows in white; this was the only white I had seen so far. Everything else was a deep brown or burgundy.

I went up the stairs to my room and when I opened the door the attic was bare; totally bare with not so much as a steamer trunk in it. The wood was dark with age and spider webs were laced about the room in crisscross fashion. Dust lay up on the floor and the windowsills and even permeated the air making the attic smell old and musty.

The ceiling windows and the wall between the study and the bedroom with its mirrored door were all gone. There was no terrace or door leading to it; there was another dormer instead. The attic looked bigger without its walls and furniture and as dark and gloomy as the rest of the house without its ceiling windows and light wood and white walls.

I had to go to one of the second floor bedrooms to look for my things and I tried the back stairs; they were gone so I went the front way and stopped off in Joeys' room to see if I would indeed find a closet there. I did and here too the light had turned dark. The walls were deep burgundy, wallpaper splashed with huge yellow blooms. Joey's cars were lined up on a library table. I left his room feeling sad.

In the room across from Joey's I saw my briefcase on the bed. A dress and petticoat had been laid out on the bed for this occasion. The dress was long flowing soft beige with a large collar embroidered with tiny violets. I dressed, finding shoes with stockings tucked in them under the edge of the bed.

I walked down the stairs and again stopped in front of Morgan's mirror. I certainly looked the part of someone from this time with my old dress and shoes, and my upswept hair with pearl combs.

It felt like 1910 and I realized for the first time the true significance of Morgan's words, "I had forgotten the feel of time at its best." Time did have a feel to it. It was not just the changes of clothing and furniture and decor and literature. It was a feeling of life gone by; the way it feels when the wind had passed, or the way music lingers after the last note is played.

I rejoined Elizabeth, Morgan, and Joey in the library where they were seated on the long red couch; I looked around the room with its hundreds of books. Here were the books Elizabeth had loved, books not yet written by writers not yet discovered. It was the most puzzling piece of the puzzle; here among the books might be my own stories, stories not yet born in my mind.

Seeing me look at the books, Elizabeth smiled. "There's a lifetime of reading on those shelves," she said, and they all got up to join me.

"Lifetimes of writing too no doubt; tell me, Elizabeth, are my books here too?"

"Books you haven't written, why Jennifer how could that be?" She teased.

We went out of the house by way of the front door, something I had not done before. I wondered why but said nothing. I was happy to be in the sun, the house was so depressing with its dark cloak of age. I hoped when our walk was over I would come home to the house of light I had grown to love.

We began our tour walking down the front lane to a gate hidden within the fence and not easily found. Trees abounded in the town as before. The road was dry and our steps stirred up a cloud of dust as we walked. Joey walked very fast and was already some distance ahead. Seeming especially happy with the dirt road, he kicked stones or twigs when he found them and when there were none, he would drag his feet laughing as he did. The rest of us would have been choking on the dust but he was always moving so fast beyond it he seemed unaffected and the air was clear when we came upon it.

The yards and streets were full of children playing. A horse and rider passed us at a slow trot. It was as if we had stepped onto a movie set. The smells were different, sharper and stronger. The air was clearer. Many of the houses had not been built yet offering larger yards for the ones that stood. I loved it all so much, especially the quiet. What was it Morgan had said? "I had forgotten the silence of a fall day before machines," and he was right.

My favorite part of it all was the wonder and the smells of the tiny store with its stove, sitting in the middle of the floor, cold and dusty on this warm day, old wood counters lined with big glass jars of penny candy, and big wooden barrels of pickles, sugar, and meat. The smell of apples and fresh ground coffee permeated the air.

We saw all of Main Street, a street I had yet to walk in my own time. It would never be this beautiful, this unspoiled for me again. Elizabeth had written of a day when it would be full of antique shops and a wonderful little restaurant and a bed and breakfast. In its old age it would be a tourist town; I was glad to see it now in its youth without the strangers lined up on Main Street.

I walked back up the street alone; Elizabeth had said good-bye to me in the store. I tried to absorb the feel not only of the era I was in but also of the one day knowing that the whole was important, the general over all whole, but that the one-day with its singular happenings was as much so. The songbird on the fence across the street, the wide eyed look of the boy in the brown hat by the tree, the sound of the horses as I neared the blacksmith shop, the fresh smell of apples and coffee in the store, the woman sweeping her porch, the blue, blue sky, the dust settled on porches and walkways from the dirt roads with children and wagons coming and going on it all day. This was something I had come to experience and to remember and write about in a way that would tell my readers how real it was, this thing called time travel.

At the end of Main Street I stopped for a wagon passing on Glendale Road. It was loaded with hay and laughing boys, sweaty and dirty from their work in the fields. The wagon pulled up and stopped at the blacksmith shop and Old Ned came outside to help unload the hay. I watched and listened to their voices carried along on the quiet of the day.

Crossing the road after a while I walked back up the lane to White House praying that it would once again be a house of light when I entered the front door. Though I had many questions for Elizabeth I also wanted time to think about what I had just experienced and time to search the library for my books.

Epilogue

1977

In 1977, I spoke before the graduating class at Morgan's old college. The exercises were held on the lawn near the statue of the thinker mentioned in *A Place in Time*. The valedictorian was Elizabeth Windom White full of promise and youth and the dreams of youth.

I wanted to take her aside and ask her if she had known that Michael and I would marry and that Michael would die on the mountain road he had dreamed of only a few days after he bought a '57 Chevy. Our son Will was born after Michael was killed and I came to think more and more that Michael had come back to me in our son. Will was his father from top to bottom; the same walk, the same doorway stand, the same hair and eyes. But more than the physical attributes had been the uncanny way he had of speaking his father's words, of having his father's loves and memories; and I wanted to ask if she knew that Will would be wounded in the war Michael and I had discussed from Elizabeth's *A Place in Time*.

I wanted to ask her if she knew about the books I would write but I couldn't. I knew she would not understand my questions. I knew that today she had no idea where life would take her, let alone how it would deal with me.

When the services were over I signed her copy of my book *The Feel Of Time at its Best*, "Elizabeth, this book was written for you," I wrote, and I encouraged her to write herself; that was all I could do — that, and remember.

It was here in the library that I had come to know that I had been Elizabeth Windom White's inspiration and she had been mine. The only question in my mind was the question of time.